Praise for *Mary's* (

Author Anne Blackburne's *Mary's Calico Hope* is a fast-paced, heart-warming read of Reuben King and Mary Yoder, two loveable, relatable, and intriguing characters who fall in love. But their destiny together won't come without obstacles; one protagonist is Amish; the other, Mennonite. The road to true love is often a bumpy path, and in this case, becoming Mr. and Mrs. King doesn't seem likely. Despite my adoration for Mary and Reuben, the further I delved into the book, the more I wondered how this author would successfully deliver a happily-ever-after. However, Gott has a way of intervening. I won't reveal the denouement, but it's a stunner! All characters, including Hope, contribute to this highly intriguing emotional page turner that I anticipate will appeal to everyone who believes in the power of true love. Five stars!!

–Lisa Jones Baker, bestselling author

In *Mary's Calico Hope*, Mary Yoder was badly injured in a buggy accident as a child and is content living in the Dawdi Haus connected to her parents' farmhouse and with her work weaving baskets and raising specialty roosters whose feathers she uses to make excellent trout lures. When Reuben King, a Mennonite doctor, comes to town, they are attracted to one another, but Mary is a baptized Amish woman, which means they are forbidden to be together. And he wants her to have surgery to improve her mobility and lessen her day-to-day pain, but she's tired of surgeries. This second novel set in Blackburne's fictional town of Willow Creek, Ohio, reminds us that God's grace and mercy is ever present, especially when we're certain we don't fit in with our community. The story will captivate readers who love Amish culture and an endearing romance.

–Amy Clipston, bestselling author of *The Heart's Shelter*

Anne Blackburne pulls a very single, very science-minded doctor into a conservative Amish community, and she pitches him headlong in love! Science and faith tangle together in this sweet romance that proves that physical limitations make no difference when it comes to matters of the heart. Ms. Blackburne is proving herself to be a valuable addition to the Amish romance genre. Don't miss out on this heartwarming read!

–Patricia Johns, *Publishers Weekly* bestselling author

THE HEART *of* THE AMISH

Mary's Calico Hope

ANNE BLACKBURNE

BARBOUR
PUBLISHING

Mary's Calico Hope ©2024 by Anne Blackburne

Print ISBN 978-1-63609-855-5

Adobe Digital Edition (.epub) 978-1-63609-856-2

This book is a work of fiction. Names, characters, places, and incidents are either products of the author's imagination or used fictitiously. Any similarity to actual people, organizations, and/or events is purely coincidental.

Cover Design: Kirk DouPonce, DogEared Design

Published by Barbour Publishing, Inc., 1810 Barbour Drive, Uhrichsville, Ohio 44683, www.barbourbooks.com

Our mission is to inspire the world with the life-changing message of the Bible.

 Member of the
Evangelical Christian
Publishers Association

Printed in the United States of America.

DEDICATION:

To my children, who are my biggest supporters!
Kelsey, Parker, Molly, Brianna, Cooper

To Linda, Karen, Elizabeth, Virginia, Jennifer,
John, Alex, Sherry, Kitrina, Pam, Martha, Janine
You believe in me and give me wings!

And to Phil, my wonderful bro-in-law/tech wiz!
Without your help, nobody would know about my books!

I love you all.

Thank you for your honesty and love.

CHAPTER ONE

"Careful, Hope, I'll squish you if you don't watch out." Mary Yoder was careful not to set one of her crutches down on the half-grown calico kitten presently making a nuisance of itself by winding around her legs.

"*Ach!* That cat is going to make you fall, Mary!"

"*Maem*, don't worry. I'm fine." The petite blond woman smiled fondly at her mother as she did her best to avoid the adolescent feline.

"You know I can't help worrying about you, Mary. I'm sure Hope is a very *gut* cat, but a fall could really hurt you."

Mary kissed her *mudder* on the cheek. "*Ja*, I know. Which is why I'm very careful. I like having Hope around. She's gut company."

Mary reached down and stroked the pretty cat, a gift from her old friend Lydia Coblentz, who had given a kitten from her cat's final litter to several unmarried Amish women in Mary's community. Lydia's only stipulation was that the cats must be indoor pets.

"If you need more company, you could move back into the main house. I worry about you living by yourself in the *dawdi haus*. How would I know if you fell and needed help?" Edie's well-meant nagging made Mary hide a smile as she leaned one crutch against the wall by the table, pulled out a chair, sat down, and laid the second crutch next to the first. It was true she wasn't light on her feet, nor could she change direction quickly to avoid an unexpected obstacle. But all things considered, she thought she did pretty well.

"I guess I could be like that television commercial *Englishers* talk about, and yell, "I've fallen, and I can't get up!"

"Mary Yoder, this is not a joking matter."

"Come on, Maem. I have to joke about some things because laughter is better than tears, ja? And I love knowing you miss me, but I'm not moving back. It's nice and quiet in my little house, unlike the main house when my *brieder* are here. And honestly, I'm more likely to be knocked down by them than tripped by Hope."

"Ach, I can't argue with you there." Edie laughed. "They are very energetic."

"Ja, that's one way of putting it."

Mary had four younger brothers—much younger, as they were the children of her mother and her stepfather. The boys were six, eight, ten, and twelve. Mary's mother had been widowed at a young age when her husband was killed in the same buggy accident that injured Mary's legs and back. Mary had been fortunate to have been thrown clear of the vehicle when it was rear-ended by a big pickup truck being driven by a drunk Englisher. She was only three years old at the time of the accident and had no memory of the trauma or the pain she'd endured during several surgeries to save her life, and her legs.

To her regret, she could barely remember her father either. She only had vague recollections of a large, strong man with a soft brown beard and laughing eyes.

Edie Yoder set two steaming mugs of *kaffi* down on the table, then filled a plate with half a dozen cookies from the cookie jar on the counter and placed them on the table. She sat down and sighed, then patted Mary's hand and smiled wryly. "I'm sorry, *liebchen*. I don't mean to mother you to death."

"I am nearly thirty, Maem," Mary reminded her mother with a small grin. "You're going to have to cut the apron strings at some point, you know."

Hope jumped lightly to Mary's lap and settled down, purring as Mary stroked her soft fur.

"Ja, ja, I know you're a woman grown, daughter. But you'll always be my *boppli*."

Mary rolled her eyes but leaned over to give her mother a kiss on the cheek, causing the cat to let out an indignant squawk. Both women chuckled at the tiny animal's ire, and Mary petted her in apology. "Fortunately for me, you have four young ones to lavish your attention on. Otherwise, I doubt you'd let me out of the house."

Edie chuckled. "You're probably right. But Mary, I don't want you to think I don't trust you or don't understand that you're a capable adult. I'm sorry if I made you feel that way."

"Aw, Maem, I understand. You worry. It's what a mudder does."

"Ja! But I'll try harder not to." The women smiled at each other in understanding and sipped their hot coffee.

"So, did you hear about Ruth Helmuth and Jonas Hershberger?" Mary wiggled her eyebrows at her mother.

"I know they've been courting," Edie responded, raising her own eyebrows questioningly.

"What? I actually know something before you do? You're slipping, Maem." Mary grinned and took another sip of coffee just to draw out the pleasure of being the bearer of gut news.

"Mary Yoder! Tell me what you know before I burst!"

Mary laughed but relented. "All right! Ruth stopped in to see us at work today, and she told me she and Jonas are getting married this fall! But you can't tell anyone, as it's a secret. She told me I could tell you."

Edie clapped her hands together and grinned at her daughter. "*Wunderbar!* I can't think of a better matched couple, for I know she's always wanted *kinner*, and he has that adorable little daughter who needs a mudder! Speaking of which, I doubt this will remain a secret for long, what with that chatty little girl doubtless in on the secret."

"Probably so. I know Abigail is happy about the situation. She and Ruth already love each other. They're very sweet together. And they both got kittens from Lydia Coblentz, from the same litter as my Hope!" At the sound of her name, the cat let out a contented chirp, and Mary scratched her under the chin.

"I heard Lydia is moving into Ruth's dawdi haus. Is that true?" Edie asked as she broke a cookie in half, nibbling around the edges until both halves disappeared and she picked up another and repeated the process.

"Ja, and Ruth couldn't be happier. She's been lonely, I expect, since she lost Levi a couple years ago, and her *grossmammi* before that. Having Lydia in the house will be like having her grossmammi back again." Mary picked up a cookie and bit into the soft, gingery goodness. "Mmm. I love your ginger snaps, Maem."

Edie glowed with pleasure and gestured for Mary to continue with her story. "And Jonas doesn't mind?"

"Ach, no! He's a gut man. He encouraged Ruth to ask Lydia to move in after Lydia's house burned down during the blizzard this winter."

Edie opened her mouth to reply, but a firm knock on the kitchen door interrupted and caused Hope to leap to the floor to investigate.

Edie set her cup down on the table and pushed to her feet. "Now, who could that be? I'm not expecting anyone, are you?"

Mary shook her head, and Hope wound around Edie's ankles and then strolled over to the door and stood looking up at it expectantly.

"Would you look at that? She wants to see who's here!" Edie exclaimed.

"So do I, Maem," Mary said with a smile. "Why don't you open the door?" She could make out the shape of a broad-shouldered man through the cream curtains hanging over the window in the door, but that was all.

"I will, I will. It's probably Germaine Stoltzfus come to talk about the pies we're going to bake for the fundraiser next weekend."

"I don't think it's Mrs. Stoltzfus," Mary said as Edie wiped her hands on her apron and opened the kitchen door. Instead of her mother's stout and matronly friend, a strange man stood at the door. As soon as he saw Edie, he smiled reassuringly.

"Good morning, ma'am. I'm sorry to intrude, but I seem to have gotten turned around, and I'm lost. Can you please tell me where the Hostetler farm is?"

Mary peered around her mother. The stranger was tall and slim, with the broad shoulders hinted at through the window curtains on the kitchen doorway. He was dressed like a working man in denim jeans rather than homemade pants—so probably not Amish, though possibly Mennonite—and a blue chambray work shirt. His lack of a beard told her he wasn't married, though that wasn't a reliable indicator if he wasn't Amish, and the thought caused a warmth to spread throughout her body. Confused, she stared at the floor. How could a stranger have this effect on her? Especially one who probably didn't share her faith?

"Sure, you're not far." Edie stepped outside to join the man on the stoop and pulled the screen door closed behind her to keep the curious kitten inside. She pointed down the road to the south. "See, you go about half a mile and turn at the big white barn with the huge oak. The Hostetler place is just a ways along on the left. It won't take you five minutes in your truck."

Mary felt a surge of disappointment. If he was driving a truck, he definitely wasn't Amish. So no beard didn't necessarily mean no wife. Although how that should affect her, she couldn't imagine, she scolded herself silently.

"Thanks. Oh, and my name is Reuben King. Please excuse me for not mentioning it before."

Edie looked closely at the clean-cut young man. "King, you say? You wouldn't be the new *dokder*, would you? Took over from old Doc Smith over in Willow Creek?"

"Yep, that's me, Mrs. . . ?"

"Ach! My manners. I'm Edie Yoder, and this is my daughter, Mary," she said, standing aside and gesturing into the kitchen.

Mary felt the stranger's keen gaze on her and slowly lifted her eyes to meet his. Her breath caught in her chest, and she felt lightheaded. "How do you do?" she murmured.

He grinned at her, his teeth flashing white in his tanned face. Little crinkles were revealed at the corners of his eyes, which Mary saw were an unusual shade of brown, almost amber. He wasn't a very young man, she mused, nor was he much older than her own twenty-nine years. He looked fit and healthy and like he must spend a good deal of time outdoors to have that natural tanned look to his face.

"It's nice to meet you, Mary, Mrs. Yoder." His voice was smooth and somehow reassuring.

You just felt like trusting the guy, Mary reflected. Handy thing in a doctor.

"Well, you may as well come in and have a glass of lemonade," Edie invited, snapping Mary out of her reverie. She stood back to let him enter. "Mary made it a little while ago. It should be gut and cold by now."

"I wouldn't want to interrupt your work," he protested.

"No problem. We just finished putting the laundry up, and we haven't started supper yet. As you can see, we are enjoying a short break. We have time to be neighborly to a new member of the community. Sit yourself down!"

She shooed him in like a mother hen with an errant chick, and he smiled again before taking a seat at the table next to Mary. She saw his glance at her crutches, and though his eyes widened slightly, he didn't intrude with questions.

Edie showed no such compunction.

"What takes you out to the Hostetler place this afternoon, Dokder?"

"Maem!" Mary said. "That's not our concern."

"Ach! I know you're right. I just want to make sure our neighbors are all right."

"I don't imagine Dr. King would be sitting here drinking lemonade if they weren't, ain't so?" Mary pointed out.

"True, true, I don't suppose he would." Edie laughed. "Would you rather have some hot tea?"

"Um, no, lemonade actually sounds perfect."

"Gut, gut, and as I thought, it's just right!" She pulled the pitcher from the propane-powered fridge and poured a generous glass of sweet, icy lemonade. "There you go! Drink your mouth empty!"

"*Denki!*" he said, savoring a sip of lemonade. A look of surprised pleasure passed over his face. He said to Mary, "This is truly excellent lemonade."

She felt herself blushing again. "Denki. It's probably the mint. It adds a nice zip." Hope, who had disappeared from the room when the doctor entered, chose that moment to zoom back in, clattering down the back stairs and whipping around the corner to disappear again into the living room.

Reuben looked surprised. "Was that a tiny tornado?"

Mary snorted, much to her dismay, but felt better when Reuben turned and grinned appreciatively at her. "*Nee*, it was my kitten, Hope."

"She behaves like a tornado sometimes, though, so it's not a bad description, you have to admit," Edie said. She ignored Mary's eye roll and continued. "So, Dokder"—she twinkled at the younger man as she pushed the plate of ginger snaps in his direction—"did your wife come to Willow Creek with you, or are you giving us a try before you decide to move your family here?"

Mary cringed. Her mother was a wonderful woman, but subtle she was not.

"Please, call me Reuben," he said, obligingly selecting a fragrant cookie from the plate. "And I'm not married, Mrs. Yoder." He bit into the cookie and made a low hum of pleasure before devouring the rest. Then he tipped up his glass to get the last drops of lemonade, making Edie beam with pleasure at his obvious enjoyment.

"I'm Edie. Would you like another glass?"

"No, but thank you very much. I've never tasted its equal." He stood and held out his hand first to Edie and then to Mary. "I'd better be getting on over to the Hostetlers'. They invited me to supper tonight as a welcome to the community. Denki for the hospitality!"

"You're welcome," Mary said softly.

Her mother accompanied the doctor to the door, opening it for him. "You're welcome to stop in any time you're in the neighborhood, Reuben," she invited. "Mary also bakes excellent cookies to go with her wunderbar lemonade!"

He looked over at Mary and smiled. "I might just do that." He nodded at them both, then trotted down the steps and over to his truck. He fired up the engine, glanced back at the house and, seeing Edie still standing there, saluted her before heading down the driveway and turning toward the Hostetler farm.

"Maem! Come inside, what are you doing?"

"I'm just waving the nice young man on his way. What's wrong with that?"

Mary sighed. "Nothing, Maem. But there's little point in informing our new town doctor of my talent as a baker. He'd hardly be interested in me. Also, you baked these cookies. It wasn't quite honest leading him to believe they're mine."

Edie waved away that small detail. "Pfft. Yours are even better."

"Still. . ."

"Still what? There's no harm done. Next time we'll be sure to give him your cookies. In fact, we should invite him to dinner here to welcome him to the community! He could see what a gut cook you are! I wish I'd thought of it before he left for the Hostetlers."

"Oh, Maem, the poor man was just here to ask directions, and we bushwhacked him. Besides, he's not Amish. And as I said, if he were, he wouldn't be looking at me for his *fraa*."

Edie turned sharply toward her oldest child. "Now, Mary, don't you talk like that! You're a lovely woman with a lot to offer any man smart enough to look past your slight disadvantage. My goodness, child, being able to walk quickly isn't the be-all and end-all of human existence, you know! And as for his faith, well, I hear he's Mennonite, and that's not so different. He might even convert!" With that, she picked up the basket of folded laundry and marched up the back stairs, muttering under her breath about her silly daughter. Mary sighed and shook her head. She'd been called worse, though not often by her mother, who had always been very supportive of her eldest child's challenges. At the same time, she'd refused to allow Mary to grow up thinking of herself as helpless or as less than other people. Consequently, Mary held down a good job making functional yet beautiful baskets for Jonas Hershberger. And she held her own when it came to household chores as well. She couldn't do everything, but then, who could?

"I don't suppose there's really any reason I couldn't marry and make some man a gut fraa, if I wanted to," she mused. The new doctor's odd amber eyes popped into her head, which she shook impatiently.

"Enough. Maem, I'm going to start supper!"

Pushing up from the table, Mary grabbed her crutches and made her determined way toward the fridge to get out the ingredients for that night's meal.

Later that evening, Reuben steered his old black Chevy pickup out of the Hostetlers' driveway and toward town and the combination house and office he was renting from Doc Smith. He'd enjoyed his supper and had found the Hostetlers, a Mennonite family, to be quite hospitable and welcoming. Of course, the fact that they had four unmarried daughters in their late teens and early twenties may have had something to do with their welcome of the young, single doctor.

"Careful, Reuben, you're becoming a cynic," he told himself. "They were a perfectly nice family, even if their conversation did tend toward cattle." He smiled as he recalled the heated debate between Mr. Hostetler—Paul—and his widowed brother, George Hostetler, about the relative merits of Angus versus Hereford beef cattle. It seemed Paul's family raised Angus beef cattle, while George's cattle were Herefords.

"I like them both, as far as a good steak goes," Reuben had mused. "And that's about all I know about either breed!"

Still, the dinner and the company had been very nice. And only the most recent such invitation he'd received since moving to town. He was slowly getting to know the various members of his new community. He'd only been in town about a month, but many people, English, Amish, and Mennonite, had gone out of their way to stop in and say hello, drop off some fresh butter or eggs, and invite him to dinner, church services, even a barn raising. He felt welcomed here.

As he passed the Yoder place, he smiled, remembering the shameless questioning of Mrs. Yoder and her pretty daughter's obvious discomfort, especially when the older woman dropped a couple of hints about Mary's suitability as a potential wife for him. He shook his head. Mothers were all the same, he supposed. His own mother, back in Lancaster, Pennsylvania, had tossed up her hands and given up hope of ever having grandchildren. "My son, the dokder!" she'd said. "You know I'm sinfully proud of you, but I still want to cuddle some babies before I die!"

Now that all the years of college, medical school, and residency were behind him, he felt ready to take a deep breath and slow down a little, maybe start to think about establishing his own home and family. Plenty of people got married during medical training, but he'd felt the need to concentrate all his efforts on becoming a physician and didn't think it would be fair to a woman to place her second in his priorities.

His thoughts drifted to Mary Yoder, who apparently needed two crutches to get around. But when Reuben thought of her, it was her gentle smile and lovely eyes that came to mind, not her physical challenges.

"She's a lot like Eliza," he mused, thinking of his younger sister with a smile. Ever the doctor, he couldn't help being curious about Mary. "I wonder what's been done to rehab her injuries," he murmured as he pulled into Willow Creek, driving down Main Street and parking in front of his new digs.

Carrying the bag of fresh sweet corn he'd been given by the Hostetlers, he unlocked the glass front door of what had once been a gracious home but now held his clinic and his living quarters. The place was owned by the previous doctor, Dr. Smith, who had retired and moved with his wife of forty-five years to Florida.

"Don't worry, son," he'd told Reuben when he handed over the keys to the building. "You'll do fine. And when you decide to stay, I'll sell you the place for a fair price, like old Doc Schwartz did me back in 1980."

"If I decide to stay," Reuben had reminded the older man, who had chuckled and said something about the Hotel California as he climbed into his car, making his wife laugh as they pulled away.

"You can check out any time you like, but you can never leave," he murmured the lyrics to the old song to himself as he checked the first floor before heading upstairs. "Doesn't seem like a month has passed already," he mused, putting the corn into the refrigerator and pouring himself a glass of iced tea to take into the living room. He plopped down onto the couch, which, like all the furniture, had come with the place, and turned on the television to see what sports he could find.

He was hoping for a baseball game, but he seemed to be out of luck there. He found harness racing and settled back with his feet up on the sagging leather ottoman. He reflected that many standardbreds, once retired from racing, ended up being purchased by Amish folk to pull their buggies. And that led his thoughts back to Mary Yoder. "I wonder when she last got checked out? Maybe there's still something that could be done."

The Hostetlers had filled him in on the terrible buggy accident that had claimed Mary's father's life and taken much of the use of her legs from her. She'd been, what? Three? Four?

"A lot of time has passed. Could be too late."

He grabbed his laptop and began researching developments in the treatment of spine, leg, and hip injuries over the last twenty-five years or so. Soon he was deeply engrossed, the television forgotten. Suddenly, a thought occurred to him, and he sat up straight. Had Mary been one of old Doc Smith's patients? If so, her records were very likely right downstairs, and he could find out exactly what was wrong with her legs. Jumping up, he hurried downstairs. He'd worry about the question of whether it was ethical to poke into the old medical records of a grown woman who wasn't currently his patient later, he decided. Right now, he was seized with an urgent need to see if he could help her. He didn't question these occasional obsessions that grabbed him by the throat from time to time. This was part of the personality that had led him to become a doctor against tall odds—so that he could help people like Mary live better lives.

With that shaky justification in his mind, he began to search through old files lining the walls of his office. He'd see what he'd see and worry about how to approach the Yoders with it later.

CHAPTER TWO

"Here, chick chick chick!"

Seated in an old metal chair, Mary tossed handfuls of feed in practiced arcs as the colorful birds she bred ran this way and that trying to gobble up as much as possible. "Ah, the sun feels gut on my face after all the rain we've had," she told the birds, who didn't bother to answer. She chuckled at the antics of the greedy birds as they hurried to and fro trying to beat each other to each kernel of grain that bounced on the ground.

"There's plenty for all of you, you know."

"So, you talk to chickens," a deep voice said. "Could be a sign of something serious."

Mary started, nearly tipping her chair as Reuben, who had made no sound as he approached, stepped forward and grabbed the chair to steady it. Her crutches, leaning on the back, slid onto the ground.

For a moment Reuben loomed over Mary, caging her awkwardly between his large body and the chair. They stared at each other as the moment dragged on, until Mary broke eye contact and exclaimed, "Ach! I'm so clumsy. Would you please hand me my crutches?"

Reuben quickly straightened and took a step back from the chair before bending to comply with her request. Mary avoided his eyes while she strove to bring the confusion caused by his unexpected nearness under control.

"I'm so sorry," he said. "You aren't clumsy. I surprised you. I apologize."

Having run out of plausible reasons to avoid it, Mary raised her eyes to his. She bit her lip. "I just didn't hear you before you spoke. I was caught up in my chore. The chickens are sort of my pets."

Reuben glanced at a second chair sitting near Mary's, and he nodded at it, seeking permission to sit down.

"Oh! Ja, of course! Make yourself comfortable. After I finish here, I'll get you a cold drink, and you can tell me why you've stopped by."

Reuben sat down, folding his tall frame into the old-fashioned metal chair. "You don't need to trouble yourself about a drink, Mary. I didn't come here to add to your workload."

"Nonsense." She dared a glance at him that revealed a mischievous twinkle in her eyes. "My mudder would insist!"

A slow smile spread across his handsome face, making Mary's heart race, and he chuckled. "Well then, mustn't disappoint your mudder! Got any more of that marvelous lemonade?"

Collecting herself once more, Mary nodded. "I do. Let me finish with my chickens, and we can go in for a glass."

She scattered the remaining feed from the bucket in her lap and laughed as the chickens zoomed around, greedily snapping it up. Then she placed the bucket on the ground, grabbed her crutches, and pushed to her feet. She was gratified that the doctor didn't try to help. She couldn't explain even to herself why such gestures embarrassed and even annoyed her, but they did, and that was a fact.

Reuben picked up the empty feed bucket. "Where does this go?"

Mary pointed with her chin to the neat white shed beside the large chicken coop. "There's a hook on the wall above the feed bins, if you wouldn't mind."

He hung the bucket on the indicated hook before taking a quick look around. Mary followed him inside and watched him visually explore the space.

His eyebrows climbed toward his hairline, and he whistled low. The shed wasn't only a storage area for the chicken feed and other tools Mary would need to care for her birds. It was also obviously a workroom. Stepping farther into the space, Reuben peered at the tools lined up neatly along a counter, as well as the boxes, baskets, and bins placed with care so that whoever worked there wouldn't need to get up to fetch anything they needed. A skylight was set into the ceiling of the space to provide additional illumination.

Hanging on a wall adjacent to the work area was an amazing collection of colorful trout flies, creatively and skillfully fashioned out of rooster feathers, fur, and twine.

"It's sort of a hobby of mine."

"This is. . .amazing! I've never seen the like."

Mary felt a blush steal over her face. "It's not that much, just a hobby, like I said. Makes me a little extra money."

He glanced at the flies again. "May I look more closely?"

She shrugged. "Sure, why not? Here, let me turn on this lantern, and you'll be able to see better." She reached around him and turned on a battery-operated lantern hanging from the wall.

He stepped closer and carefully plucked up a small compact lure with upright wings made from rooster hackle feathers and a long, double tail and a small hook. He examined it, then turned to her. "What kind is this?"

She bit her lip. "That's a dry fly. It floats on top of the water, like an adult insect. It's my favorite lure to make because you can see the trout take it. I was going for a mayfly with that one, but there are several different types."

He nodded and replaced it carefully, picking up another small lure, this one green and brown, fat and heavy with its bead head and thicker hook. It obviously wouldn't float. He turned it this way and that before turning to look inquiringly at Mary.

"That one is a wet fly. It imitates the newly hatched stage of an insect and is designed to bump along the bottom like a nymph searching for food in the gravel or sediment. I also make streamers, heavier lures that jerk along just under the surface of the water—really hard for a hungry fish to resist. And I make emergers, which imitate an insect just trying to break free from the water through the surface film to become an adult. There are other types of fly-fishing lures, but I like these best to fish with, and to make."

She gestured to a line of colorful lures, some with long feathers trailing from tightly tied centers, others stubby and weighted to sink to the bottom. No two were alike, but each conveyed the essence of a water insect in the various stages of aquatic insect life. "I have a lot of fun making these, and the fact that I raise my own roosters makes it even more satisfying."

"Mary, these are amazing. Where did you learn to make them?" He reverently trailed his index finger along the row of rooster-tailed trout lures.

She felt heat creeping up her neck and face, and she hoped the shadowy workspace hid her reaction to his praise. "My *grossdaddi* taught me to fly-fish and showed me basic lure-making techniques. I got really interested in my teens and found books on the subject at the library and on the internet. After I read everything I could get my hands on, I started creating my own designs."

Reuben let out a low whistle. "Wow, I'm impressed. And you raise the roosters for their feathers?"

"Ja. My roosters are bred specifically for their feathers. But we eat them too, of course, as it would be wasteful not to."

He nodded thoughtfully. "Do these feathers come from the birds outside?" He stepped back outside and surveyed the satisfied-and-healthy-looking flock of birds still scratching around in the grass and dirt for any missed feed.

"No. Some of those are my laying hens, you know, for eggs, and the rooster for that flock, Henry. And also the hens from my feather line not currently sitting on eggs. My feather roosters are all inside the big barn in individual cages. You can't let them run free, or they'll peck each other's feathers out."

"That would be counterproductive, I suppose," he commented, looking toward the big barn across the spacious barnyard. "May I see the rest of your operation?"

She shrugged. "Why not? Come on. We can get that lemonade afterward."

They strolled in companionable silence across the wide space, and when they reached the large white barn, Reuben opened the door and stood aside for Mary to pass through before him. She nodded her thanks and maneuvered inside. He followed and was surprised to find the space well-lit with overhead lights illuminating several dozen roomy wire cages along two walls. In the center of the room were several dozen more spacious cages containing brooding hens or hens with chicks.

"Wow, I'm seriously impressed," Reuben said. "I didn't expect anything this grand. You're a serious breeder, aren't you?"

Although she felt another blush stealing across her cheeks, Mary held her head up proudly. She'd worked hard on her line of hackle roosters, and she wasn't going to pretend otherwise.

"Ja, I am. I have a waiting list of people who want to purchase fertilized eggs from me."

"I'm not surprised. These birds are just beautiful." He strolled quietly along the line of rooster cages, each separated by several feet to keep the birds away from each other and reduce stress. "Mary, this is amazing. I didn't know we had anything like this in the area. Nobody told me. Don't people know you do this?"

She grimaced and shrugged. "No, not really. I mean, people know I breed roosters and make lures, but I don't go around advertising how valuable these birds are. I wouldn't want people to think about stealing them."

"Ja, I can see that." He crouched down to study a particularly glorious bird. "This fellow is just gorgeous."

She smiled, genuinely pleased. "He's part of an experimental breeding program I'm trying out. He's from the third generation, and I think it's going to be a winner. I'll probably give the breed a name with the next generation."

He turned to stare at her. "Wait. You've created a whole new breed of chicken?"

"Well, I'm working on it. The genetics are pretty complex, but as a physician you no doubt understand how all that works?"

He nodded, and she continued. "Ja, probably better than I do. Anyway, you breed for the hackle feathers, which are the most important for creating the dry fly lures. This all goes back to just a couple of breeders, who really pioneered this entire industry. There are only half a dozen companies in the country creating really gut lures. And I'm trying to break in and join their ranks. I'm considered a bit of an upstart, especially because I'm a woman, and these people don't even know I'm Amish." An impish smile played around her generous mouth at the thought. But when she saw Reuben's face blank and his eyes suddenly become riveted on her lips, she recalled herself and snapped herself back to the subject at hand. She'd wonder what that meant later. "But my results speak for themselves. My lures float just right on or below the surface of the water, and they turn very satisfactorily when you cast them. It all translates into catching a lot of fish, with a pretty piece of craftsmanship."

Feeling a bit embarrassed at his momentary lapse when Mary had smiled so winsomely, Reuben tried to follow the topic so he wouldn't look like a green kid getting his first glimpse of a pretty girl, but he found himself forgetting about how impressed he was with her enterprise and simply admiring how simply lovely she was. He'd noticed the other day when he'd met her that she was very pleasant looking, but the kitchen had been dim and he'd been standing outside in the bright sunlight, looking in. Once he'd been invited inside, Mary had kept her head down much of the time, shyly avoiding his attempts to catch her eye. Consequently, he hadn't really appreciated her beauty, noticing instead her crutches and her labored movements in the brief time he'd been there—purely a professional observation, based on his training as a doctor.

Now, under the bright lights inside her poultry barn, with the look of eager interest in her subject matter shining on her intelligent face, Mary was more than just pretty, she was stunning. Reuben was surprised he'd failed to notice the other day. But then, when a professional problem caught his interest, he often wore blinders to all else.

Which reminded him—he hadn't come here today to admire her chickens or her lures, no pun intended. He'd come to discuss what he'd found in Dr. Smith's medical records.

And he wasn't at all sure he'd receive a positive response from this remarkable woman, who obviously didn't let her disability slow her down in the least.

Unsure how to proceed, he decided he might as well just dive right in. If she was offended, he'd be sorry. If she was angry, he'd deal with it.

"Um, Mary, I'm very impressed with your operation here, and I'd love to see more and learn about it in greater detail another time. But today, I actually came over to discuss something more specific, if you have a few minutes?"

She looked at him carefully, the enthusiasm dimming noticeably in her eyes. He had the uncomfortable feeling people didn't often indulge her interest in her birds, and he wished he'd held his tongue and let her talk more about the chickens, and waited for another time to broach what was certain to be a touchy topic.

"Ja? Well, sure, we can go inside and have that lemonade now, and you can tell me what's on your mind, Dokder. You'll have to forgive me if I went on too long about my little hobby here."

He grimaced as she turned and headed for the door. He'd struck a nerve, and again regretted the bad timing. But now there was no help for it, so he followed her from the barn, pulling the door closed firmly behind him. He wouldn't want to be responsible for letting a predator inside that particular chicken coop!

Now he just had to find the right way to present his idea to Mary, and he had no idea what he was going to say.

CHAPTER THREE

"Mary, I really did enjoy seeing your breeding operation, and I would love to hear more another day. Really, I mean it."

Mary kept walking laboriously toward the house, seemingly ignoring Reuben as he trudged along in her wake. When they reached the kitchen door, he hurried around her to open it, and she stopped and narrowed her eyes at him.

"Dokder King, I appreciate your kindness, but there's no need to pretend an interest you don't feel. I'm used to people finding my fascination with those birds to be a bit, well, odd. No need to feel bad about it. Now, let's go in and have that lemonade, and you can tell me why you came."

She preceded him into the kitchen, and he followed, knowing he'd messed up but not sure how to fix it. He'd have to leave that for another day, he decided, stepping into the cozy interior of the farmhouse and hanging his hat on a hook by the kitchen door. The pretty calico kitten he'd glimpsed the other day was snoozing on a cushion by the stove. It pried one eye open to peer at them before settling back down to its nap.

"Sit yourself down."

"Can I help with anything?"

Mary hung her crutches on a hook beside the propane-powered refrigerator, put her hands on the counter, and let her chin drop to her chest. Reuben couldn't see her face, but he had the feeling she was gathering her thoughts. He started to speak, hoping to salvage the visit, but Mary held up one hand to stop him, and he closed his mouth and held his peace.

She sighed deeply and turned slowly to look at him, resignation on her pretty face. "Look, I apologize for being a bit prickly. It isn't often I get a new victim to show off my chickens and lures to. Denki for your interest." She smiled, and he couldn't help feeling it was a bit forced.

"My interest is real, Mary. Your lures are works of art, and the roosters are beautiful. I'd like very much to see more of your operation another day."

She stared at him with a look of frank skepticism in her cornflower blue eyes. "Really?"

"Ja, really," he said. "I have no reason to lie to you."

He could see her considering that, and hoped she'd accept his word, which was only the truth. Finally, she nodded, and a small, embarrassed smile crossed her face. "Well then. How about that lemonade?"

"I'd like that." He sat back and breathed a sigh of relief as she turned to open the refrigerator door and hefted a large glass pitcher of lemonade, which she placed on the counter. She filled two pretty blue glasses Reuben thought looked like handblown Mexican glass with the cold beverage, then turned back to Reuben.

"You may carry the glasses and the pitcher to the table if you like. I'll get some cookies I baked this morning."

He scrambled up from the table and hurried to carry out her request as she took a blue earthenware plate down from another cabinet, opened a cookie jar shaped like a rooster, and placed a handful of delicious-looking cookies onto the plate, which she nudged in his direction. He took the plate and put it on the table as well before returning to his seat.

Mary left the crutches where they were, steadying herself on the back of a chair and taking a seat across from Reuben. Looking around, he realized the kitchen was set up to be convenient for her to use without having to move all around to complete a chore.

"Shall we thank *Gott*?"

He nodded and bowed his head, silently giving thanks for both the lovely snack he was about to enjoy and for the company of this unusual, sometimes prickly, and very interesting young woman. When he finished, he raised his head to find Mary watching him. He smiled.

"Well, these cookies look scrumptious. What are they?"

"They're peach cobbler cookies. I got the recipe from the *Taste of Home* cookbook and played with it a little bit. They're gut alone or as an ice cream sandwich."

He picked one up and took a bite. His eyes grew large as the flavor of fresh peaches and rich butter flooded his mouth.

"Oh my gosh, these are amazing!" He took a sip of lemonade and smiled blissfully. "Mary, not only do you make an art out of tying fishing lures, but you're an artist in the kitchen as well!"

She smiled at him and took a bite of her own cookie. "Go on and butter me up. It can't hurt," she joked.

Reuben lost his train of thought as he found himself pulled into the simple joy of Mary's smile. Her blue eyes crinkled at the corners and a dimple appeared in her right cheek. He watched her enjoy a bite of cookie, and swallowed as pleasure washed over her mobile features. Then her eyes met his, and her smile turned into a puzzled frown.

"Um, do I have something in my teeth?"

He shook himself, embarrassed at his lapse. "What?"

She giggled, a sound he hadn't heard the normally self-contained young woman make before.

"You were just sitting there staring at me. I figured I must have something caught in my teeth."

"No, no, sorry. I got lost in thought. Um, about what I came to talk to you about today." He stuffed the rest of his cookie into his mouth and washed it down with icy lemonade while he composed his thoughts.

She quirked an eyebrow.

He took a deep breath, thinking Mary was nothing like you'd think at first glance. Where was the shy woman he'd first met? Replaced by a much more interesting woman, he reflected.

"Okay, I hope you take this the right way—whatever way that is. The fact is, I. . .may have overstepped my boundaries, but I felt it was for a gut cause."

"Goodness, this does sound serious. I don't offend easily. Just say whatever it is, and I'll tell you if this time is an exception."

He nodded. "It's. . .it's about your legs, Mary. I think there may be a way to make your legs work better, if you'll just trust me."

Mary gasped with surprise. She didn't know what she'd expected to hear, but that wasn't it. Although, come to think of it, the man was a doctor, so what else did she think he'd want to talk to her about if not her health? It wasn't as if he were there to court her.

But she still felt unaccountably let down, as if he'd somehow led her on and then disappointed her. Which absolutely was not the case, was it?

She thought back on the past half hour. She had to admit to herself that he'd said nothing at all to give her any cause for the disappointment coursing through her, but she still felt like crying.

"Mary?" Reuben's voice broke into her thoughts, his obvious concern making her feel even worse.

"Oh! Now I'm the one woolgathering." She forced a smile.

He wasn't fooled. "I'm so sorry. I'm *doppich* sometimes when I get excited about something."

She bit her lip. Good manners dictated that she put him at ease. "You're not clumsy. I just didn't see that coming. I'm not sure why. I'm not generally slow. And why else would you come to see me?"

When he started to protest, she held up a hand. "Dokder, please, we both feel *deerich* enough."

"Why should we feel foolish? I admit to being a bit *verhuddelt*, but I don't feel foolish, and neither should you."

"I'm sorry to confuse you, but really, let's move on. What do you think can be done about my legs after all these years? I doubt there's an exercise I haven't tried. I still stick to a strict daily physical therapy regimen to keep from stiffening up. And not to be rude, but honestly, why do you care?"

He looked surprised. "Why do I care? Well, because I'm a doctor, and because you're an amazing woman, and if there's anything I can do to lessen your pain and improve your mobility, then why wouldn't I want to do so?"

"You think I'm amazing?"

"Well, ja. Despite the fact that you're in pain pretty much all the time, and that walking is more of a chore for you than for most people, you don't slow down for a moment. You don't merely exist—you live. You could give most people lessons."

Mary's mouth dropped open, and she stared at the doctor, who now looked a bit embarrassed at his impassioned little speech. He shrugged and smiled sheepishly. "Well, it's true. You set a very gut example."

Reuben's words made Mary feel good, even if he was only interested in her as a patient. She hadn't honestly expected such an interesting, vibrant man to see her in any other way. And if that stung just a wee bit, well, it was nothing she hadn't felt before, and nothing she couldn't ignore and put behind her.

Determined to get over her silliness, she smiled at him and handed the plate of cookies across the table to him. "Okay, Dokder, let's hear what you've got."

He took another cookie and studied her with a wary expression. "Then, you're not mad at me?"

She shook her head. "No, I'm not mad, I'm curious. You have to understand, I was injured when I was very young. I've seen many, many physicians, and I've gone through more than my share of surgeries. Believe it or not, I'm much better than I was early on. . .much better than any of those physicians expected me to be. I count myself blessed."

"You count yourself blessed?" He looked amazed.

"Well, ja. . ."

He interrupted. "For goodness' sake, Mary, stop calling me dokder. My name is Reuben. Please use it."

Mary was taken aback. "All right. Reuben. I was just being polite. After all, we don't know each other very well. And you are a dokder."

"That's true. But I'm not your dokder, and I don't intend to be!"

"You. . .don't?"

He looked surprised at his own outburst, but after a moment, he shook his head. "No. This sort of thing is not my field. But I confess that I did look at your old records in Dr. Smith's old files. Please *vergib mir* if you feel I overstepped. But I really want to help."

Mary wasn't sure how to feel about all this. He'd gone into her old files? That seemed intrusive. On the other hand, he was the new town doctor, and the files were now his, weren't they? And since old Dr. Smith had been her doctor since birth and Reuben had taken over his practice, didn't that, in fact, make Reuben her doctor?

But maybe she didn't want him to be. Maybe she wanted him to be something else entirely.

She shook her head and mentally pulled back on her reins. Not going there! Then she noticed that Reuben seemed to be waiting for her to say something. She reviewed the conversation to figure out what he'd said last. Right. The files.

She blew a puff of air from her lips and shrugged. "Well, it seems to me that from a certain point of view—a very legitimate point of view, most would agree—you had every right to review those old files. You took over Dr. Smith's practice, so it stands to reason you also took over Dr. Smith's patients, ja?"

Mary thought Reuben looked a bit dismayed yet relieved all at once, and it was all she could do not to laugh at him.

"So, now that you know I'm not angry, please go on. What is your idea? Do you really think there's more that can be done?"

"Well, I can't be sure because, as I said, this isn't my specialty. But medicine continually marches forward, and breakthroughs are made daily. I'm not saying you'll walk normally, and I'm not saying you'll be pain-free. But I think it's possible that you could have a significant improvement in both areas. You could experience improved mobility and a reduction in your everyday pain level. Would you be interested in exploring that?"

He sat back and waited.

Mary absentmindedly picked up another cookie and bit in. On the surface of it, who wouldn't want those things? But anyone who had been through what she had would understand that one didn't just jump into more surgeries, more recovery time, more time lost at work—time lost from her life. And without any guarantee of success. Doctors had told her before that they could help, and the last two surgeries she'd endured hadn't really made much difference, but they'd been hard on her, and by extension, on her family and on her church community, which paid for them.

On the one hand, she appreciated his concern and didn't want to appear ungrateful. On the other, she just hated the idea of going through all that a surgery entailed again.

"Are you just talking about new exercises? Or would I have to go through another surgery? Because I do not want to do that!" She shuddered a bit at the thought. "The last one was very difficult and didn't offer me much relief. So what's the point in wasting time and money when I'm used to being the way I am?"

He blinked and looked away for a moment, as if gathering his thoughts. Then he looked back at her and frowned. "I can understand your hesitation, but if you could be better, feel better, isn't it worth a try? You'd have to be brave, but I think you are."

She just stared at him while thoughts and feelings swirled through her head and heart. He thought he could understand how she felt? She doubted it! He looked very fit, and she'd admired his easy, loose gait. He had no experience with what it was like to use crutches to get around, or of the pain that was so much a part of her life that she sometimes forgot about it. She felt herself becoming angry, and as sometimes happened when her temper became engaged, the normally soft-spoken young woman snapped, and spoke her mind in a very decided manner.

"I'd have to be brave? Ha! I'd like to know what you think brave means, if not going forward every day into a world where everyone else I know can just stride right out! Or dance or run. I couldn't play jump rope games as a child. I can't ride a horse. And most women my age are married with *bopplin* of their own, while I sit there admiring every new baby, my heart secretly breaking, always good old Aunt

Mary, always happy to hold someone else's boppli so they can go have fun! But I get up every day and do it again. I know what courage is, Dokder! It's smiling when your heart is breaking so you don't force your troubles onto other people. Don't tell me you understand, with your perfect body. You understand nothing about my life! Nothing!"

His eyes widened in dismay, and Mary felt bad. She knew—knew!—his intentions were gut. But he'd really touched a raw spot. Her face grew hot, and she felt the sting of tears in her eyes. She feared that if she tried to speak again, she'd cry or yell, and neither was an acceptable response to a man who was really just trying to help, even if he'd revealed his lamentable ignorance in the process. And he was a doctor!

She shook her head, disgusted with herself and disappointed in him. She suddenly felt exhausted, and she just wanted him to leave.

I won't feel guilty for being upset with him. I won't!

Mary sat up straighter and squared her shoulders. She could see that Reuben was at a loss for words, but fortunately, she now felt ready to supply her own. When he started to speak, with a look of confused dismay on his handsome face, she held up a hand.

"Wait, please. Let me speak first."

He nodded, and she paused to gather her thoughts. Then she dove in. "Look, I know you mean well. I do. But what you don't seem to understand is that my life is gut as it is. I'm not a burden on anyone."

"I never meant to imply. . ."

"Please let me finish. I earn my own living at the basket company, and then there's the money I bring in from my lures and rooster pelts. I'm a help to my mudder and *vader*, with the *youngie*, my brieder. I am a member of this community and of my church, and I like my life. Understand?"

When she looked at him expectantly, he nodded slowly, but when he would have said something, she again raised her hand. "Reuben, I don't know you. But you seem to be confused about what bravery is. Since I was four, I've been different from everyone else. People have always stared at me, either with pity at the poor little crippled Amish girl, or with the disgust some people feel for anyone they deem not normal.

"You're right, it hurts a whole lot just to get around. But I'm used to it. This community has already spent many thousands of dollars on surgeries that didn't miraculously turn me into a 'normal' girl. I can't ask them to spend anymore. And I can't have you giving my parents, especially my mudder, false hope again that her little girl can be a normal woman. I know I'll never get married, never have children of my own. But I refuse to feel sorry for myself. Got it?"

He nodded dumbly, and she pushed to her feet, grabbing her crutches and swinging toward the door, which she yanked open with more force than she'd intended. Refusing to let him see her embarrassment, she looked at him pointedly. "Gut. Then that's all I have to say. Good day, Dokder."

He stood awkwardly and walked toward her. "Um, I've obviously misstepped rather badly here. I'm really sorry for upsetting you. Can you forgive me?"

She held her head high and gave a stiff nod. "Of course I forgive you. Gott says we must forgive others as He forgives us. Besides, I know you meant no insult. You just don't know what you're talking about."

He bit his lip, then gave a nod. "Ja, you're right, I don't. And you've given me plenty to think about. I'm going. But in return, I want to give you something to think about, okay?" He dug into his coat pocket and pulled out a copy of an article, which he handed her. "It's a copy of an article I read a couple years ago in the *Journal of Family Medicine*. It addresses advances made in the treatment of spinal injuries like yours, suffered in childhood years ago. After you read that, if you're still not interested in hearing more, I'll leave it alone. If you do want to learn more, you can let me know. I won't bother you about it again, okay?"

He shoved the papers into her hands and strode past her and out the door. She watched him go, feeling a pang of regret that she would probably never speak to him again. She was surprised when he stopped halfway down the path through her yard. He paused a moment, his back to her, then turned and met her eyes, seemingly unsurprised to find her standing there.

"For the record, I'm not just here as a doctor. I happen to find

you interesting and attractive. So you can just think about that too."
He walked to his truck, climbed in, looked at her once more before
nodding at her, and then did a three-point turn and drove away down
the road toward town. A soft form rubbed against one of Mary's
ankles, and she glanced down to find Hope winding herself around
her legs. Bracing against one crutch, she reached down and scooped
up the little cat, holding her against her chest as she stared blindly
out into the farmyard.

"Well, little one, I'm not sure what to think. He says he finds me
interesting and attractive." She stifled a giggle at the strangeness of
the feelings Reuben's revelations had bubbling in her belly. "There's a
lot standing in the way of any possible romance between us, not least
of which is that he isn't Amish. But I have to confess to a tiny little
bit of hope and excitement. Do you think I'm a fool?"

Glancing at the article Reuben wanted her to read, she shook her
head. "Well, I guess there's no harm in reading this. It doesn't mean
I'll go farther."

She put the cat down, sat at the table, and began to read.

CHAPTER FOUR

Mary was sitting at the table woolgathering, absentmindedly stroking Hope's silky head, when her mother walked up behind her, startling her. She jumped a bit, and the cat gave an indignant squawk and jumped down to stalk away, tail in the air. Both women laughed at the kitten's antics.

"Gracious, Maem! You startled me!"

"Gracious, Mary! What are you doing sitting here staring into space?"

Mary laughed in spite of herself. Then she blew air between her lips and looked at her mother. "Nothing in particular. Dokder Reuben stopped by for a visit a bit ago. He was sorry to miss you and sent you his regards."

She picked up her forgotten cup of coffee, now quite cold.

"Oh?" Edie took Mary's mug and emptied it into the sink before pouring them each a fresh cup. She sat down next to her daughter and handed her the coffee. "What did the gut dokder want?"

Mary nodded her thanks for the fresh coffee and took a cautious sip. She frowned, considering what to say in answer to her mudder's question. She would never tell a lie, but sometimes full disclosure felt unnecessary. She decided to compromise.

"He has been going through the records he inherited from Doc Smith and came across the files about my accident and subsequent treatment. I guess he felt guilty about that for some reason, so he came here to tell me what he'd done."

After blowing on her hot coffee, Edie put the cup down on the table with a gentle *click* and looked at her daughter skeptically. "Really? A dokder felt guilty for going through the medical records in his own practice? Come, Mary, I've been your maem for almost thirty years, and I can tell when you aren't giving me the whole story."

Mary tried to look affronted. "Maem! Do you think I'd lie to you?"

"Not lie, no."

Mary breathed a sigh of relief, but it was premature. Her mother smiled knowingly and continued. "But I know perfectly well that you'd edit the story a bit if you thought it would make it easier for me to hear. So let's have the rest of it. Why did he come here today? Hmm?"

Mary rolled her eyes. She should know better than to try and fool her mother, who was pretty shrewd for an honest woman.

"Fine. He thinks there may be some new procedure that might let me walk more easily. He brought me an article he found on the subject, and he wanted me to read it."

Edie sat back in her seat with a sigh. "Ah. Now I understand why you're feeling grumpy. It's been quite a while since the last surgery, and that one didn't make much difference, did it?"

"No, it didn't," Mary confirmed. "But it cost the community plenty, and it caused you and *Dat* considerable trouble. I don't want to go through that again!"

"Your dat and I are not the ones who suffered through the surgery, *liebling*, not directly. That was you. And if you don't want to listen to what this young dokder has to say about new possibilities, then that's your business, and we won't interfere. Though if there were really something new that could help you get around better, with less pain, then it might be worth hearing about."

"It's not that I don't want to listen to him, Maem! But he might be wrong. He told me this is not his field. He only found some article in a medical journal, and now he's bound and determined for me to look into it, never mind how much trouble it'll cause in our lives and routines!"

Her mother chose a cookie from the plate still lying on the table and bit in, chewing contemplatively. She swallowed and drew a slow, deep breath, then let it out. "Mary, this is your business. All I'm saying is, dokders learn about new things by reading their journals, right? So, maybe just learn a little more before you decide against it, ja?"

Mary felt her eyes fill with tears, and she blinked furiously to keep them from falling. But her mother reached out and patted her hand where it rested on the table. "There, there, child. You don't need to make up your mind tonight. Let's start supper. Your dat and the boys will be in soon from chores, and they'll be powerful hungry." Edie indicated the papers sitting on the table. "Is this the article he wants you to read?"

Mary nodded, and Edie picked up the papers, folded them, and handed them to her daughter. "Well then, put them away where they'll be safe for now."

The older woman pushed herself to her feet and bustled about, gathering supplies for supper. Mary shoved the article into her apron pocket, then rubbed her eyes with her palms and began peeling potatoes her mother set before her. After a few minutes of silence, she looked up to find her mother regarding her.

"What?"

"Nothing, I'm just thinking."

"Maem, it would be expensive."

"You let the elders worry about that. We help each other in this community."

"Well, I've had my share and then some."

"Nobody's keeping count."

They worked in silence a bit longer, and then Mary bit out, "Maem, it would be so difficult. How can I. . .we. . .go through all that again? How?"

Edie put down the tray of dinner rolls she was preparing for the oven and walked over to sit beside Mary. She took her hand and smiled into her eyes. "But liebling, don't you remember what they say about difficulty?"

"I know, but. . ." Mary started to say, but her mother shook her head and smiled. "Difficulty is a miracle in its first stage, Mary. You just have to have faith."

Mary was silent for a moment, and then she looked at her mother. "I feel as if we're past the first stage, Maem."

Edie laughed softly. "Well then, you should be getting to the miracle pretty soon, ja?"

Mary shook her head in wonder at how her mudder could help her see things from different perspectives.

"Ja, I suppose so." Mary pulled the article from her apron pocket and smoothed it on the table. "I read this before you came in. It's interesting, and yes, it is something new. How about I read it to you while you make dinner, and then we can show it to Dat and see what we think?"

"*Oll recht*, you read it to me and I'll finish peeling the potatoes. Then we can talk about it. Maybe it won't work for you, but maybe it will."

"All right," Mary agreed, and while her mother puttered around in the cozy kitchen of their farmhouse, she read aloud about a relatively new procedure that might make her life a little better—or maybe not.

CHAPTER FIVE

The following week, Reuben was sitting in his office in town making notes in a patient file when his nurse practitioner, Rita Smythe, poked her head in the door.

"Whew! What a day. Mrs. Miller's ride finally arrived, and they just left. He had a flat tire that held him up."

"I thought it seemed pretty quiet in here all of a sudden." Reuben smiled. "Those Miller kids are full of energy, that's for sure!"

Rita, a petite brunette in the final trimester of her first pregnancy, grinned. "You're not kidding. Gut thing her sister-in-law, Elizabeth Miller, came with her to help ride herd on the kids. She works for Sophie Miller as a mother's helper when they go out. Seven little boys! Everyone needed shots, and the littlest has the sniffles. Of course, it's not Mrs. Miller's first rodeo, so she wasn't worried about the little guy, but with number eight due any day she wanted to get this bunch squared away. I was relieved it wasn't anything serious. Chicken pox is going around, and the Millers don't need that right now." She pressed her hand against the small of her back.

Reuben kicked back in his chair and scratched his chin thoughtfully. "Aren't they all vaccinated?"

"True. So any case would be mild. But let's not borrow trouble for Mrs. Miller. I wanted to tell you I'm leaving. I'll lock up on my way out."

"I'm leaving too. I need dinner, and I haven't had time to shop. I'm going to let Rebekkah talk me into her famous baked steak and mashed potatoes tonight."

"It would give me indigestion." Rita grimaced, walking out the door before her boss and checking the mailbox as he locked up. "Everything does these days."

He dropped his keys in his pocket and smiled at her. "Won't be too long now."

"Another six weeks at least. Forever. I'm huge. Maybe it's twins." She handed him a letter, the only mail that day. "Personal correspondence. People still write paper letters?"

He peered at the return address, and his face lit with pleasure. "My little sister does. I think I'll sit here on the porch and read this before I head to dinner. See you tomorrow, Rita. And if your back is bothering you, get that husband of yours to sit or stand behind you and massage gently with his thumbs. That'll help. And you can try heat or ice—whatever works."

She smiled and waved, then waddled toward the parking lot on the side of the building while Reuben settled into one of the comfy cushioned wicker chairs that had come with the building, and happily tore open his letter.

As he read, his eyebrows rose, and he grinned at his sister's humor. It seemed she was tired of their mother's increasingly pointed hints about finding a husband and was thinking of coming to see him for a visit. "I'd love that," he murmured as he turned the page over. He had three bedrooms above the practice, two of which were currently unused. Eliza would be a ray of sunshine in what Reuben suddenly realized was his very empty, and somewhat lonely, home.

He folded the letter and stuffed it into his pocket, deciding he'd write an answer inviting her to come as soon as she'd like when he returned from dinner. Whistling, he strolled the short distance to Rebekkah's Kitchen, thoughts of her tasty baked steak making his mouth water.

A block away, Mary Yoder stood to the side of her buggy as a helpful boy loaded a large bag of cat food into the buggy's trunk.

"Thanks for the help, Peter," she said as he closed the buggy's rear hatch.

"No problem, Mary." The tall, lanky youth smiled. "Need help with anything else?"

She shook her head. "No, I'm fine, denki. I'd better get home and feed Hope. I can't believe I ran out of cat food! She thinks she's starving, of course."

He laughed and turned to walk back into the store, when suddenly a cry of "Watch out!" rang through the parking lot, and the young man turned, eyes widening in alarm as he saw something behind Mary.

"Look out!" he cried, starting in her direction.

Before she could maneuver around to see what was happening, a pair of strong arms wrapped around her and jerked her to the side, and she found herself falling to the parking lot. She heard something that sounded like "Oomph!" as she landed, but instead of hitting the hard pavement, she landed on something—or someone—much more yielding.

That someone groaned, and alarmed, Mary scrambled to remove herself from what she realized was a man. She rolled slightly to the side but didn't manage to free herself fully from the tangle of arms and legs because she jarred her hip, causing her eyes to sting for a moment with tears. "Oh!" she whispered, looking around to see where her crutches had ended up, and trying to figure out what had happened.

"Miss! Are you okay? I'm so sorry. They just got away from me, and I couldn't catch them!"

Still a bit disoriented, Mary turned her head to see a middle-aged Englisher dressed in blue jeans and a neat gray work shirt hurrying toward her. "What?"

The man reached her at the same time as several other Good Samaritans, and he reached down to offer her a hand. She shook her head and suddenly found herself grasped by strong hands from beside her. She glanced around in alarm and discovered that the soft mass she'd landed on was none other than Reuben King, who grunted and said, "Mary, if you're okay, do you mind shifting off me? I can't breathe, and I don't want to dump you onto the hard pavement."

"Oh, Reuben! I'm so sorry! I have no idea what happened. How did you end up down there?"

"If you'll just let me shift you a bit, I'll explain."

The frantic workman, meanwhile, had picked up her crutches and was holding them out to her, but there was no way she could stand up from the ground without help. What a pickle!

"Mary, if you'll let me help you, we'll get the doctor out from under you and get you back on your feet," a calm voice offered. Mary glanced at the speaker and saw the minister from the Baptist church squatting down next to her, concern in his kind brown eyes.

"Oh! Pastor Dan! Denki, I would appreciate a bit of help. But please, don't yank me up."

"How should I help you?" he asked, slowly standing and looking down at her.

Reuben, meanwhile, had shifted himself to a sitting position, and Mary was fairly embarrassed to find herself sitting on his lap, and more people were coming over to see what all the fuss was about. The workman, who turned out to be a delivery driver for a food company, kept apologizing and explaining that two of his big barrels full of cooking oil had gotten away from him and rolled across the parking lot.

"I'd help, but I'm kind of trapped," Reuben joked, obviously trying to lighten the mood. "But I'd recommend holding out both hands and letting Mary grab onto your forearms. You can grasp hers in return, and slowly, gently, help her stand without yanking, okay, Pastor? I'll boost her from here. Is that all right, Mary?"

"Ja, that'll work," Mary said, hating to be the center of so much attention and just wanting to get in her buggy and drive home. "I'm strong. I can pull myself up if you give me your hands."

The pastor nodded, and a moment later she was standing. With a relieved sigh, she accepted her crutches from the worried driver.

"It's okay, I'm fine," she assured him.

He took off his hat and scratched his head, not convinced. "Miss, if those barrels had hit you, they'd have flattened you! I'm so sorry!

Nothing like this has ever happened to me before! How can I make it up to you?"

Mary just shook her head and watched Reuben climb gracefully to his feet, unaided, and brush himself off.

"That man is a hero!" the driver exclaimed. "He saved your life for sure. Or at least, kept you from getting hurt."

It seemed everyone in the small crowd that had gathered outside the grocery store had something to add, and the buzz of voices filled Mary's ears until she couldn't think.

She grimaced and put a hand to her head, and the deliveryman cried, "You are hurt! Oh no!"

"No, I'm really fine, it's just that I would like to sit down for a few minutes. Please, don't worry about me anymore. No harm was done."

Pastor Dan looked at Mary and then at Reuben, and leaned in to quietly say, "Say, Doc, maybe if you took Mary over to Rebekkah's for a bit, she could have something cold to drink and maybe a bite, until she gets over the shock. We wouldn't want her driving right now."

Reuben nodded. "That is a very good idea, denki."

Mary looked sharply at Reuben. He'd used the Pennsylvania Dutch term for "thank you," but he wasn't Amish. Was he? Come to think of it, this wasn't the first time she'd heard him use words from the language spoken by the Amish. She'd figured he'd just picked them up, but something about the way he said "denki" sounded like it was a part of him, not a borrowed word.

Unaware of her confusion, Reuben turned to Mary. "How about it? I was headed to Rebekkah's for dinner anyway. Why don't you let me get you something to eat, and then we'll get you home?"

Mary looked around at all the curious or concerned faces and wanted nothing more than to be safe in her own kitchen, but she knew the pastor was right. She wasn't in any condition to drive just then. And she was a bit hungry. To further embarrass her, her stomach picked that moment to let out a loud growl, and Pastor Dan smiled. "Sounds like your belly likes the plan, anyway." He looked around. "Okay, everyone, Mary is fine, as you can all see. Thanks for coming over to see if you could help, but thankfully no help is needed. You'd better get those barrels into the restaurant before someone helps themselves to them," he told the deliveryman, who glanced over at where the heavy barrels had come to rest against a sturdy wooden fence, amazingly doing no damage to it or apparently to themselves.

He nodded. "Okay, if you're sure you're okay, Miss?"

Mary nodded, and he reached into his pocket and pulled out his wallet, grabbing two twenty-dollar bills and thrusting them at Mary, who accepted them reflexively.

"At least let me buy you dinner. It'll make me feel better, really!" Before she could refuse, he'd tipped his hat and hurried over to get the first barrel, which he started rolling over toward the restaurant across the parking lot. The restaurant owner, meanwhile, was hurrying across the lot to help.

The people all murmured words of encouragement to Mary, and relief that she was unharmed, and wandered away to continue their days. Reuben indicated that Mary should lead the way, and she turned toward Rebekkah's Kitchen, just a short distance away.

Inside, they were greeted by a hostess, who seated them immediately, as the dinner rush hadn't gotten underway yet.

"Denki for suggesting this," Mary said in a low voice. "I'll be fine, but there's no harm in taking a few minutes to regroup, is there?"

"Absolutely not," Reuben agreed. "And honestly, I'm happy for the company. I'm used to the bachelor life, but eating alone gets old."

A server approached the table to take their orders. Reuben chose the baked steak dinner with mashed potatoes and green beans, while Mary decided on chicken and gravy over noodles, with a side of peas.

"Pure comfort food." She smiled as the server hurried off to put in their order and fetch their drinks. "Nothing like it sometimes!"

He nodded. "Are you certain you weren't injured? I took you down pretty hard."

She took a few moments to take stock and then shook her head. "I may be a bit sore in the morning, but I believe you took the brunt of it, cushioning me the way you did. I should be asking if you're hurt!"

He smiled wryly and stuck one leg out from under the table. "My jeans didn't fare very well, I'm afraid. I must have landed on this knee."

She looked at his leg and exclaimed in dismay, "Reuben! You've torn your pants, and you're bleeding! Why didn't you say you were hurt? I could have found someone to take me home while you saw to your injury."

He grinned at her. "Nice to know you care. But honestly, it looks worse than it feels. I just scraped my knee. I'll survive, even if the pants won't."

She was distressed and unsure what to say. He had endangered himself to keep her from harm—this man she hardly knew. "But you could have been seriously injured! Then how would you have worked? You should go home and take care of that before it gets infected."

"Who's the doctor here?" he asked, and when she flushed with embarrassment, he shook his head. "Mary, I'm fine. I'm hungry, and I don't want to miss out on Rebekkah's famous baked steak. Stop fretting, okay? When I saw those barrels rolling your way and knew you didn't see them, I was more concerned with getting to you before they flattened you like a steamroller than with anything else. Then I was worried I'd hurt you when I knocked you out of the way. I'm glad you're uninjured, and frankly, a little scraped knee is a very small price to pay. Okay?"

Reluctantly, Mary nodded. "Fine. But you're being totally honest with me, aren't you? You'd tell me if you were hurt worse than that scrape?"

He looked at her serious expression and smiled gently. "Ja, I promise, I'd tell you. I'm fine."

Mary sat back, regarding him for a few moments. He'd done it again, used an Amish word, apparently without thinking about what he was saying, which seemed to suggest the language was very familiar to him.

"What is it?" he asked when she kept staring at him.

She opened her mouth to ask how he was so familiar with Pennsylvania Dutch, but at that moment the server returned with Reuben's iced tea and Mary's strawberry lemonade, and before she could say anything, there was a small commotion by the door, and

Mary turned to see what was happening. She groaned when she saw her mother and stepfather hurrying inside and looking around frantically.

"Oh boy, I'm in for it now," she mumbled as her mother spotted her and hurried over, followed closely by her husband.

"Mary! There you are! Are you oll recht? Imagine my worry when Mrs. Jones called from the grocery store and told me you'd nearly been mowed down by some runaway barrels! Your father and I called the neighbor for a ride and came as fast as we could."

"You made really gut time, considering this only happened about fifteen minutes ago!"

Edie ran her hands over Mary's arms and squatted down to run them over her legs.

"Maem! Please, stop. You're embarrassing me. Goodness! I'm fine!"

Edie sat back on her heels and regarded her daughter, only then seeming to realize she was treating Mary like a child. Her cheeks turned pink, and she reached a hand up toward her husband. "Ach! Help me up, Joe, I've gone and forgotten myself. I'm sorry, Mary, it's just that I lost my head when I heard what had happened!"

Mary rolled her eyes. "Maem, it's fine. I understand, but the barrels did not run me over. Dr. King got me out of the way. I'm fine."

Mrs. Yoder sat down in the booth next to Mary and beamed at Reuben. "You saved our daughter's life! How can I thank you, young man?"

Mary's stepfather patted her mother on the shoulder. "There now, Edie, you can see Mary is fine." He glanced at Reuben's knee and pursed his lips. "Though perhaps the same can't be said for the young dokder. Did that happen in the accident?" Reuben covered his knee self-consciously with his hand, and Joe grinned at him. "Too late, I already saw it!"

"Well, yes, I scraped it when we fell, but it's really fine. Hardly hurts at all."

"Looks kinda purple to me, son, and your pants are done for," Joe said.

"Oh well, they died for a good cause."

There was an awkward silence, broken when Mary snorted helplessly through her nose. She immediately covered the offending feature with her hand, eyes wide, and Reuben, looking at her from across the table, couldn't help it. A snort of his own escaped, followed by a snicker, and Mary burst out laughing. Mary's parents stared at them for a moment as if they'd lost their minds, and then Joe Yoder poked Reuben in the shoulder. "Move over, Doc. I think I fancy some of Rebekkah's baked steak."

Edie shook her head. "You two are a puzzle, that's for sure."

That only set Reuben and Mary laughing again, and it took a minute for Mary to get herself under control. She wiped tears from her eyes and heaved a sigh. "Ach, that actually felt really gut. I needed a gut laugh."

"I guess so!" Edie sniffed as she picked up a menu and opened it up to the entrée section.

Mary noticed then the bills clutched in her hand, and she started laughing again.

"What is it?" Reuben asked, and she held up the money.

"I guess dinner is on the food truck driver!" She giggled. "Maem, Dat, I've got the check tonight! I guess I profited from my little misadventure after all!" She laughed again, and Reuben explained how the driver had thrust the money at Mary and hurried off. Her parents agreed it was the polite thing to do to allow him this small penance and got back to the serious business of choosing their meals.

Reuben smiled at Mary, and she felt something shift in her chest, very close to the region she believed housed her heart. Confused, she stared down at her lap. Her parents were engaging Reuben in conversation, which gave Mary a few moments to examine this new feeling. It was almost as if she and Reuben had made a special connection. But that was just plain fanciful, wasn't it? Handsome, single doctors did not make special connections with physically challenged spinsters. It was ridiculous for her to get her hopes up like that. Ridiculous! She hadn't even allowed such thoughts to flit through her head for years and years, ever since she'd told herself as a young woman not to hope for a "normal" life with a *mann* and kinner. True, her mother had tried to tell her she was being too hard on herself, that her personality, work ethic, and—Mary couldn't help but roll her eyes at this one—pretty face made up for whatever she lacked in mobility.

Her mother had told her any man would be fortunate to have her as a fraa, but Mary didn't fully believe her mother, who was, it had to be admitted, biased in her daughter's favor.

No. She'd faced facts as a young woman and decided to make a gut life for herself without dreaming impossible dreams of married happiness and, most improbable of all, kinner of her own. She didn't specifically know she couldn't have children, but she was sure it was unlikely. The doctors had said they just didn't know. Her mother had said she should leave it up to God.

Mary thought she'd do well to put such dreams away so they couldn't haunt her and so she could get on with making a different sort of life for herself, a life in which she was useful to her parents, to her siblings, to her boss, and to her friends. A life devoted to helping those she loved and to serving God through her faith community.

A life that didn't involve any risk to her deepest hopes and heart, she now admitted to herself, still staring at her hands, clenched tightly in her lap.

And all of that didn't begin to touch the crux of the matter—the fact that even if Dr. Reuben happened to be attracted to her, they could have no possible future.

She'd been baptized into the Amish faith when she turned eighteen.

Reuben was not Amish. According to the *Ordnung*, the written and unwritten rules of her community, she could not marry a man who was not Amish. To do so would mean certain shunning—a fate she could not even contemplate.

To be shunned, or placed under the bann, was to be separated from the Amish community. A person who had knowingly broken an important rule of society, usually having been given more than one opportunity to atone and get back on the right path, might ultimately be shunned. They would not be allowed to eat with or ride anywhere with members in good standing. Probably nobody in the community, or other Amish communities, would hire them. They would be isolated from their community, which was a terrible thing for people accustomed to living in community. Ultimately, the hope was that shunned members would come back, publicly confess their sins and ask for forgiveness, and determine to live by the community's rules, the Ordnung. Then they would be welcomed back with open arms and hearts. But sometimes they left. For good.

Mary shuddered. It was not to be contemplated.

Unless Reuben chose to become Amish, they could not possibly have a future together.

And why would he want to give up everything he's worked so hard for to be with me?

Mary shook her head, denying the attraction she felt for the Mennonite physician. *I'll simply ignore this, and it'll go away in a few days. Poof! Problem solved.*

Satisfied she'd come up with a solution to her little problem, Mary lifted her eyes and tuned in to the conversation taking place between Reuben and her parents. She could conquer this tiny infatuation. After all, she'd always known she'd be alone. This would not be a problem.

And yet, there was that traitorous little glow undeniably surrounding her heart. A glow that suggested maybe forgetting about Reuben wouldn't be as easy as she hoped.

CHAPTER SIX

"Ah, there you are!" Edie Yoder's voice pulled Mary from the magazine she was reading about poultry breeding. Marking her place with her finger, she reluctantly looked up from the page, squinting against the late afternoon sunlight streaming in through the west-facing windows of the screened porch off the living room of the Yoders' farmhouse.

"Sorry to interrupt your reading, but my ride to the quilting meeting will be here soon. We're stopping at the grocery store on the way for a few things. Do you need anything?"

Mary tipped her head to the side while she considered her pantry. "I am about out of garlic cloves and gingerroot. Oh, and flaxseed. I'd appreciate it if you picked some up. Thanks!"

"No problem. That's why I asked. Gingerroot, hmm? Are you going to bake some cookies?" She wiggled her eyebrows at her daughter, making Mary laugh.

"Ja, I am, but they're for church on Sunday. You'll have to wait until then, if you want one."

"If? One?" Edie struck her breast dramatically with a fist. "Mary, you wound me! Your own mudder, and you won't let me have just a few...maybe a dozen...before Sunday?"

Mary giggled. "Oh, Maem. You know I'll give you a dozen. If I don't, you'll just come in and try and sneak some anyway."

Edie smiled sheepishly. "Well, I can't help it if Gott in His wisdom made me love ginger snaps unreasonably."

"And all other sugary foods!" Mary laughed. "It's the least I can do since you're picking up the main ingredient, anyway. So denki, and have fun at your quilting meeting."

"Oh, I will. Charlene Byler is bringing some apple cider she and her mann made last fall. The trick will be to keep myself to one glass, it's so delicious."

"Don't forget your reading glasses."

"Nonsense. My eyes are fine. It's just those tiny little stitches! White thread on a white background. I'm getting too old for this."

Mary smiled sympathetically. Her mother was a bit proud of her perfect vision…which didn't seem so perfect anymore. But she wouldn't consider getting an eye exam to see whether reading glasses wouldn't be cutting it for much longer.

"Maem," Mary ventured, but her mother held up a hand, stopping Mary before she could get started nagging her about her eyes. Again.

"I know what you think. And maybe you're right, and I do need real glasses. But I just hate to go down that road. I've seen it before. You get reading glasses, and the next thing you know, you need a stronger pair. They ruin your eyes! The pair I have is just fine, denki."

Mary blinked at this reasoning. "Um, that's like saying my crutches cause me to limp. It doesn't make any sense."

"Hmmpf." Edie gathered her sewing bag from the floor, her cheeks a bit pink. "I know what I know, Mary. If people wouldn't insist on ridiculous things like ten white stitches per inch on a white background, I wouldn't have this problem. Well, I'll pick up your groceries, and I'll be back around nine. Dinner is in the oven. You're in charge of feeding time at the zoo!"

"Maem, wait!"

"Ja? I need to hurry."

"Um, maybe since you're going anyway, you could pick up some cherry ice cream? And put it in the freezer at the quilting?"

Edie smiled. "I suppose I could. But I'll have to watch that Ida Smythe like a hawk, or you'll never get a taste! Now I must go. *Gut nocht.*"

She hurried out the door, and Mary smiled to herself. Her mother loved her little brieder to pieces, but she wasn't wrong about feeding the four youngie seeming a bit like the time they'd all gone to the Cleveland Zoo and watched the monkeys get their dinner. They were very energetic eaters. And so were Mary's brothers. When her mudder was at the table, she brooked no nonsense. But when she was out during dinner, such as tonight, things were a bit more relaxed. Mary's stepfather wasn't as worried about manners and messes as his fraa.

Mary marked her place in her magazine and pushed to her feet to go organize dinner. She knew manners were important, of course. But sometimes, a lighter, fun atmosphere could also have its place. And that place would be tonight around the Yoder table.

Twenty minutes later, Mary was questioning the wisdom of her previous opinion as she ducked a carrot tossed across the table by her *bruder* Daniel. But unfortunately for Daniel, their father had seen the flying tuber, and even his tolerance for boyish shenanigans had limits.

"Daniel Yoder! You will not waste the gut food prepared for you by your mudder and your *schwester*. No more of that behavior, or you'll get three extra days of pig mucking duty."

"Aw, Dat!" the boy whined, but Joe Yoder was no rookie to such attempts.

"No more, Daniel. Eat your dinner, and then go do your chores. You too, boys," he said, nodding at his other three sons, who nodded obediently and cleaned their plates, glad not to be the ones under the paternal microscope. They then cleared their dishes to the sink and trooped out the door to do their chores, grabbing their little hats on the way.

Mary knew that once they were outside, they'd grumble and get up to some horseplay, but it was all in good fun. They were gut boys.

She sat at the table enjoying a cup of kaffi with her stepfather, chatting about their days. She finished her piece of raisin pie—one of her favorites—and was thinking about getting up to do the dishes when there was a knock on the wooden screen door. She caught her stepfather's look of surprise, which turned quickly to one of speculation, and turned to see whose arrival caused such a reaction.

Reuben was standing outside on the stoop, smiling in at them. "Sorry, am I interrupting your dinner?"

Mary couldn't help smiling in return. "No, we were just finishing. Would you like some pie?"

"Depends. What kind?"

"Raisin. And I have fresh whipped cream."

"Well, then, yes! Who would be deerich enough to say no to that?"

"You'd have to be foolish indeed to pass up Mary's raisin pie. Are you going to invite him in, Mary, or will you be serving his pie and kaffi outside on the stoop?" Joe asked with a small smile.

"Oh! I'm sorry, please come in!" She closed her eyes and shook her head.

Reuben opened the screen door and stepped inside. "Don't mind if I do."

Mary noticed that Reuben wiped his feet on the doormat, something her brieder often forgot to do, before stepping over to the table and taking a seat. Her stepfather was cutting a large serving of pie and placing it onto a plate. He handed it to Reuben, and Mary passed him the whipped cream.

"Wow, my timing is good!" Reuben spooned a dollop of homemade whipped cream onto his pie.

"I'll make a fresh pot of kaffi." Mary started to stand, but her stepfather held up a hand.

"No, sit, daughter. I'm finished anyway and need to go out and supervise your brieder before they get up to mischief. I'll make the kaffi."

"Denki," both Mary and Reuben said together. They looked at each other and laughed.

Joe put a fresh pot on to brew, then grabbed his hat off its hook and plopped it onto his head. "That was a very gut supper, Mary, denki!"

She nodded and he walked outside, calling for the boys.

"What did you have?" Reuben asked around another mouthful of pie.

"Pork chops, mashed potatoes, and carrots."

"Beats my grilled cheese sandwich and tomato soup."

"I love that meal, actually."

"Well, so do I, but it's not as good as pork chops and raisin pie!"

"Kind of depends on your mood, though, ain't so?"

He pondered this as he chewed the last bite of pie, his eyes slipping over to the pie pan which still held about half a pie. Mary noticed and, with a smile, asked, "Would you like another piece, Dokder?"

He grinned sheepishly. "Well, if you insist."

"Oh, I do!" she said, cutting him a second, generous piece and placing it on his plate.

"Then I'll have to be polite and eat it, I guess!"

Mary poured Reuben a cup of the fresh coffee, and then she moved to the sink, where she began washing dishes. "So, I noticed you used a Pennsylvania Dutch word again a bit ago. That's several times that I've heard."

"Nibby?"

"Curious."

"Careful—you know what they say about curiosity and what it did to the cat."

"What cat was that anyway?"

He shrugged and finished off his second piece of pie and then took a large sip of fragrant coffee. "I have no idea. The one in the adage, I guess."

A sharp "meow" punctuated his words, and he gave a startled glance at Mary.

She took one look at his face and burst out laughing. "Oh! You should see your face! You thought that was me!" She laughed even harder when he just looked confused and glanced around the kitchen, obviously seeking the source of the sound.

"Well, I wasn't sure," he said. "It sounded like a cat, and I thought maybe you do an amazing imitation. You could be into animal sounds, for all I know."

She wiped her eyes and chuckled. "It was my little cat, Hope. You met her the other day, remember? She's under the stove."

He peered at the woodstove in the corner of the kitchen and grinned when he caught sight of a calico tail whipping back and forth on one side. "Ah, I see it now. Good hiding place."

"Ja. She discovered it when she was just a kitten. And she never got very big, so she still fits. But it's a bit tight now, so she only goes under there when she's startled."

"Sorry if I startled her."

"Just ignore her, and she'll come out in her own time."

He nodded and sipped his coffee. "This is very gut kaffi."

"Aha! There you go again! You must have been studying the language since you arrived, nee?"

He stared into his coffee cup for a few moments, as if deciding what he wanted to say. Then he looked at her and shook his head. "Nee."

"Nee?"

"Nee. I didn't need to study the language, because I grew up speaking it. I was raised Amish, in Pennsylvania."

Her mouth dropped open, and she stared at him, flummoxed. "But. . .but you're a dokder! You can't be Amish."

His mouth lifted a bit at one corner. "No, I'm not Amish anymore, at least, not in practice. I suppose you can't really stop being something you've been all your life, though, can you?"

A terrible thought occurred to Mary, and she raised one hand to her mouth.

"Now you look as if your favorite rooster died. If you have a question, go ahead and ask it."

"Well, if you used to be Amish, but you aren't now, does that mean you were. . .shunned?" She whispered the last word.

Reuben's expression was very serious as he slowly shook his head. "No, I was not shunned."

"Thank Gott!" she said, sinking back against the counter and placing a hand over her heart. "For I don't know whether the community would use your services had you been!"

"I'm sure they wouldn't," he murmured. "But I wasn't shunned. I chose not to be baptized because I knew since I was a young child I wanted a different path."

"To be a dokder?"

"Ja, and to do that, I had to leave the community."

"Oh, Reuben, that is so sad! Your poor parents! They must be heartbroken!"

He sighed. "It's not as if I'm dead, Mary. I simply didn't get baptized, and it's not as if I'm living a life of wild sin. I became Mennonite, which is the next thing to Amish, as you well know."

"Well, ja, I suppose."

"And I see my family regularly. It's not so far in the truck. In fact, I got a letter from my little sister the other day. . .the day you nearly got mowed down by the barrels of cooking oil. . .and she wants to come visit."

"Oh, that's nice. How old is she?"

"Eliza is seventeen. I think our mudder is hoping she will meet some interesting young men here. Nobody has caught her fancy back home."

Mary smiled understandingly. "But she's still very young. Surely your mudder isn't worried she'll never marry?"

"Well, I haven't yet," Reuben said. "Maem is getting impatient. Eliza is more interested in seeing new places and having adventures than settling down and having a family right now. I convinced Maem that visiting me beats a wild *rumspringa*. So she's coming to stay with me. I'll go get her in a couple weeks."

"Nice. I look forward to meeting her."

"That's actually what I was hoping. She'll need to make some friends here if she decides to stay for a while. And you know everybody!"

"Well, I grew up here."

"Yes. So, is your curiosity satisfied?"

"Sort of. How did you go about becoming a dokder?"

"Well, it wasn't easy. When I told my parents, they were not very happy. They thought I'd go into the hardware business with them. I'm the oldest son. I think for a while they counted on me outgrowing my interest in medicine. But that didn't happen. Fortunately, my younger brothers are very interested in nuts and bolts, where my interests tend more toward tonsils and ingrown toenails."

"Yuck. So what happened when you told them?"

"There's that curiosity again," he teased. Her face turned pink, and he smiled. "You're pretty when you blush, Mary."

She turned an even darker shade of pink, and his smile turned gentle. "You're not used to having men tell you you're pretty, are you?"

Her mouth opened and closed a few times until, feeling she must look like a beached carp, she snapped her teeth together and got herself under control. "Well, I. . .no. I guess not."

"The men around here must be blind and half-witted."

Feeling out of her depth, Mary did what she did best—she played down the entire situation. "Well, aren't all men? Now, you were telling me about how you became a dokder. Please go on."

She turned and began energetically scrubbing dishes, and he smiled at her back. "Well, even though my parents weren't thrilled with my decision, they supported me. I had to attend public high school when I finished eighth grade at the Amish school in my community."

"Really? How did that go? Were you prepared?"

He rubbed his beardless chin and thought about it for a few moments before lifting a hand and making a so-so gesture. "Academically I was surprisingly well prepared. I was the same age as the other kids entering high school and had studied pretty much the same subjects. There were some things I had to start from scratch on, such as keyboarding, since I'd never used a computer. But when it came to math, history, reading, spelling—the basics—I was well-versed. Unfortunately, science, the subject most necessary to my goal, was something I'd had little training in. But neither had most of the other freshmen at my high school. I started in earth science, aced that, then moved on to biology, chemistry, and advanced biology and genetics. I squeezed physics in as a summer course at a local community college."

"This sounds fascinating and terrifying at the same time!"

"Ja. Socially, I was not prepared for what I found at the public high school. I did not fit in at all. Even though these kids had grown up in Pennsylvania's Amish country, with the exception of a few farm kids who had Amish neighbors, they didn't know many Amish kids personally. Unfortunately, none of them were my neighbors."

"Were the kids mean?"

He shrugged. "Some were, some weren't. Mostly, people leave you alone if you do them the same favor. But there were some bullies who seemed to need to prove how tough they were by taking on the new kid."

"The weird, different kid?"

"Ja."

She sighed. "I've been there. Not that any bullies ever physically hurt me, but words can be vicious too."

"Because of your injury?"

"Of course. And I was way behind in school. Even Amish kids can be mean."

"You're not telling me anything new. Plenty of Amish kids were mean to me after I 'turned traitor' as some of them said."

She was instantly angry on his behalf. "And we're supposed to be pacifists!"

He laughed. "Right. Supposed to be, but there's always someone willing to take cheap shots, in any culture."

"So, did you actually have to fight?" She was both fascinated and appalled at the thought.

"It didn't come to that, but it was a near thing a couple times. I generally walked away from conflict. I'm not sure my parents would have let me continue if I'd gotten into a fight. It would have been proof that I was being irredeemably corrupted. Mostly, I kept my head down and just really applied myself to my schoolwork."

"So you attended public high school." Mary could hardly imagine such a thing. "How did that work? Did you need special permission from your bishop?"

"Ja, once I convinced my parents I was serious, they applied to the council for permission for me to attend public high school. I was a little young for rumspringa, but I believe that was the loophole they used to make it happen. It was agreed that I could attend school, but as I was so young, I was not to embrace other English ways. Since we didn't have electricity at home, let alone a computer, I got into the habit of going directly to the public library after school and doing my homework. Then I'd head over to my parents' hardware store and help out there before riding home with my mudder to do farm chores while she made supper every night."

"And that worked out?"

"Surprisingly well. Of course, the whole time my parents were hoping I'd outgrow my 'phase' and realize I actually wanted to take over the store when they retired. When I graduated from high school, the real trouble started."

"Because obviously you didn't outgrow your desire to become a dokder?"

"Right. I was eighteen when I graduated, and the bishop told my parents that it was time for me to make a choice. I had to decide either to be Amish and give up my dreams, or to continue along the path I was on and become English."

"You were still so young!"

He shrugged. "Old enough to marry. Old enough to be considered a grown man."

"You hadn't been baptized yet, so they didn't have to shun you, right?"

"Right, which helped a bit. But they wouldn't pay for college, obviously, since that isn't what we do."

"I've heard it's very expensive. . ." she ventured, not wanting to become too intrusive by coming right out and asking how much it had cost and how he'd managed. But she was dying to know!

"Very. But I'd proven to be an apt pupil, and I won a full scholarship to Penn State, including room and board."

She clapped her hands together. "Wunderbar gut!"

He smiled. "Yes, it was. I worked part-time at a hardware store in State College while I was in undergrad. And I took out loans and such to pay for medical school. I wanted a change of scenery, so I attended medical school at Ohio State in Columbus and took advantage of a program they had at the time for minority grants to help pay. Being Amish, it turned out, was considered a cultural minority."

"Handy."

"Yep. The rest is history. After medical school I did a residency in family medicine and pediatrics, and then I looked around for a practice. I knew I wanted something small and rural, and when I heard about Dr. Smith's practice being up for sale, it felt like Gott's will that I return to my roots, after a fashion. And here I am."

"What about your family? Are they reconciled to your choice now?"

"Yes, I think becoming Mennonite helped. I didn't turn wild and embrace a hedonistic lifestyle, after all."

"That probably did help."

"Ja. And my next younger bruder, John, is going to take over the store when my parents retire."

"Is he your only bruder?"

"No, no. I have three younger brieder, and three younger *schwestern*. It's a full house."

"And all the boys are working in the family business?"

"Yes, and one of my schwestern. The youngest one, save Eliza, is Meg. The older one, Samantha, is married and expecting her first child."

"How exciting! Your parents' first grandchild?"

"Yes," he said dryly.

She quirked a brow. "And that's. . .gut, nee?"

He smiled wryly. "Ja. Except now that my mudder has gotten a taste of impending grandmotherhood—if that's a word—she wants more."

Mary covered her mouth to hide a laugh. "Ah. So as the oldest son, you're on the hot seat now?"

"Good guess. My mudder has started hinting that since I'm done with my studies and settled down, I should find a nice Mennonite girl, get married, and make her some grandbabies. I'm not sure whether she's fine with my choices or just making the best of things. Can't put the chicken back into the egg, right?"

Mary laughed. "My mother has finally given up on trying to match me with every single man who comes to town. Thank goodness! It was exhausting. And who's going to marry me anyway, I ask you?" At Reuben's frown, Mary held up a hand. "No, no, it's fine. I don't have a poor self-image or anything. I'm just realistic. I can't do all the hard physical work necessary to be a farmwife. And that's what most Amish men need."

"There are Amish men who aren't farmers," he pointed out. "At least, not solely farmers. My mother isn't really a farmwife. Sure, my father farms a bit of land but not much. The hardware store is really his focus. He doesn't have time to be a farmer. He leases our fields to sharecroppers and has a hired man come in when he needs help with his beef cattle. I think he enjoys walking behind the horses for a day or two in the spring and calling it a job well done. Other than that, Maem has a few chickens and a kitchen garden. That's it. They're shopkeepers."

"Ja, my boss is like that. He farms a small amount of acreage but mainly focuses on his basket business. However, there aren't many such opportunities around."

"Actually, I believe that with the Amish population growing, especially here in Ohio, there are more younger sons branching out into businesses such as roofing and siding, timber, shopkeeping, and all sorts of things which have no land at all."

"Yes, but truly, I'm fine with my life the way it is."

Reuben found himself unaccountably relieved that Mary didn't jump at the thought of finding a husband. For some reason, the idea of her marrying depressed him. Part of it was that he didn't like hearing her put herself down, sure—but another part, if he were to be honest, found her very appealing, and he wished there were some way they could explore a possible relationship. But since she'd been baptized in the faith, and he had chosen to leave it, they might as well be a fish and a bird. Sure, they might fall in love, but where would they live? He was being selfish wanting her for himself when there didn't seem to be any possible way. *Time to change the subject*, he thought with a small shake of his head. "Speaking of which," Reuben said, putting his coffee cup down and looking her in the eye, all trace of humor gone from his expressive face. "Have you given my suggestion any thought?"

Mary actually squirmed in her chair, and Reuben thought she looked a bit like a schoolgirl who hadn't done her assignment. He held back a smile lest he offend her.

"Honestly, Reuben, no, I haven't had time."

He raised a skeptical brow. "Haven't had time? Or avoiding the issue?"

She puffed out an exasperated breath and pushed to her feet, grabbing her crutches and walking to the door. "This has been a lovely visit, but I have chores to do, Dokder." She opened the kitchen door and stood to one side, clearly hinting that it was time for him to take his leave.

He looked down at his empty plate and cup, shrugged, and stood. Without looking at her, he stood and started out the door. But he stopped next to Mary, took a deep breath, and looked her in the eyes. He considered what to say, aware that her reluctance could hold her back from measurably improving her life, but at the same time, acknowledging to himself that he must respect her decision, whether or not he agreed with it. But he couldn't help trying one more time.

"Mary. If you read through that material and still don't want to move forward, I'll leave off, I promise. But how do you know this isn't the right move for you if you don't at least check into it?"

She looked away, across the farmyard. In the distance, the boys were calling back and forth to each other as they did their evening chores. She swallowed and then looked back at Reuben.

"Actually, I did read it. And so did my parents."

"That's terrific! Unless. . .you have decided that it still isn't for you?"

She worried her lower lip with her teeth before slashing a glance at him and then looking at her shoes. "It isn't that we didn't think it sounded like it might work, exactly."

"Then, what? Please talk to me. I want to help, truly."

Her eyes brimmed with tears, and it was all he could do not to reach for her.

"I'm. . .afraid."

He nodded. "Of course you are."

Her nostrils flared and she drew breath to throw out an angry retort, but he raised a hand, stopping her. "Mary. I don't mean you're a coward. Far from it! The proof is in all you've accomplished! All you can do! I only meant that anyone with any sense would be a bit afraid of the idea of being put under and letting someone cut into them. Especially since the results of this type of surgery are never guaranteed. I don't think you run the risk of being worse off than you are now, but whether you'd see any improvement? It's a gamble."

Obviously deflated, Mary let out her breath. "Sorry. I can get a bit prickly about this stuff."

"Really? I hadn't noticed," Reuben said, straight-faced.

She gave a reluctant smile and shook her head.

"Look, I'll think about this and pray about it. But no promises, okay?"

Relief and gladness spread through Reuben, but he worked to keep his emotions off his face and remain professional. The last thing she needed at the moment was the complication of his confused feelings for her added to the situation.

"A fair hearing is all I can ask for. If after thought and prayer and talking it over with your parents and maybe the bishop you're still adamantly opposed to the idea, I'll drop it. It's your life. But if you want to know more, well, then I'll find out what the next step would be. Deal?"

She nodded. "As long as you promise that if I say no, that's it."

"I promise." He gazed down at her and became distracted by her perfectly shaped, peony-pink lips, before calling himself once more to order and jerking his glance away. He gave her a firm nod. "Okay, then. Let me know what you decide."

With that, he headed out the door to his truck, climbed in, and started the engine. He jockeyed the truck around while she watched, and before he headed down the driveway, he rolled the window down and called out, "And thanks for the coffee and pie! It was delicious!"

As he pointed his truck toward town, Reuben felt elated that Mary had agreed to at least explore the possibility of further treatment. He couldn't recall feeling this happy about something since getting his acceptance to medical school—a moment that had justified his hopes and put to rest his secret fears of inadequacy. He still suffered occasionally from imposter syndrome—the Amish boy playing at being a dokder.

"It doesn't mean she'll go through with it, or that if she does, that it'll help," he murmured. "And you'd better keep your priorities straight, Reuben. She's not interested in you as a man. She's looking to you for sound medical advice. Don't cross the line, for goodness' sake!"

But in truth, he'd told her he didn't want to be her doctor, and he really, really didn't. If she chose to pursue this, he'd find a specialist and pass her to him or her, and maybe then he could consider being more to her. Maybe a friend. Maybe. . .something more.

Impatient with himself, he turned on the truck's radio and spent the rest of the drive singing along to oldies but goodies.

Mary watched Reuben's truck disappear onto the main road and soon became aware of the good-natured bickering and jibing that meant her brieder were returning from the barn. Knowing they'd be hungry all over again after doing their chores, she turned back to the kitchen, where she got out a pitcher of fresh, cold milk from the fridge and put a big plate she filled with cookies and slices of cheese on the table. She sliced up a couple of apples and added them to the plate and called it a job well done.

Hope wandered into sight and gave a small meow. Mary placed a sliver of cheese in the little cat's food bowl and scratched her between the ears. Hope gobbled up the cheese, but then, hearing the boys stomping up the steps to the kitchen porch, she made herself scarce.

"Coward," Mary called after the retreating cat. Hope flicked her tail and disappeared through the cat door between the main house and the dawdi haus as the back door burst open and the boys poured noisily inside.

"Cookies!" Isaac, ten years old, and second-oldest brother, cried. "You're the best, Mary!"

"Wash your hands before you touch those. And take off your boots and put them in the mudroom, since you've been in the barn."

"Yes, Mary," intoned her brothers, sitting down on the floor to take off their boots before carrying them dutifully to the mudroom off the kitchen, then hurrying back to splash a bit of water on their grimy hands.

"Use soap," Mary chided. Groaning, the boys shouldered into the sink, washing thoroughly, drying their hands on the dish towel, and then sitting down at the table. Their father came in the door and said, "Remember to thank the Lord for your snack, boys."

They bowed their heads for a few seconds and then hungrily attacked the plate of cookies, cheese, and apple slices and drank down their first glasses of milk before asking for seconds. Mary refilled their glasses and smiled as they polished off their milk and every crumb of the food.

"Cookies, apples, and cheese," her stepfather murmured. "Interesting combination."

"Satisfying on more than one level and gives them more than just sugar and fat."

"I didn't say it was bad, just…unusual. But I think I'd like some too."

She grinned and got out the cheese and cookies and a fresh glass, which she filled with milk for him. She tossed him an apple and sat down to enjoy a cookie with him.

"There you go! Enjoy!"

He smiled. "You're a gut girl, Mary. Denki."

"Okay, boys, head upstairs and take your showers before getting into your pj's," Mary said. "I'll come up in a bit to tuck you in, since Maem is out at a quilting."

There was a bit of grumbling about showers, but they headed upstairs, and soon Mary heard the shower running.

"They're gut boys," Joe said, taking a big sip of milk and then savoring a slice of extra-sharp white cheddar. "Mmm, I love the little crunchy bits in this cheese."

"Ja, me too." She joined him at the table and savored a slice of cheese herself. "And they are gut boys. But I confess the end of the day is always a bit of a relief."

He chuckled. "Now you sound like your mudder."

She smiled. "Well, there you go."

"That dokder fellow seems taken with you, Mary," he commented casually as he polished off a cookie, then chased it with more milk.

Shocked, Mary snapped her head up and stared at her stepfather. Could she have heard right? "What do you mean?"

He shrugged. "Just that he comes around here a lot, and he seems to like spending time with you. Which shows he has gut sense, you ask me."

"But. . .but. . .he's not Amish. Anymore, I mean. He's Mennonite now. He used to be Amish but not anymore," she stammered.

"Really? That's interesting. Used to be Amish you say? Hmm." He wiped his mouth with a napkin, then washed his dishes and then set them into the dish drainer. He put the milk away too. "Well, I think I'll go upstairs and supervise the showers, or pretty soon we'll have water coming through the ceiling."

"He's just trying to convince me to look into another treatment for my spine and legs. He isn't interested in me as a woman."

"Hmm," he said as he grabbed his apple and started up the stairs.

"Dat!" she called, and he turned and looked at her, an innocent expression on his face.

"Ja?"

"I mean, since he isn't Amish, I couldn't consider him." She gestured vaguely with her hands. "As a husband, I mean. I'd be shunned!"

He looked at her a moment, then did a little facial shrug. "Not if he returned to the church you wouldn't. He wasn't baptized, right?" She shook her head.

"Well, then, he could come back, couldn't he?"

"But. . .but he's a dokder! He can't be Amish anymore, can he?"

"Who knows what might be possible or allowable, if he asked? Maybe pray about it, child. You never know."

Whistling, he mounted the steps, while Mary sat and stared after him, astonished. Reuben, interested in her? Ridiculous!

Or. . .was it? Mary remembered how he'd looked at her before he left earlier. And he had been coming around a lot.

"But no!" she exclaimed. "He's only interested in me as a patient, hoping I'll get that operation. This is just silly. I'm not going to think about him that way—as a man."

But thinking about Reuben's smile, and about the fact that he obviously cared about her... Even if she was reading too much into it—how could she think about him at all and not think about him as a man?

"Ach! Dat is right. I need to trust in Gott and ask Him for His guidance in this. Actually, in both things—how I should think about Reuben and whether I should consider pursuing further treatment."

Making sure everything in the kitchen was tidy, she took her crutches and headed for her little home in the dawdi haus.

CHAPTER SEVEN

Several days flew by, and Mary found herself too busy with work and home to make a decision. She'd placed the papers on the coffee table in her tiny living room in the dawdi haus, and each time she passed the table she felt a confused mixture of guilt, resistance, hope, and resentment. If she were honest with herself, she'd have to admit she was oddly reluctant to learn more about the procedure—reluctant to be tempted, maybe.

"Ach! Enough! I don't have time for this foolishness." Grabbing up the brochures, Mary crossed the room and, opening the drop-down door of her grandmother's old secretary, thrust them inside and snapped the door closed. "There! Now they won't be staring at me every time I cross the room. I'll make a decision when I'm ready."

Mary exited her little home by the front door, which had a ramp leading down into the farmyard not far from the kitchen door in the main house, left over from her grandparents' occupancy. She made her way toward the barn, intending to feed her chickens. She was halfway there when the kitchen door banged open and her maem poked her head outside.

"Mary! *Guder mariye!* Have you seen your brieder? I need them to try on their new pants so I can get them hemmed before Sunday."

"Sorry, Maem, I just came outside. I'll see if they're in the barn."

Edie threw up her hands, muttering something about rascals, making Mary smile as she continued to the barn. She'd just unlatched the door and was about to go inside when the sound of tires on gravel caused her to pause and glance toward the road. The sight of Reuben's truck rolling down the driveway sent a surge of pleasure through Mary, followed by a wave of confusion. She wasn't prepared to deal with such feelings toward the handsome Mennonite doctor.

Drawing her dignity around her like a comforting cloak, she prepared to inform the doctor that he might as well stop pestering her. She'd inform him when her mind was made up, and not before.

But when Reuben jumped out of his truck and caught sight of Mary standing by the barn, the sunny smile that spread uninhibitedly across his face disarmed her, and for a moment she couldn't remember what she was determined to say to the man.

"Good morning, Mary!" Reuben strode over to where she stood, stopping a few feet away and smiling at her. She couldn't stop an answering smile from sliding over her own face, and she felt like a simpleton. Sternly reprimanding herself, Mary schooled her face into serious lines. And she knew what she had to do, not only because she really felt her life was fine as it was, but also in hopes the doctor would stop coming around so frequently, thus innocently filling her with hopeless dreams. She took a deep breath and met his eyes.

"Good morning, Dokder. I'm glad you stopped by, for I must tell you I've come to a decision."

"A serious decision, by the looks of that frown."

"Well, yes. I'm afraid I've decided not to pursue further treatment for my condition. Thank you for your interest. You've been most kind."

He stood looking at her for a few moments, then shook his head and looked away. "Huh."

She looked at him uncertainly. "What?"

He stared at the ground, not meeting her eyes. And she felt her uncertainty grow and her anger spark. "What do you mean by 'huh'?"

"I just. . . Well, I guess I expected a different answer. I thought you'd go for it in the end."

Mary's mouth opened and then closed. She looked up at the sky and drew in a long, slow breath. Then she looked him squarely in the eyes. "Reuben. You have no idea what it's like to live in my skin. How can you have any expectation at all? How can you have any idea what I'd think or say about anything?"

He had the grace to look a bit ashamed, and he nodded an affirmation of her feelings. But before she could feel vindicated, his mouth firmed and his penetrating gaze returned to hers. "Did you at least read the material I gave you?"

"Yes, Dokder. But. . .I've made up my mind, and that's all there is to it."

"It's Reuben," he interrupted. "You agreed to call me Reuben. "Remember?"

Mary felt the sting of tears in her eyes, something that never failed to infuriate her. The normally peaceful and sunny-natured young woman hated to cry, especially in front of others. So she always turned to anger to deal with the embarrassment. It was one of the few things that could make her lose her temper—which was nothing to sneeze at once unleashed.

"Ja, I do remember. But, Dokder—" At his raised eyebrow she relented with a tired sigh. "Reuben, then. The only relationship we have is that of casual acquaintances. I listened to your opinion, and if you don't like my decision, you can just deal with it. My body is my own, and nobody is going to tell me what to do with it or imply I'm somehow letting them down because I don't want to go through yet another painful surgery with a long recovery time that will keep me from living my life! And with no guarantees! Right? You can't make me any promises that this surgery you want me to undergo will help one little bit, can you? Well?"

It was Reuben's turn to stand there with his mouth hanging open in surprise, looking like a landed fish. "Um, well, no. There are never any guarantees in medicine."

"As I thought! Well, I'm perfectly fine and happy the way I am, and if that's not good enough for you, get back in your truck and drive back to town! I never asked for you to keep coming around here. I never asked for your medical advice, Dokder! So what do you think of that?"

He looked miserable as he stared at her. "Mary, I'm sorry. I crossed a line. Can you forgive me?"

Before she could answer, a shout from around the enormous old building drew her attention. She stopped and craned her neck to see who was yelling.

Just then, Nathan, her eight-year-old brother, pelted around the side of the barn closely followed by Isaac, who had just turned ten. Both boys were running as if they were being chased by an angry swarm of bees, yelling at the top of their lungs.

Mary frowned. Where were Daniel and Simon? "Boys! Where are you going? What's wrong? Where are your brieder?"

Hearing her, they veered toward her and nearly ran her down in their haste. Reuben reached out and caught the two boys, stopping them before they crashed into their sister in their agitation and, Mary could see once they got close, fear.

Nathan had tears streaming down his face, and he was babbling too fast for her to understand. She took him by the shoulders and gave him a firm shake. "Nathan! Isaac! What's wrong? Slow down! I can't understand!"

"The pond!" Isaac gasped, placing his hands on his knees as he caught his breath. "Simon fell into the pond, and Daniel tried to reach him, but he fell in too, and it's the deep part and he can't touch! We need to get help!"

Mary gasped. Daniel, at twelve, was a decent swimmer but not good enough to rescue a panicking six-year-old. She grabbed each boy by the arm and spoke firmly, keeping calm so they wouldn't panic even more. "Boys! I need you to listen! Dat is in the field across the road, tedding the hay. Maem is in the kitchen. Isaac, go get Dat. Nathan, get Maem. Tell them what's happening! I'll go to the pond. Hurry! There's not much time!"

The boys ran off, and Mary turned toward the pond. Reuben stopped her—she'd forgotten he was there!

"Mary, where is the pond? Hurry! Seconds count in a drowning."

Mary's hand flew up to cover her mouth at the terrible word, but she knew he was right. "Over there, past the cornfield! Oh Reuben, hurry!"

He squeezed her arm, then turned and ran across the farmyard and through the cornfield.

Mary followed as fast as she could. But it was a fair distance off, and she knew the chances were slim she'd get to the boys in time to be of any help. Using her crutches to swing herself along, she reached the edge of the plowed cornfield and grimaced. Her crutches would sink in the plowed soil. She'd have to slow down. Behind her, she heard her mother calling out, and she could hear men yelling from across the highway. Shading her eyes, she saw her dat and the neighbor who was helping with the hay, Ben Lapp, running full-out at an angle, already crossing the cornfield. She could see that Reuben had nearly reached the pond.

Feeling useless, she started across the field as fast as she could go. She saw first Reuben, then Joe, jump into the pond, Ben standing on the shore in case he was needed. She'd made it about three-quarters of the way across when one crutch suddenly sank into a deep hole she hadn't noticed in her haste, and before she could catch herself, down she went, face-planting into the rich soil.

Furious with herself, she spat out dirt, pushed herself to her knees, and used the crutches to shove to her feet. As she made it to her feet, desperate to get to her brieder, her mother and two younger brothers ran up next to her.

"Boys! Help your schwester!" Edie shouted as she ran past Mary, and Isaac and Nathan both stopped by their big sister and walked slowly with her the remaining distance to the pond as Reuben and Joe lifted the boys out of the water, Ben reaching out a hand to haul them up onto the grassy bank before helping each of the men in the same way.

Simon was coughing uncontrollably, and Daniel was white as a ghost and looked terrified but unharmed.

"Oh! Thank Gott! Thank Gott! You made it in time," Edie cried, falling to her knees and grabbing Simon in her arms. The little boy clung to his mother as he coughed and threw up pond water and dripped all over her. She didn't seem to notice. She turned and reached for Daniel, who was sitting on the shore a few feet away, looking very frightened but manfully sniffing back the tears Mary could see wanted to come.

"Come here, Daniel," Edie said, pulling her oldest son into her arms and rocking him along with the baby. With that, Daniel's stoicism ended, and the boy cried silently into his mother's shoulder.

Mary limped closer and stood by with her brothers and the men, giving a silent prayer of thanks for the safety of Daniel and Simon.

Joe cleared his throat and wiped away moisture from his face before setting his hand on his wife's shoulder. "Okay, the boys are fine, Edie. Gott took care of them until we could get here."

Turning to Reuben, he reached out and shook the doctor's dripping hand. "Dokder, I can't express my gratitude. If you hadn't gotten here so fast, Ben and I might have been too late. Denki!"

Edie raised a tearstained face. "Yes! Denki, Dokder!"

Clearly embarrassed, Reuben cleared his throat. "Well, I guess it wasn't Gott's will that the boys join Him in heaven today. I was glad to be His instrument."

"Well said," Ben commented.

"Ja," Joe said, wiping his face again with a big, work-roughened hand as Edie hugged the boys again. "Okay. Let's get these two back to the house and get everyone dried off. Edie, I imagine you have some hot chocolate and zucchini bread?"

Edie wiped her face and nodded, smiling. "Ja, of course. I hope you men can stay for breakfast as well. It won't take me any time to whip up a batch of sausages and scrapple. And I can make buckwheat pancakes too. It's a gut day to celebrate!"

"Pancakes!" the boys yelled, all tears forgotten.

Joe reached down and helped Edie stand and then took Simon from her and set the boy on his shoulder. He gave Daniel a pat and turned to walk back to the house. He stopped when he saw Mary standing there with the other boys.

"Mary, you would have gotten here just a few seconds later. It probably would have been soon enough. Denki for trying. Were you hurt when you fell? I saw you as I was running. I'm sorry I didn't stop to help you up."

While Mary appreciated his kindness, she couldn't share his optimism. Even if she'd reached the pond in time, what then? Would she have reached a crutch to the boys? What if they were too far out? She couldn't swim, had never learned—just one of the many normal, everyday things she'd been deemed unable to do, either by others or, in some cases, by herself. She mustered a smile for her stepfather. "Denki. I'm fine, Dat."

Joe smiled at her and continued to the house with Edie, who gave her a one-armed hug on the way by, followed by Ben Lapp and the two boys who hadn't fallen into the pond. Mary stood and watched them all start across the cornfield, and she shook her head.

Reuben, whose presence she'd nearly forgotten, came to stand beside her. "What are you thinking, Mary? Your brothers are safe, but you look so sad."

"I wouldn't have been enough," she whispered before starting slowly back to the house, favoring her right knee, which she'd wrenched when she fell.

He fell into step with her. "Says who?"

"I wouldn't have gotten there in time, Reuben. And even if I had, I can't swim. I wouldn't have done them any good. Thank Gott you and the other men were here! Even my maem can swim! And she's twenty years older than I am, but she still beat me to the pond."

Deciding to play it safe, she veered left to take the long way around the plowed field, with Reuben striding along silently beside her. They arrived back in the barnyard well after everyone else had disappeared into the house. Disgusted with herself, she turned toward the barn to feed her chickens. Reuben stopped her with a hand on her arm.

"Mary, please don't be so hard on yourself. You don't deserve such a harsh judgment."

She eyed him incredulously. "I don't? When my pigheaded refusal to even consider your suggestion could keep me from being a lot more helpful in the future?"

"No, Mary, this was an extreme situation, not a normal test of your abilities. You're very capable in many, many ways. You gave it your all, which is a testimony to your character. Many people would have sat down at the edge of the field and quit. But not you."

Her expression softened, and she managed a small smile. "Denki, Reuben. But the truth is, it's fear, plain and simple, that's kept me from agreeing to this new procedure. Fear of pain. Fear of failure. That's it. Just. . .fear."

"Fear is a good instinct. It keeps us from doing something that could hurt us."

She rolled her eyes, and he couldn't help smiling. "Ha! Now you're just being nice."

"Well, I like being nice to you. I like you."

The smile slipped off her face as she gazed at his kind face. "Oh, Reuben," she sighed. "I like you too. And I'll try to be more worthy of your faith. If I can get even a little better, I might be able to be of use to someone in a real way, instead of having to stand by helplessly and maybe watch someone I love get hurt or die."

He stopped and turned to face her, placing his hands on her shoulders. "Mary, don't speak of yourself like that. You're far from useless. You're essential to a lot of people. Your family, obviously. And I heard your boss talking about you the other day. . ."

"My boss? You know Jonas?"

He shrugged. "His daughter is a patient. Your name came up, and he couldn't say enough about what an excellent job you do on the detail weaving requiring fine motor skills."

"Oh, that's nice."

"You seem surprised to hear someone speak well of you. Why is that?"

"I don't know. I guess I just don't think of myself as being. . ."

"Important?"

"Ja, maybe."

"Well, you are. As for courage, we never know what life has in store. And there are always going to be things too big for anyone, even the strongest person, to overcome. There are grown men who don't have your courage and strength. It's just different."

She smiled at him but looked a bit flustered. She fluttered her hands. "Denki for that. Now, go inside and let Maem give you dry clothes and feed you. It's the least you can do!"

"The least I can do?"

"Ja. Let her fuss over you to make up for not jumping in the pond herself, Reuben."

He laughed. "Well, when you put it that way, how can I refuse? Does she have pie?"

"Oh ja. She always has pie."

He laughed and turned toward the house. "I'll see you in a bit?"

"Ja, after I do my chores." She watched him go inside, then, determined, she got on with her chores. Whatever else happened in life, chores always needed to be done.

Half an hour later, Reuben was showered and dressed in some of Joe's clothes. Edie had insisted on washing his, promising to return them later in the week. He was seated at the kitchen table in the Yoders' warm, welcoming home, enjoying some hot kaffi and a slice of zucchini bread slathered with apple butter from last fall. He could get used to this, he thought.

The kitchen door opened, and Mary made her way inside. She smiled at Reuben and took a seat at the table. Breakfast was nearly ready, and Reuben could hear the two swimmers upstairs, getting dressed after their quick bath. Nathan and Isaac were already seated at the table, enjoying bread and apple butter.

"Anything I can do to help, Maem?" Mary asked.

"No, no, I've got it. Joe, bring those boys down and come eat!" Edie called to her husband, turning to place heaping platters of pancakes, sausages, scrapple, and scrambled eggs onto the table. Mary looked around. "Where's Ben?"

"He said he needed to shower and dress at home, since your father's clothes wouldn't fit him. He's already had breakfast and said he'd be back in an hour to take up where they left off tedding the hay."

Reuben was unsurprised that Ben would prefer showering at home. He was a big man, with a good fifty pounds on Joe. Mrs. Yoder was right, Reuben reflected—Joe's clothes wouldn't come close to fitting him.

Joe and the boys joined the table, and even though unusual circumstances had led to some of the party having already started eating, heads were bowed and God was thanked for sparing the boys and for the food on the table, as well as for gut friends.

Reuben felt a little awkward when Joe and Edie both looked at him with emotion filling their eyes and again thanked him for his role in rescuing their boys.

"You seem to be making a habit of rescuing our kinner, Dokder!" Joe said. "Denki for being there for us—again!"

"Now, eat up!" Edie cheerfully directed, scooping food onto her younger sons' plates as Joe started passing platters around the table. *You'd have to go a long way to find someone who could outcook Mrs. Yoder,* Reuben thought, happily taking a serving of pancakes and topping them with fresh butter and real maple syrup.

As he enjoyed his breakfast, he studied Mary, enjoying the natural way she interacted with her half brothers, mother, and stepfather.

He was very happy she'd decided to at least consider the procedure which might make her life easier. That was really all he could ask. But he found himself more determined than ever to avoid developing a doctor-patient relationship with her. Sure, he could give her advice, friend to friend, and help her connect with the medical specialists she'd need in Columbus or Cleveland, most likely, but as he watched her he realized that his interest in her was anything but clinical.

Now all he had to do was convince the stubborn woman that his admiration for her was genuine and sincere. Oh, and figure out a way for a baptized Amish woman and an unbaptized former Amish man to explore a relationship without getting the woman excommunicated.

Because Reuben had become quite sure that pursuing a relationship with Mary was what he wanted to do, if it was at all possible.

He'd leave it up to God for now and just enjoy being with her—and her mother's excellent cooking.

CHAPTER EIGHT

Mary was seated in her little living room in the dawdi haus a couple of mornings later, once again looking over the brochures Reuben had given her.

She was seated in a cozy antique armchair dating to the 1940s, big and comfy with lovely wooden trim and feet. It had been reupholstered at least twice that she knew of, and the current robin's egg blue, while not the most practical color, made Mary happy every time she saw it. There was a matching footstool too. The pieces had belonged to her grossmammi, who had bought them at auction when she and Mary's grandfather had moved from the big house into the newly built dawdi haus years before.

Mary reached for the glass of icy lemonade sitting on a quilted coaster on a cherry side table next to her chair. Mary had made the coaster for her grossmammi as a teen.

She shook her head as she examined one of the brochures, with a cover featuring a pretty English girl walking with a cane and looking as if she hadn't a care in the world.

"Hmph. I doubt I'd get results that good," Mary muttered, opening the brochure to review its contents. Before she could dive in, a perfunctory knock sounded on her door, followed by her dear friend Lydia's voice calling out.

"Hello! Are you home, Mary? I came to check on that kitten!"

A grin spread over Mary's face at her friend's greeting.

"In here, Lydia! Come in! Hope misses you, and so do I."

Lydia Coblentz, an elderly Amish woman who'd recently moved into her friend Ruth's dawdi haus, stumped into the room, leading with her handsome, hand-carved cane—a gift from her late husband.

"It looks as if you were expecting me!" Lydia chuckled, lowering herself carefully into a rocking chair across from where Mary was sitting. "You've got an extra glass set out!"

"I never know who might stop by, so I brought out a glass in case. I'm so happy it's you! Help yourself!"

"Don't mind if I do. Denki." Lydia poured herself a tall glass of lemonade and sat back with a sigh. "It's mighty gut to sit with a friend on a hot summer day. I'm glad you're in. Do you work today?"

"Nee, it's my day off. I finished my chores and thought I might tie some new lures this afternoon. But first I have some reading I've been meaning to get to."

Lydia's sharp glance took in the brochures on the table, and she looked at Mary with raised eyebrows. "Interesting. You're thinking about having another surgery, child?"

Mary squirmed a bit in her chair, unaccountably uncomfortable with the subject. "Well, I'm considering it. Dr. King wants me to look these over."

A wily smile spread over the old woman's weathered face, making her resemble one of the apple-head dolls Mary had seen for sale in the tourist shops.

"Dr. King, is it? The handsome new dokder in town? I have to say, he's easy on the eyes, ja?"

Mary's mouth dropped open. "Lydia! Goodness, he's a nice man helping out a patient, that's all."

"Ah, you're one of his patients?"

Mary frowned. "Well, no, not really."

"You are or you ain't," Lydia said, taking a sip of her lemonade and sighing with pleasure. "Mmm. Mary, you make the best lemonade in Holmes County."

Mary rolled her eyes. "Anyway, it's not like it would be a miracle cure or anything. Reuben said it could—*might*—improve my mobility and reduce my daily discomfort."

"Reuben, hmm? But we'll save that for later. By discomfort, I assume you mean pain?" She nodded at Mary's small shrug. "Well, then what's to think about? If I could have a surgery that would give me back some of the mobility I had ten years ago and take away some of the pain of simply getting old, I'd jump on it. You're stubborn is what you are, child. Always worrying about inconveniencing others, instead of occasionally thinking about yourself."

"Oh, really? Well, you could have that hip replacement Dr. Smith always nagged you about, Lydia." At Lydia's dismissive gesture, Mary frowned. "Why not? How is it any different? Here you are trying to convince me to have a procedure with uncertain results, when you know a new hip would take care of much of your trouble, Lydia! That's a proven procedure, not some new, experimental one. You're the stubborn one!"

"Now you sound like Ruth. She's been after me to get that hip replacement. But I'm seventy-five years old! What do I need with a new hip?"

"You should listen to Ruth! She's a sensible girl who cares about you. And seventy-five isn't old. Think how much more help you could be to Ruth and Jonas if you could get around better. And of course, they may have more kinner after the wedding."

"Hmm. You're not wrong. But I hear it's a difficult recovery. I'd have to go in for physical therapy for several weeks afterward. I don't know. It's a big decision."

"Exactly what I've been telling Reu. . .er, Dr. King. In my case, it'll cost the community money without the guaranteed good results your hip would get you. How can I do that? Plus, I'd miss work, and it would create more work for Maem and Dat." She huffed out a breath. "I guess we both have some thinking to do."

Lydia sat up, her eyes sparkling. "So, if I agree to have my hip replaced—not that I'm saying I will, just *if*—then would you agree to have your surgery? We could recover together!"

"What, in the same house? Wouldn't that make a lot of work for either my maem or Ruth, depending on which house we chose?"

Lydia looked thoughtful. "I hadn't actually meant in the same house, although come to think of it, that could be fun! Both dawdi hauses have two bedrooms. We could keep each other company."

"Maybe. But we're getting ahead of ourselves. I haven't said I'll do this."

Lydia reached for a brochure with one hand and a cookie from a plate on the table with the other. "Well, let's see what this is all about." She dug in her apron for a pair of reading glasses, and when she put them on, Mary giggled.

"Those aren't exactly plain, Lydia!" The glasses were green with blue polka dots.

"Shhh, they're my little rebellion. I don't use them at services. It's between me and Gott." She frowned at Mary and started reading.

Mary smiled fondly as her friend perused the brochure. She picked up a second pamphlet and read through it herself. After a few minutes, they traded pamphlets and spent the next few minutes reading up on the latest in spinal repair surgery aimed at increasing mobility and reducing pain in the legs and back of people with traumatic spinal injuries.

When they were through, they put the papers on the table and sat back, each lost in thought. After a few minutes, Lydia raised her gaze and met Mary's. "Well, that's a lot, I admit. And as you said, no guarantees."

"Ja. They make it sound pretty safe, though. But I'm sure it isn't without risks."

"What is?" Lydia shrugged. "You need to think about it. And pray about it. Gott always knows what we should do. We just need to open our hearts to hear Him."

Mary smiled. "Ja, of course, you're right. And will you open your heart to listen to what He has to say about your hip?"

Lydia gave a belly laugh, which made her sound much younger and clued one into what a fun person she was, just in case they didn't already know. "Ja, ja, I will pray about it. And I'll come back here in a few days with my decision. At which point, I expect you to have also made a decision, young lady."

Mary sighed. "Oll recht, I agree to think and pray. And I'll talk to my parents and the dokder."

Lydia sat back. "Gut! Now, where's my little Hope?" At the sound of her name, Hope popped her head up from her bed in the corner of the room. Seeing Lydia, one of her favorite people, she gave a happy meow and hopped up onto her lap, where she began kneading her apron and accepting pats and scratches, as was her due.

"She sure loves you," Mary commented.

"I'm her grossmammi, after all! I enjoy visiting all of my grand-kittens and seeing their human mamas."

"How is everyone? Is Ruth getting excited about her wedding?"

"It's little Abby who can hardly contain herself! She's helping to sew a new frock for the special day."

"How sweet! She's a lovely child. I'm so happy she and Ruth and Jonas found each other."

The two friends settled in for a comfortable chat about mutual friends, and when Lydia left an hour later she admonished Mary not to forget her promise.

"I heard about your near mishap a few days ago, Mary. I heard you fell trying to reach your brieder. I'm so grateful to Gott that you weren't hurt and that they are safe. But this is one of those things, you know—one of those things that happens that makes me think maybe Gott puts things into our paths to help us make decisions. If you could get around better, you wouldn't have fallen. And if you'd needed to reach those kinner, well. . .maybe you'd be more able to do so if you have that surgery. That's all I'm going to say!"

She let herself out the door and waved cheerfully as she climbed into her buggy. As Mary watched her drive down the driveway, she reflected that what Lydia had said was only what she herself had thought.

"I think what Gott actually places in our path are honest friends who light a fire under us when we're hesitating to go where we need to go." She smiled as she closed the door. "I will pray. And I will talk to Reuben. That's all I can promise for now."

CHAPTER NINE

Two days later, Mary had essentially made her decision, but before she talked to Lydia or her parents, she decided to have a conversation with Reuben.

It was early afternoon, and since it was Saturday, Mary knew her maem would be busy baking pies for tomorrow's church services. She took the breezeway between the main and dawdi hauses and opened the door to her mudder's kitchen, waiting while Hope scampered through, pausing to make sure the coast was clear of noisy young boys. Mary could tell from the relative quiet in the house that the boys must be outside somewhere, most likely with their dat.

"Well, hello!" Edie threw an absent-minded smile at Mary as she took two steaming, fragrant pies from the oven and carefully replaced them with two uncooked ones. "What are you up to on this fine day?"

"Afternoon, Maem. I've been thinking about Dokder King's suggestion about undergoing another surgery, and there are some things I want to discuss with him. May I use the buggy? I shouldn't be too long. I'll certainly be back in time to help you make supper."

Edie waved at her daughter while setting the timer for the pies. "Of course you may use the buggy. Take Sebastian, if you don't mind. He's been feeling a bit restless and could use the exercise. Besides, I think Daisy Mae needs her left rear shoe replaced. I need to remember to speak to your dat about it."

Mary wrapped a light shawl around her shoulders, made sure her *kapp* was tied neatly and securely, and headed out to hitch up the horse. She met Joe and the boys on her way out to the barn, and they made quick work of the chore for her. Before she knew it, she was turning onto the road and heading into town.

Alone with her thoughts, Mary wondered if she was making the right decision as she second-guessed herself yet again.

Nothing new about that! she thought, shaking her head at her own foolishness.

Sighing, she clucked to Sebastian, who trotted happily down the road, showing off a bit of the spirit that had made him a winner at the racetrack for two seasons before a pulled hamstring ended his career. He had healed well but not well enough to win races. As a gelding, he had few career options and was fortunate to be purchased by Joe and trained as a buggy horse. Mary was inordinately fond of the big standardbred.

"You're a gut boy, aren't you, Sebastian? Trot on, there you go."

Sebastian snorted and trotted smartly toward town. Mary almost wished the big animal would slow down, since she wasn't quite sure what to say to Reuben, assuming he was home on a Saturday afternoon. Should she have her crow fried? Or maybe boiled? A small smile tugged at the corner of her mouth. Reuben might tease her for changing her mind, but the important thing was that he'd help her find out whether she was a gut candidate for the surgery. If not, that would be that, and she could walk away knowing she'd done her best.

But if she was a good candidate—terrifying thought!—then she'd need the Mennonite doctor's help to navigate the English medical system. And she couldn't think of anyone who would be a better guide. In a short time, she'd come to trust Reuben. She knew he wouldn't let her down if he could possibly help it.

Having just returned from a trip to the market, Reuben finished putting away his groceries and realized he was thirsty.

"It's a hot day. I need lemonade."

He took the canister of powdered lemonade out of the cabinet, peeled open the protective foil, and coughed a bit as a waft of powdered tartness poofed up from the can.

"Gah! I hope it tastes better once I mix it with water."

Soon he had a pitcher filled with lemonade and ice cubes, and he poured some into a tall tumbler, which he lifted to his lips and carefully tasted.

He shrugged. "Okay, so it's not as good as Mary's homemade, but it's not terrible." Determined, he guzzled down the glass, then poured another, which he took outside to sip on the front porch.

As he settled onto one of the rockers, the sound of hooves clip-clopping down the street caught his attention. Mildly interested—the sound was commonplace in Willow Creek, and he'd gotten used to it again—he glanced up in time to see a buggy pulled by a big chestnut gelding turn into his parking lot.

"Well, speak of the devil, and you'll hear the flop of his wings!"

He rose from his chair and moved casually toward the buggy, which had pulled into a parking area. The driver opened the door and stepped carefully out.

"Hello there! Have you come to judge my lemonade-making skills?"

Startled, Mary turned too quickly and almost lost her balance. She grabbed Sebastian's reins to steady herself and frowned fiercely at Reuben. "Are you trying to make me fall down and look *narrish*?"

Contrite, Reuben hurried forward. "Of course not! I'm sorry. I thought you'd seen me when you turned in. Here, let me take your bag."

"I've got it, thanks," she said, hooking the sturdy leather backpack her stepfather had made over one shoulder before taking up her crutches and turning toward Reuben. "Excuse me?"

He didn't move, but stood looking down at her, glass of lemonade in hand. "Are you here to see me?"

She rolled her eyes. "And who else would I be coming to see? If you'd step aside, I could go up on the porch and have a seat."

Grinning, he moved aside, and she made her way to the porch, up the steps, and over to the rocking chairs. Setting her backpack down on the low table set in front of the three rocking chairs, she lowered herself into one and sighed. "Now, are you going to offer me a glass of lemonade? Or do you plan to drink yours in front of me while I melt from the heat?"

Chuckling, Reuben opened his front door. "Bide a spell, and I'll go get you a glass."

The door banged closed, and Mary smiled. She leaned back in the comfy chair and set it rocking with a small push of one foot. Closing her eyes, she listened to the drone of cicadas and let the heat of the day lull her into a half doze, enjoying a rare moment of having absolutely nothing to do.

"Here you go! Drink yourself dry! But don't expect it to be as good as yours. It came from a can."

"Beggers, choosers," she said, taking the glass and sipping gratefully. She drank half the glass before coming up for air. "Ah. Denki, that hits the spot."

"So, it's okay?"

She looked surprised. "Ja, of course. It's cold and wet. I'm pretty thirsty." She finished the remainder of the glass and then eyed the pitcher on the table. Taking the hint, Reuben filled her glass again, and then his own.

"I guess it isn't too bad," he conceded. "It's just not as good as yours."

"I prefer to think of them as two different drinks. That way I can enjoy this stuff without comparing it unfairly to homemade."

"Huh. I like that. That's a really good way of thinking. You have a pretty good attitude, Mary. I suppose that's been a help to you."

"Or maybe I developed a gut attitude in response to having a disability."

He shrugged, sipping his lemonade. "I guess it doesn't matter which came first. Only that you have found an admirable way of viewing the world."

Apparently uncomfortable with his praise, she set her glass down and reached for her bag. Unzipping it, she dug around inside until she said, "Aha!" Then she pulled out the brochures he'd given her. Suddenly her visit made sense. She'd come to a decision about the surgery.

Reuben was surprised by how much he cared about whether or not Mary had decided against the procedure. He really cared about her and about the quality of her life. He said a silent prayer, asking God to give her courage to move forward. He believed this procedure could help her live a better life, and whether he would be part of that life or not didn't matter. He just wanted her to live with less pain and to be able to get around more easily.

He licked his lips and stared at the brochures Mary was clutching in her hand. Then he raised his eyes and met hers.

He couldn't tell from her expression what she'd decided to do. She'd make a good poker player.

Doing his best to hide his strong feelings, he reached for the brochures, but she pulled them out of his reach. Was she playing a game?

His eyes widened. "Didn't you come to return those to me? It's okay, I understand. There's a lot of risk, and the possibility of a good return on it is too low. No worries."

She raised her eyebrows and stared at him a few moments before speaking. "Wait. You think I'm here to tell you I've decided not to go through with the procedure?"

He blinked in confusion. "Well, haven't you?"

One corner of her pretty mouth quirked up, and she shook her head. "No, Reuben. I've decided to do it. I'm here so you can help me decide what to do next."

"Mary! That's wonderful news!" He reached for her hands and captured them in his much bigger ones. Squeezing gently, he let his happiness at her decision wash through him and shine out of his eyes.

"Well, I didn't know you'd be this pleased!"

"I'm very pleased—for you." He felt very proud of her for her courage in the face of the unknown—and worse, in the face of the previous painful surgeries she'd endured. "You are a remarkable woman, Mary."

She smiled up at him. "Well. Denki."

For the space of several breaths, they just sat there, holding hands and looking at each other. The sound of a buggy passing in the street snapped them out of their brief reverie, and Mary frowned.

"I did tell you I would consider it, remember?"

"Ja, I just didn't dare hope."

She shrugged. "Hope away. I'm going to give this one more shot. What have I got to lose?"

Admiration welled within him for her. "Um, the third brochure went over that. . ."

She laughed. "Oh, right! It did explain exactly what I could lose. But I'm not going to worry about it. Reuben, I'm putting it in Gott's hands. And I'll put myself into yours and let you guide me through this."

His mouth fell open a bit as he was struck with humility at her faith, both in Gott and in him.

"I hope you won't be disappointed again, Mary," he whispered.

"Honestly, Reuben, my expectations are pretty low, so it would be hard for me to be disappointed."

At that, he sat up straight and laughed. "Okay, then! I guess that's a healthy outlook. Anyway, I'll help you through the medical hoops, but I won't be acting as your physician. I'll help you find a specialist, and then I'll be emotional support for you and your family."

She nodded. "Denki, Reuben. That will be very kind of you."

He opened his mouth to inform her that kindness had little to do with his motivations, when their conversation was interrupted by a small open buggy paused in front of the house, and the friendly call of, "Yoo-hoo! Guder middag! Don't you two look cozy sharing lemonade on the porch on a hot day?"

"Oh bother," Mary muttered before pasting a smile on her face and calling back, "Good afternoon to you, Mrs. Schwartz! Ja, it is super hot, and the dokder was kind enough to offer me a glass."

Speculation glittered in the older woman's eyes, and Reuben could almost hear her thinking she had a hot scoop to take to the next quilting frolic.

"How kind! And you happened to be strolling by and he invited you up?" Her eyes darted to where Mary had parked her buggy.

"Ah. . ." Mary started, but Reuben cut in.

"And I'd love to invite you up for a glass too, Mrs. Schwartz. In fact, while you're here, why don't I go in and get those vaccines we were talking about the other day? It won't take me five minutes, and I really do think you should have them."

He felt a guilty satisfaction at the woman's look of alarm. He'd been counting on it.

"Oh dear," Mrs. Schwartz said. "If I only had time! But I must be off! You two young people enjoy your visit. Goodbye, now!" She flicked her reins, and her horse trotted down the road smartly.

Mary looked at him with amusement. "What was that about?"

He bit his lip. "I'm afraid I can't really discuss it. Doctor/patient confidentiality, you understand. But. . .I will say Mrs. Schwartz has a fear of getting a shot unusual in one so. . .mature." He grinned.

Mary grinned back, and they sat looking at one another for a few seconds until Mary snapped herself out of it.

"Goodness, what am I thinking? I can't be sitting here holding hands with a single, handsome man. People do like to gossip! In fact, Mrs. Schwartz is possibly the biggest gossip in the community."

"You think I'm handsome?"

"Is that all you heard in that entire sentence?" She shook her head. "Men."

He threw back his head and laughed. It was quite infectious, and Mary was soon laughing along with him. "Hopefully you're still laughing tomorrow when all the gossips in town are discussing the Mennonite dokder and the Amish spinster holding hands on his front porch. They'll have us married and me under the bann before we know it."

He frowned. "I hadn't thought of that. Mary, could there be serious trouble for you over this?"

She shrugged. "If anyone comments, I'll simply tell them what we were doing."

"And what were we doing?"

"Why, you were obviously supporting me with compassion and the benefit of your medical experience. Innocent."

"Right, obviously." Reuben wasn't sure why he felt a little deflated at this clinical assessment.

Mary continued, "Some people will forever be looking for something to wag their tongues about."

He sighed. "I don't want to cause you harm. And you are baptized, and I left the faith. That makes things pretty complicated."

She looked at him warily. "Things?"

He felt like squirming, much as he had as a child caught doing something he shouldn't. "You know, if we were interested in. . .getting to know one another better. . .there's no easy path for that for us."

"Right," she said. "So let's not even worry about that. Let's focus on what I came for. What's the next step now that I've decided to move forward with this?"

He sat back and frowned at her. His emotions were in a whirl. How could she so calmly dismiss the attraction they obviously felt for one another? She watched him so calmly—or did she? Looking at Mary, Reuben saw something in her eyes, something sad that hinted at buried hopes and dreams. Maybe she wasn't as indifferent as she seemed? The thought cheered him. He'd have to consider it later.

He sat back, determined to bide his time and not spook her. "Okay, the next step is to find a specialist. I have some contacts at the Cleveland Clinic I can call if you like, see if we can get you an appointment for an assessment."

She nodded firmly. "Ja. Let's do it. Now that I've made up my mind, I want to get moving on this. If it's possible that I could walk better, I don't want to wait until it's almost too late again. Next time, you and my vader might not be handy to save the day."

He smiled at her. "Okay. It's Saturday evening. They'll be closed tomorrow. I'll call Monday morning." She looked dismayed at the delay, which he could understand. It was no doubt frustrating to make such a difficult decision and then have to wait to put it into action. But she, more than most people, probably knew just how much "hurry up and wait" there was in the medical world.

"Okay then, we have a plan! Congratulations, Mary. I'm impressed with your courage. I just hope this procedure makes a measurable difference in your pain level and mobility."

"Me too. But Gott will take care of me. Of that, I'm sure."

Reuben felt humbled by her unwavering faith, in spite of all the hard things she'd endured. Many people would have decided God wasn't there, or that if He was, He didn't have time for them. But not Mary. She just kept going, rich in the fullness of her belief in God's love for her.

"Well, I'd better get home. I'll need to help prepare supper. And I'll talk to my parents about this tonight, and I suppose to Bishop Troyer soon, to be sure I can get the community's support."

She pushed to her feet, and Reuben also stood.

"If for some reason the community can't pay for this, there's financial help at Cleveland Clinic based on income. I'm quite sure you'd qualify. In fact, maybe you should apply and see how much they'll cover before asking the community to pay."

"We'll see. Denki, Reuben. I will talk to you soon."

"I'll walk you to your buggy."

"That's not necessary."

"My maem would have my hide if I forgot my manners, Mary. Don't shame me in front of my maem."

She let out a little snort that Reuben thought might be an attempt at covering up a laugh. "Your maem is hundreds of miles away. She won't know."

"I would know." He grinned and accompanied her down the steps and along the path to where she'd left her horse and buggy. He opened her door and watched as she tossed her bag inside, then climbed in with a practiced air. He was once again impressed with her ability.

He untied the horse from the hitching post and stood back as Mary waved, and then he watched her competently drive the buggy away down the street.

He stood with his hands in his pockets, staring after her even after she'd turned a corner and disappeared. He'd call the specialist he'd already found first thing Monday. There was no need for Mary to know he'd already looked into this just in case she decided to move forward. What she didn't know couldn't hurt him.

As for the rest—was there any possible future for a baptized Amish woman and a lapsed Amish man, now a Mennonite doctor?

He shook his head. He couldn't see a way that wouldn't end up with Mary losing her church and her family and friends. He'd better forget about that. Unless he was willing to give up his practice and rejoin the church and be baptized, he just didn't think there could be a path forward.

Tipping his head back, he let his gaze drift through the green leaf canopy of the ancient oaks planted more than a hundred years before in the tree lawn before his house and practice. They were majestic, lasting. He found his thoughts turning to eternity, and to God.

"Lord," he prayed silently, "it seems I want to have my cake and eat it too. How ironic is it that when You finally send me a woman I think I could love, she's out-of-bounds for me? I've tried to turn my feelings from her, but I'm struggling. Please, Father, if there is no way forward for us, help me to overcome these feelings. But if there is a way, then please help us see it. Your will be done."

He closed his eyes for a moment, just breathing.

The sudden blast of a horn as a vehicle turned fast into his parking area jerked him back. A blue Subaru Forester screeched to a halt, and the front doors popped open. A man jumped out of the driver's seat, and a woman holding a screaming child jumped out of the passenger seat.

"Doctor! Our son has cut his foot on a piece of broken glass! He's bleeding!" the man cried as he hurried around to take the heavy child from his wife and bring him to Reuben.

"Let's have a look. What's your name, buddy?"

The child sniffled and looked at him with tear-filled eyes. "Paul."

"Okay, Paul, I'm not going to hurt you. Let me have a look." He peeled back the paper towel Paul's father was using to keep pressure on the wound, and immediately blood welled from an inch-long cut that looked fairly deep.

"Well, Paul, you did a number on your foot, all right. Folks, carry him inside. I'll stitch him up, and he'll be good as new."

"Will it hurt?" the child asked, fresh tears falling down his chubby cheeks.

"A little, son, but afterward I'll give you a popsicle, okay?"

The child looked interested in the popsicle, but Reuben knew the next half hour would be tough. But in the end, this child would fully recover from his injury and walk normally. Not all children were as fortunate, he reflected.

He was hoping that with God's grace, Mary's quality of life was about to take a turn for the better.

CHAPTER TEN

"Of course the bishop approved the surgery, Mary. Why on earth wouldn't he want you to have a chance at better health? Honestly, sometimes I don't know what you're thinking!" Mary's friend Jane Bontrager shook her head as she washed up dishes and Mary sat at the Bontragers' big wood block kitchen counter drying them. It was after Sunday services, which had been held at Jane's family's farm, and with a number of visitors from Lancaster, Pennsylvania, in attendance, they kept running out of dishes.

Jane turned and piled another heap of plates on a towel set on the table, and Mary picked up the top one and dried it off with a hand towel, which was quickly becoming wetter than the dishes.

"I need another towel, please."

Jane moved to a drawer next to the sink and pulled out two. "Here you go. This should take care of it. There aren't many left, and I think this is the last batch."

"So. You really don't think I'm being. . .selfish?"

"There you go again, Mary. No. I don't think you're being selfish. I do think you're being silly." She put the final plates on the pile on the table, grabbed a dry towel, and began drying them alongside her friend.

"Silly?"

"Ja! Look. If I needed a surgery, would you begrudge me?"

"Of course not! But it's like my tenth surgery, Jane. It's expensive!"

Jane turned to face Mary, her face betraying her exasperation. "Mary. You are a member of this faith community. We take care of each other. That is what we do. First surgery or tenth, if you need it and we can afford it, you get it. Understand?"

Mary sighed and wiped at tears brimming in her eyes. "Ja. I understand. Denki, Jane. I guess I just needed to hear it from someone who isn't my mom."

Jane chuckled. "I can understand that. But I'm biased too, because you're my friend and I love you." She tossed the towel down. "Can you finish up here? I need to go check on my sister's kinner. I promised to keep an eye on them while she and her husband spend a little grown-up time with their friends."

"Sure, no problem. I'm almost done here, then I'll go out and see who's still here."

Jane gave her a quick hug. "And stop worrying so much! Bishop Troyer would say, 'Trust Gott to take care of you!'"

Mary giggled at her friend's terrible imitation of the old bishop's deep voice. "Go!"

Jane went. Mary thoughtfully picked up another dish and began drying it.

"Your impudent friend is right, you know," a familiar, deep voice said from behind her.

"Oh! You startled me!"

"Well, don't drop a plate. I don't want to have to face Jane's mudder if I caused you to do that!"

Bishop Troyer settled his slightly stooped form on a chair across from Mary. "I overheard what she said to you. I'll ignore her attempt at acting as it wasn't that far off." He chuckled.

"I'm sure she didn't mean any disrespect, Bishop."

"Of course not. Nor did she realize I was right around the corner. And remember the old saying—if you listen through the wall, you will hear others recite your faults."

Mary smiled. "Ja. But she'd be mortified."

"We won't tell her. Look, Mary, we can afford this surgery as a community, especially with the financial aid available from the Cleveland Clinic. And I spoke with Dr. King earlier. He seems to feel there is a gut chance it will help you move around more freely and with less pain. That sounds like reason enough to try to me."

She nodded. "That's what I thought too, Bishop Troyer. And as my parents agree, we've given Reuben...um, Dr. King...the go-ahead to talk to the specialists to see if they'll see me. It all may come to nothing, you know. I may not be a gut candidate, for whatever reason. I'm not going to get my hopes up."

The bishop sat back and surveyed Mary through narrowed eyes. "Well, then, we'll wait and see. There is another issue I wish to discuss, Mary."

"Yes, Bishop Troyer?"

"I feel a bit awkward talking to you like this, given the fact that you're no rebellious teenager in the middle of your rumspringa." He cleared his throat and looked uncomfortable, and Mary felt a twinge of trepidation. This didn't sound good.

"In fact, you've always been a most prudent and obedient child. But I feel I must warn you that you may be in danger now."

Her eyes widened and she stared at the bishop. "In danger? From what?"

He cleared his throat again and gave her a stern look. "From temptation."

"Temptation? I don't understand."

He sighed. "To speak plainly, Mary, it's been noticed that you've been spending time with the new dokder." He stopped and looked at her expectantly.

She nodded. "The new dokder. Yes. . .of course I have, as he is helping me to get this surgery. I have to spend time with him."

"Mary, it's been noticed that when you're with him, the two of you don't act like a doctor and patient. But rather, you act like a courting couple."

Mary's mouth dropped open. "A courting couple? That's ridiculous. No disrespect meant, Bishop."

He regarded her steadily for a few moments. "Is it ridiculous? You're a lovely young woman. He has eyes. Moreover, he grew up Amish, so our ways are familiar to him, and part of him probably yearns for that familiarity—that sense of belonging."

"He's not under the bann."

"I know, but he left the faith. He's an Englisher now."

"He's a Mennonite. That's not really an Englisher."

"Close enough. He drives a truck, lives in a house with electricity, has a phone. And do I need to remind you that you chose to be baptized in the faith? If you decide to go with this man, marry this man, you will be shunned."

Mary's eyes filled with tears. "I hadn't seriously thought of marrying him. I mean, I may have daydreamed a bit. But I fully understand the vow I took, and of course I honor it."

He looked even more uncomfortable. "Mary, I'm not enjoying this conversation. Some people need to be scolded roundly to jolt them back onto the right course. You've never been like that." He patted her hand and reached into his pocket and offered her a clean white handkerchief. "But Mary, I understand what it's like to be alone and lonely."

"But I'm rarely alone, Bishop."

He waved a hand. "Ja, you live with your parents and brieder. But you are a woman in her prime, and of course you wish for a husband. It doesn't seem fair that this man who attracts you is not one of us. You may wonder, why would Gott send this man to tempt me?" He shrugged. "We cannot know His ways or His reasons. But we do know our ways, and this man is not for you, Mary. You're both adults, and you both made your choices. Now you must live with that choice. Do you understand?"

She dashed a tear away with the back of her hand. "Ja, I understand. If I break my vow, I'll be shunned and lose everyone I know and love, and my whole way of life. I'd never do that, Bishop Troyer. But you're right. It does seem unfair. I've never met a man I liked so much before. And who seems to like me too." She shook her head and blew her nose. "But don't worry, I won't succumb to temptation. I'd never leave the community."

"That's a gut girl." He patted her hand again. "I know it isn't always easy." He stood. "I suggest you pray very hard for Gott to help you overcome your feelings for this man and to soothe your heart. Who knows? You might yet meet a nice Amish man who'll see what a wonderful young woman you are."

He walked to the door and opened it. "I'll see you later, Mary. Please remember what I said and be more circumspect. You don't want to attract the eyes of the gossips."

She nodded, miserably, and he went out.

And she felt bereft.

CHAPTER ELEVEN

Mary rode home from services that afternoon with her family, pondering the bishop's words. In truth, she felt depressed. Although she knew nothing could come of her attraction to Reuben, it felt gut to find a man to whom she was attracted and, even better, to know that her interest was returned.

Yet it was foolish and wrong of her to continue to entertain such feelings—for they could only lead to her ruin.

More than once, she saw her mother glance back at her where she sat in the back of the buggy with two of her brieder. She knew from the worried look on her mudder's face that there would be questions later. Goodness, for all she knew, the bishop had aired his concerns to her parents! What a humiliating idea. She felt heat crawl up her cheeks at the thought and turned her face to the window so nobody would notice her blush of shame.

She heaved a sigh. Time would tell. She spent the remainder of the ride home holding back tears. And it didn't go unnoticed by her mudder, she was certain. An uncomfortable conversation loomed ahead.

Joe and the boys disappeared into the barn for chores when they got home, and Mary and Edie went inside to start supper.

Mary felt her mudder's eyes on her as she went about her chores, and finally she put both hands on the counter, took a deep breath, and looked at her mudder.

"Okay, Maem, you want to say something. Just get it off your chest."

Edie was standing across the large farm kitchen, a jug of milk in her hands, worrying her lower lip with her teeth. She nodded and set the milk on the counter, then walked to the table and sat down. "Sit, Mary. You're right, I need to tell you what happened today after services."

Mary sat and braced herself for an accounting of the bishop's conversation with her elders. Her mother frowned and then surprised Mary by saying, "That busybody Amelia Schwartz is causing trouble, gossiping about you and the dokder! As a gut Christian woman, I must forgive her, but I'll admit I'm having a hard time. I've been praying all afternoon, but it's preying on my mind!"

Mary's mouth fell open, and she stared at her mudder, unsure of how to respond.

"Um, this is not what I expected you to say, Maem."

"What did you think I was going to say?"

"Well, that the bishop had talked to you and Dat about this. He...he talked to me after lunch." She swallowed, still ashamed at being called to task like a naughty child.

"He did, did he?" Edie frowned again. "Well, what did he say?"

"He said that there had been talk about the dokder and me, that we were acting too familiar. He was worried I would be tempted to leave the community and wanted to remind me that if I did, I'd be put under the bann, since I've been baptized. As if I could forget."

"Interesting. The talk, no doubt, started with Amelia Schwartz. But having heard it, or probably, having had her force it on him directly, he has to act on it." Edie sighed. "I'm sorry, lieb. I know you would never act in an unseemly way."

"I assumed, at my age, that I could talk to a friend, outside on his porch, without being reported like a teen getting out of control on my rumspringa. Goodness, I never even had a rumspringa! Anyway, I thought I was considered trustworthy enough to talk with a friend outside in plain view without raising eyebrows. I guess I was wrong."

"Nonsense. Of course you're considered mature and trustworthy by most people in the community." Her lips pressed together. "We are talking about one busybody who took it upon herself to run to the bishop and tell tales. Then he had to say something to you. I wouldn't spend much time worrying about it. I just want to be sure you knew it was out there."

"I knew, because Bishop Troyer told me so himself. He warned me not to give in to my attraction. That I need to pray and that as *en alt maedel*, I might be especially prone to succumbing to temptation, due to my lonely state. It was so embarrassing!"

Edie reached across the table and took Mary's hand. "First, you're not an old maid. You have time to find a mann, if you want one. Second, I'm sure he meant no offense. He's elderly, and it's a delicate topic, nee?"

Mary nodded reluctantly. "Ja, I suppose so."

"Ja. Finally, if you are attracted to this man, pray about it. Don't just give up as if there were no hope. Remember, Gott can do anything. With Him, many things that seem impossible *aren't*."

Mary smiled at her mother. "Are you telling me to go against the bishop's advice, Maem?"

"Nee, nee. I'm just saying, Gott may know a way you and the dokder could be together that is not apparent yet to us mere humans. That's all. And, I trust you completely. So try not to fret about what some people may say. You know the truth of what is in your heart. Hold your head up and look that Amelia Schwartz right in the eye and smile next time you see her. It'll make her wonder what you're up to." Edie patted Mary's hand and stood up. She picked up the milk and started making gravy for supper.

"Maem! That seems almost. . .rebellious."

Edie stirred milk and flour into the sausage drippings to make sausage gravy and pursed her lips. "Not at all. I wouldn't suggest rebelliousness toward the bishop or the community. You know that." She stirred energetically for a few moments before looking up with something of a twinkle in her eye at Mary. "But Amelia Schwartz is not a church or community leader, and you don't have to heed her. Just be your usual sensible self. Pray about this and see what happens.

That's all I'm saying. Be open-minded so the Lord can work His will through you. Remember, Gott promises that in all things He works for the good of those who love Him." She waved the spoon at Mary. "Now, let me get this supper going. Why don't you go on over to the dawdi haus and take care of your own chores, or get some rest. I saw how you worked at lunch today, while I relaxed. Supper will be ready in an hour. Come on over a little before that, and you can help me get it on the table, ja?"

Mary felt a bit dazed as she nodded, picked up her crutches, and walked through the breezeway to the dawdi haus. Her maem had given her a lot to think about!

A short time later, Mary was darning a sock in her living room when a knock sounded on her door. She raised her eyes to the door and was surprised to see Reuben and a young woman through the window. She waved at him to come in, and he opened the door and stepped inside, followed by the woman—really just a girl, Mary saw once she was in the house.

"Guder middag, Mary," Reuben said. "I hope you aren't busy right now? I wanted to introduce my schwester to you."

Mary smiled at the young woman, whom she'd guessed to be his younger sister. "Absolutely! Please, come in and sit, both of you."

They sat down on the sofa facing her chair in front of the fireplace, and Reuben smiled fondly at the pretty girl he'd brought to meet Mary. "This is Eliza, my baby schwester. Eliza, this is my friend, Mary."

Eliza rolled her expressive brown eyes at her brother and laughed. "Baby sister! I'm seventeen! But it's so nice to meet you, Mary. Reuben has told me so much about you. I'm actually a little *naerfich* to meet you!"

Mary frowned at Reuben. "What on earth could he have said to make you nervous to meet me? There's no need for that! I've been looking forward to meeting you ever since he said you'd be coming, a few weeks ago. Welcome to Willow Creek!"

The younger woman glowed with pleasure and smiled back,

showing off charming dimples.

"Denki! I've really been looking forward to coming. Reuben drove over home yesterday and spent the night, and we came back together this afternoon, after services. I'm looking forward to settling in and then hope to find a job in town."

"So you're planning to stay awhile?"

Eliza nodded. "Ja. Maem and Dat think I'm husband hunting, but the truth is, I'm not ready to settle down yet, and my favorite bruder is less likely to nag me about it than my parents are."

"Favorite bruder, ha! If John were here, you wouldn't call me that." She twinkled at him. "That would depend."

"On?"

"On which of you I needed something from."

He threw back his head and laughed, and Mary smiled at the interplay between brother and sister. They were obviously very fond of each other, much as she was of her younger half siblings.

"We have services this Sunday. Would you like to attend with me?"

Eliza beamed at her. "Ja! That would be wonderful gut!"

"That's really nice of you, Mary. Do you want me to drop her off here before services?"

Mary considered. "No, services are at the Millers' this weekend. We have to go through town to get there anyway, so we'll pick you up on our way."

"Now I'm a little naerfich about this!" The younger woman laughed, but Mary could see in her eyes that she wasn't entirely joking.

"Don't worry. It's a very nice community. You'll be welcomed by everyone."

"Thank you so much, Mary! I'll try to fit in."

"I'm sure you won't have any trouble." She smiled at the girl and then caught Reuben's eye from where he sat slightly behind his sister. He smiled warmly at her, and she was suddenly confused and felt a blush steal over her cheeks. This had to stop!

She glared at Reuben when Eliza bent down to retrieve her bag, and he mock-glared back at her, the scoundrel.

"Well, bruder, we'd better get going if we're going to make the grocery store before it closes. I really need a few things to get settled in." Eliza stood and faced Mary. "Denki so much for your welcome and for inviting me to services! I already feel as if we're friends."

Mary smiled. "Me too. See you in a few days."

Reuben opened the door for his sister, who stepped through and walked toward the truck parked in the driveway. He looked after his sister, then turned hurriedly to Mary. "Thank you very much for making her welcome. It means a lot to both of us."

"Honestly, it's nothing. And...we need to talk, Dokder. Soon. It's important."

He frowned. "We're back to dokder again? What's wrong?"

"Not now. But please stop by sometime soon, when you're alone."

He nodded. "I will, soon. And...it's not nothing, to her or to me." With a jaunty salute, he turned and headed to the truck.

Mary watched them drive away, and she frowned. She needed to warn Reuben about the wagging tongues. Gossip could hurt his practice. And she needed to let him know, once and for all, that there could be nothing between them. No matter what her mudder thought, she just couldn't see a way. *As stubborn as he is, I'll have to make my point very clear. I can't spend any more time with him. It'll just encourage him to keep trying. In the end, it'll hurt us both.*

With a heavy heart she closed the door on the sight of Reuben's truck receding down the driveway and, as far as she was concerned, on any hope of a relationship with the man. Straightening her shoulders, she grabbed her crutches and headed over to help her maem with supper.

CHAPTER TWELVE

Sunday morning Mary's stepfather pulled his buggy to a stop in front of Reuben's home and office in Willow Creek. Before anyone could get out to knock on the door, it opened, and out stepped Reuben and Eliza.

Mary drank in the sight of Reuben, dressed nicely in a pair of khaki pants and a short-sleeved green button-up shirt to attend church services in the Mennonite church outside town. He looked toward the buggy, and she drew back from the window, not wanting to have to face him yet, even at a distance. He frowned but then focused on her mudder, who was waving cheerfully from the front passenger seat. He smiled and waved and said something to Eliza, who smiled and hurried to the buggy.

"Make room for the girl," Edie said over her shoulder as Eliza climbed into the back with Mary and two of her brieder. They scooched over, and Eliza pulled the door closed behind her.

"Guder mariye!" Edie said, smiling into the back seat as Joe pulled the buggy away from the curb.

"Guder mariye!" Eliza chirped, turning to wave once more at Reuben, who stood on his porch watching them go. Mary snuck a peek at him, then turned to smile at his sister.

"Guder mariye, Eliza. You look very nice today."

Eliza smiled and glanced down at her lavender dress. She was wearing the heart-shaped cap worn by women from Lancaster County, Pennsylvania, the ties hanging loose to her shoulders, and Mary thought she looked very fresh and pretty. "Denki, Mary. So do you."

Mary smiled back. She did feel that she'd put herself together nicely today, donning a new leaf-green dress she'd recently finished sewing. "Denki back!"

"So, Eliza, I'm Mary's maem, Edie. And this is my mann, Joe. We're happy to meet you and glad to take you to services today. Welcome to Willow Creek!"

"It will be so much easier going somewhere new with your *familie*. I feel as if Mary is already a gut friend. Reuben speaks so highly of her, and of all of you."

Pleased to hear it, Edie smiled at the girl. "We'll introduce you to everyone, and you'll soon stop feeling like a stranger. So, what's in the bag?"

Eliza glanced at the bag tucked between her feet on the floor. "I didn't want to show up empty handed, so I baked some brownies last night. Will that be okay?"

"Brownies!" Simon cried. "My favorite!"

"Mine too!" Ben said. "Can we have one?"

"After services, boys," Joe said sternly, not taking his eyes from the road. They'd left Willow Creek behind and were traveling down the state route in the narrow buggy lane, cars and trucks whizzing past on the left. Ahead were several other buggies, all headed toward services.

Soon they turned off onto a smaller township road, and it wasn't long before the buggy made the turn into the lane leading to several Amish farms. Services were to be held at the Miller farm. Joe pulled into the driveway, and there were several buggies ahead of theirs.

"It's a nice day, so I'll park here in the field, and we'll walk to the house. It's not far. Okay, Mary?"

"Ja, no problem, Joe."

They parked at the end of a line of buggies in the field and climbed out. The boys ran ahead, and Edie followed quickly. Joe made sure Mary had her crutches and her backpack and hurried after his fraa and *sohns*, leaving Mary and Eliza to walk together more slowly.

"What a lovely day!" Eliza enthused, smiling around at everything.

"It is. And you'll like Elizabeth. She's a friend of mine, and this is her family's farm."

"Oh good. Nothing makes you feel more at home in a place than making friends, right?"

"Well, I've always lived here, and I've known most of these people my whole life. But I suppose you're right."

"I always lived in Lancaster too, but other people were always moving to town, and I observed that the ones who seemed happy were the ones who put themselves to the trouble of getting to know the community and fitting in." She shrugged. "The ones who kept to themselves didn't seem as happy. Of course, maybe I'm getting the buggy before the horse. Maybe the ones who kept to themselves were just unhappy people who wanted to be left alone?"

"Could be. I think happy people are naturally friendlier. Anyway, that's what I've observed."

Before they could talk more, a cheerful voice called out, and they looked down the lane and saw a young Amish woman driving a pony cart their way. "Anybody want a lift?"

Mary laughed. "There's my friend Elizabeth now. She must have seen my parents or brieder and come to collect us with her little cart. Guder mariye, Elizabeth! Yes please, because your pony is so cute!"

Elizabeth pulled up beside them. "Ho, Goldie! That's a gut girl!" Her little brown cart, with one bench just big enough for three slender young women, was pulled by a fat little Haflinger pony. "Climb in and I'll drop you right at the kitchen door!"

Mary climbed in first, followed by Eliza. Elizabeth clicked her tongue at the mare, who trotted smoothly down the drive toward the big white farmhouse.

"This is Dr. King's younger sister, Eliza. She's come to stay with him for a while from Lancaster, Pennsylvania."

Elizabeth glanced curiously at the young woman. "Really? How long will you stay here?"

Eliza shrugged. "I'm not sure. I just wanted a change of scene, and I'm blessed to have a bruder who will let me stay with him."

"Well, welcome to Willow Creek! I'm sure you'll love it here, and maybe you won't want to leave! Maybe you'll find a mann while you're here!" Elizabeth giggled.

"Eliza is only seventeen, Elizabeth. She's not looking for a mann yet. But she is looking for a job. Do you know of anyone hiring?"

"Hmm. Let me think." Elizabeth drove the pony cart up to the kitchen door and pulled to a smooth stop. Eliza and Mary climbed down, taking their bags with them.

"Denki for the ride, Elizabeth. It was very nice to meet you!" Eliza smiled.

"You're welcome! And if you're looking for a job, you could try the bakery in town. That's where I work, and I think we're looking for a part-time counter worker in the early afternoons."

"Really? What would I do?"

"You'd serve customers after the lunch rush. Make kaffi, serve rolls, donuts, that sort of thing. We have internet and comfy chairs, so people come in there to work and people watch. And eat our excellent baked goods, of course!" Elizabeth giggled again.

"I could do that. And I really like baked goods. How do I apply?"

"Stop in tomorrow morning. Actually, it's an easy walk from the dokder's. Is that where you're staying?"

Eliza nodded. "I'll ask Reuben how to get there. Denki, Elizabeth. I'll come by in the morning. I'm excited!"

"Let's take these things into the kitchen, Eliza. It's nearly time for services to start," Mary said.

"Oh! I need to put Goldie in the pasture. I'll see you girls later!" Elizabeth clucked to the mare, who trotted off toward the barn. Mary led the way up the steps into the kitchen, where she introduced Eliza to the women who were gathered there. Then a young boy poked his head in the door to say the elders were ready to start services, and they all made their way to the big barn, where backless benches had been set up for the day's worship service.

Inside, Mary smiled at several people before sliding onto a bench next to a pretty woman with red hair peeking out from under her prayer kapp, and a little girl about five years old sitting next to her.

"Guder mariye, Ruth, Abigail!" Mary whispered, settling on the bench with her crutches on the floor in front of her. "This is Dr. King's sister Eliza, visiting from Lancaster, Pennsylvania."

"Guder mariye, Eliza, it's gut to meet you," Ruth said. The child smiled and said hello, and Eliza wished them good morning. Then the elders entered the barn, and talking was done. As she raised her voice with her fellow worshippers in the opening hymn, she heard Eliza enthusiastically joining in. Mary thought that Eliza had a very natural way with new people and that the younger girl would have no problem fitting in with the Willow Creek Amish community.

Three hours later, Mary and Eliza stood and stretched a bit to loosen up after sitting for so long. Ruth gathered up a sleepy Abigail. Elizabeth Miller hurried up to them. "Let's all sit together! I'll introduce you to some other young people, Eliza."

"Abigail and I are going to join Jonas for lunch, but denki for including us, Elizabeth. I'd love to visit some more after we eat? I think there's going to be volleyball later."

"I love volleyball!" Eliza enthused. "Are we staying a bit? I'm fine either way."

"Ja, we'll be sticking around for a bit. You can join in the games after the meal. See you later, Ruth!"

"Come on, girls, let's go see if we can help get lunch on the tables." Elizabeth led the way into the house, followed by Mary and Eliza. The door had just closed behind them when a lovely gray tabby cat jumped off a chair and wound her way around Elizabeth's ankles.

"There you are! I wondered where you'd gotten to. Are all these people worrying you?" She picked up the cat and stroked her lovingly. "This is Petite Souris, my little sweetheart."

"Petite...what?" Eliza asked, reaching out to scratch the gorgeous cat just under her chin with the tip of a finger.

"It means *little mouse* in French," Elizabeth said. "She reminded me of a tiny mouse when she was little."

"Why the fancy name, though?" Eliza wondered.

"Lizzie wants to be a fancy French baker someday, ever since she visited New Orleans," Mary said with a smile for her friend.

Elizabeth laughed self-consciously. "Ja, I do. That's why I work at the bakery in town—to learn the trade. Someday I will open my own place. But for now, my Petite Souris is the only fancy French thing around."

"She's no fancier than any of the other kittens I gave to you and your friends," Lydia Coblentz said from behind them. "But I admit, she sure is purdy!"

"Guder mariye, Lydia!" Mary and Elizabeth chorused. "We'd better go help the others with the food!"

Setting the cat back on the chair, they hurried into the kitchen to join the other women in getting the food ready and carrying it outside where it was set on long tables in the shade. There was plenty for everyone, and before long they were able to take their plates to a picnic table under the shade of a big maple tree in the Millers' yard.

Elizabeth had been called away by her mother to help with a couple of younger cousins, but she'd promised to get Eliza when it was time for volleyball. One of the Miller boys carried Mary's plate at his mudder's request, and he placed it with a flourish onto the table.

"There you go, Mary. Do you need anything else?"

"No, denki for your help, Benjamin. Go enjoy your own lunch."

He touched his hat, smiled at Eliza, and hurried off to join the other teen boys.

"He's cute," Eliza said. "Did you say he's one of Elizabeth's brieder?"

Mary smiled. "Ja, but he's only fifteen."

Eliza laughed and shrugged. "Oh well, I'm not seriously looking anyway. Maybe by the time he's old enough, I'll be ready to consider finding a mann!"

"Just keep an open mind and listen to what Gott is urging you to do, and you can't go wrong," Mary said.

"That's what my maem says. But I think that she's hoping Gott will urge me to get married sooner rather than later." Their eyes met, and they held a serious expression for a few seconds before Eliza's dimples appeared, and she and Mary started laughing at the same time.

"That's a happy sound!"

Mary turned in surprise at the deep voice and saw Reuben standing nearby, his arms folded across his chest and a smile playing around his lips.

"Reuben! What are you doing here?" Eliza cried.

"My services finished before yours, so I thought I'd come over and say hello."

"Have you eaten?" Mary smiled shyly at him.

"No. I meant to, but I got involved in a couple chores and realized if I didn't get over here, I'd miss my chance."

"Well, I'm glad you came! Go get something to eat and come sit with us," Eliza urged.

Reuben frowned and looked at Mary. "I don't know, Eliza. The lunch is for the members of the Amish community. I'm afraid I don't qualify, and I didn't even attend worship. Seems kind of sketchy to show up afterward and eat a free lunch."

Mary smiled. "I don't think anyone will mind. You're the new dokder in town, after all. Those who haven't had a chance to meet you will be happy for the opportunity. You'll probably end up giving out all sorts of free medical advice. Go ahead and fill a plate. I promise, it's okay."

"Well, since you put it that way, I guess there isn't any harm."

"I'll go with you." Eliza jumped up from the table. "I'm ready for dessert! Mary, can I get you anything?"

"If there is any rhubarb pie, I'd like a slice of that."

"Got it. Whipped cream?"

"Of course!"

"Come on, Reuben, you can carry Mary's dessert. Let's hurry. There are a lot of people here, and all the gut desserts will go fast. We should have gotten it when we got our lunch!" The young woman hurried toward the food tables, and Reuben looked back at Mary and gave a helpless shrug.

"I've got my orders—better follow the general!"

"Remember, rhubarb pie!" Mary called after his retreating back. He gave a thumbs-up without looking back, and she watched him join his sister at the dessert table and peruse the choices. "I hope there's some left."

"Some what? Wait, let me guess—rhubarb pie?"

Mary gave a start at the voice directly behind her, then rolled her eyes when Lydia moved into her line of sight and took a seat next to her at the picnic table.

"Lydia! Are you trying to frighten five years off my life?"

"Of course not, child. Besides, you're made of sterner stuff than that. Is that the handsome dokder?"

Mary nodded, watching Reuben choose his own dessert and then accept a plate from Eliza, who was balancing two plates of her own, plus a glass of what looked like milk.

"And who's the youngster? I noticed her with you earlier in the house."

"Oh, that's Reuben's schwester, Eliza. She's visiting from Lancaster County, Pennsylvania."

"Is she now? That's nice. How old is she?"

"Only seventeen, but her mudder was after her to marry, and she's not of a mind to yet, so she asked her bruder if she could come visit. I think her mudder assumes she's looking for a mann here, but she's looking for a job and an adventure, if you ask me."

Lydia shook her head. "Such drama! I don't have the energy for it. Oh, here they come, and it looks like they cleaned off the dessert table! My goodness. Maybe they'll have something for me."

"I wouldn't be surprised."

"We're back! And look at what we got! They had your pie, Mary, and some fresh homemade whipped cream. I got you a nice big dollop."

Eliza placed several dishes on the table and plopped down across from Mary and Lydia. Noticing Lydia for the first time, she blushed. "Oh! Excuse my manners! I didn't notice you there, I was so busy watching my feet so I didn't drop all these plates. I'm Eliza King."

"From Lancaster, yes, I heard," Lydia said. "I'm Lydia Coblentz. Has anyone claimed that peanut butter pie?"

Reuben sat down next to his sister and looked at the pie in question.

"No, I don't think so. Why did you grab that one, Eliza?"

She shrugged. "It seemed like a gut idea, and turns out, it was! Here you go, Lydia!" She handed over the pie and a clean fork and napkin. "I'm sorry, I didn't bring anything for you to drink."

"That's fine, child. You didn't even know I'd be sitting here. I'll take the pie and be grateful."

"I think someone is coming around with kaffi," Mary said, looking across the lawn at a couple of women who had started circulating with pitchers of iced tea and kaffi.

"Gut! That'll do when they get here. So, Eliza, tell me about yourself. What are you doing here in Willow Creek?"

Eliza had just taken a big bite of pie, and her eyes widened as she chewed it as quickly as she could, washing it down with a gulp of milk. "Sorry! Um, just seeing somewhere new and spending time with my big bruder. And I'd like to find a part-time job while I'm here."

"Elizabeth Miller suggested she apply at the bakery, Reuben," Mary said. "It's just a couple blocks walk from your house, downtown. Next to the Amish furniture store."

"I know where you mean. We can drive by it on the way home today if you like, and you can see where it is."

"Oh, I guess it makes sense for me to ride home with you and save the Yoders the trip. Sure, Reuben, that will be gut. Denki!"

"It wouldn't be any trouble, really, but I think it's a gut plan to see where the bakery is. I believe they open at eight." Mary took a small bite of pie and sighed with pleasure. "Oh my, this is gut! Must be Mrs. Stoltzfus' pie. She's the best in the district, but don't tell my maem I said so!"

Eliza giggled and ate another huge bite of her own apple crisp.

"Time was, I made an excellent rhubarb pie," Lydia said, the distant look of reminiscence in her eyes. "The trick is to use the right thickener. Some people like cornstarch or flour. But I prefer tapioca starch. Gives it a little more sweetness."

"Why do you need a thickener?" Mary wondered as she took another bite and savored the sweet/tart flavor and the flaky crust.

"The water content in the rhubarb," Lydia said, pointing her fork at Mary and nodding wisely. "There's a lot of water in the rhubarb, so to counter that you use the thickener, or you end up with a soupy mess."

"Ah, I see. I'll remember that. Seems to me Maem uses flour, but she rarely makes rhubarb as she doesn't like it. Says it's a texture thing."

Lydia nodded. "Rhubarb isn't for everyone. And that's fine with me! More for me."

"Should I have gotten you rhubarb? I can go back," Eliza said, half rising from the table.

"No, no, child. I love peanut butter. Fact is, I like them all! That's why I'm as round as Elizabeth's little pony, Goldie!"

Eliza giggled and Mary shook her head. "Not by a long shot, Lydia. Goldie is pretty round!"

"I believe she's expecting a foal," Reuben said, squinting at the golden pony with the flowing butterscotch mane and tail, currently munching sweet grass in the pasture next to the barn. "And not too long from now either."

"Well, that explains it!" Lydia laughed, finishing her pie. Eliza finished at the same time and stood to gather up the empty plates and utensils.

"I'll clear this up, and then would you introduce me to a few of those young people over there?" Eliza asked, pointing with her chin at a small cluster of teens and young twenties sitting in the grass under an oak tree at the side of the house.

"Sure, I'd be glad to." Mary smiled. "Just come get me when you're ready."

"Okay!" Eliza hurried toward the house with her burden of dirty dishes, and Lydia blotted her lips with a napkin. "That's a gut girl there, Dokder. She should do well here."

He smiled. "Denki, Lydia. I believe you're right. Maybe she'll get a job at the bakery tomorrow, and that will help occupy her. She has a lot of energy!"

"Could she work part-time at your office?" Mary wondered, then blushed at her impertinence. "I'm sorry, that's none of my business."

"Nonsense. It's a good idea, except for one small problem. Eliza doesn't like doctors' offices. She faints at the sight of blood."

"Goodness! Then it wouldn't be a gut fit for her at all!" Mary frowned. "How did one sibling end up a dokder and another is afraid of blood?"

"She witnessed an unfortunate accident as a child. A man working in the hardware store got distracted while using a piece of equipment, and he cut his hand very badly. She happened to be there that day, sweeping up after school the way we all did as youngies, and she saw it happen. There was a lot of blood. And the man freaked out a bit, yelling and cursing, and then he fainted. It was a lot for a young girl to see. I think she was seven or eight. Since then, the sight of blood takes her out. Boom."

"Well, that would do it, I suppose," Lydia said. "Good thing she doesn't have to work in your office!"

"The thing is, she hasn't enjoyed working in the hardware store ever since. And my parents have tried everything, even therapy, which you have to admit is pretty unusual for an Amish family."

"Very unusual, though my mother and I both went to a therapist following the accident," Mary said. "It helped my mudder, although I was too young to remember going. Maem said I slept better after a few sessions. I was having very bad dreams."

Lydia patted her hand. "And who could blame you?"

Reuben nodded. "Well, therapy didn't do the trick for Eliza. She'll work in the store but not near the power equipment. She prefers to run the register up front or tend the plants in the garden center. And those things are necessary, so it's worked out. But it would be nice if she could overcome that phobia."

Lydia shrugged. "Who can understand how the mind works, young man? I expect she'll get over it when she has to, and not before."

"I hope so. Ah, she's waving at us. Do you want me to go with you to introduce her around?"

"Nee, you and Lydia visit. I see a couple people headed this way. They probably want to meet you. Enjoy the shade and your iced tea. I'll be fine."

She pushed to her feet and headed over to where Eliza waited impatiently for Mary to introduce her to the other young people. Mary smiled. She remembered being that age. A person simply thrummed with energy at age seventeen! Fortunately, by twenty-nine that had simmered down to a low buzz. Laughing at herself, she walked with Eliza to the group of young people and introduced her around. Everyone was happy to meet the pretty girl from Pennsylvania, and soon they'd invited her to stay for the singing that would be starting after an afternoon spent playing volleyball and lawn games. She looked at Mary, who shrugged. "You'll have to ask your bruder. But remember, you want to see where the bakery is."

"Oh, are you going to apply for the counter position?" a freckle-faced young woman asked, smiling eagerly. "I hope you do! I work there, and we really need someone friendly and outgoing, and I can just tell you'd be perfect. I'm Jane Bontrager, by the way. And this is my bruder, John."

A young, beardless man in his early twenties smiled shyly at Eliza, who grinned back. "Nice to meet you both. Yes, I'm going to apply there tomorrow, Jane. Maybe we'll work together!"

"Hey, there's a volleyball game forming up. Let's go play, and I'll tell you about the bakery!" Jane pulled Eliza by the hand, and they ran off to where a net was strung up across an open space, followed more slowly by Jane's brother. Mary turned and headed back to where Reuban and Lydia were still sitting at the table, having been joined by several other adults in the time she'd been with Eliza.

"I think she's going to fit in just fine," she said as she sat down across from Reuben. "She's naturally friendly. And she's already made a friend—Jane Bontrager. They're playing volleyball."

"Oh, Jane and her bruder, John, are very nice young people," Lydia said. "And she works at the bakery. She'll be able to give Eliza all the details. Now, I could do with a cup of kaffi. Dokder, would you mind getting an old woman a nice fresh cup?"

"If I see an old woman, I'll be happy to. But meanwhile, would you like a cup?"

Lydia laughed and slapped his hand. "Oh, you're a charmer, all right. You sound just like my young friend, Ruth Helmuth. She always says that. And I would love a cup."

Reuben smiled and stood up. "Mary, would you like anything?"

"I could use more lemonade, denki."

"Anyone else need a fresh drink? No? Okay, I'll be right back." He walked toward the house and returned a happy wave sent his way by Eliza, who was obviously having a great time playing volleyball. Mary watched him, a smile tugging at her lips, until a sharp, stern voice broke into her thoughts.

"So, what brings the dokder here today? He's not Amish that I've heard. Maybe he's interested in someone here who is?"

Mary turned her head and saw with dismay that Amelia Schwartz had arrived. The unpleasant woman stood with her arms folded beneath her ample bosom, a frown marring a face already made old before its time by deeply etched lines of discontent. Mary reflected that the woman had wasted no time injecting her poison conjecture into the previously peaceful group's conversation.

Mary was trying to think what to say when Lydia beat her to it. "Now, Amelia, none of your idle prattle please. As usual, you don't know what you're talking about."

Amelia sniffed loudly before casting a triumphant look Mary's way. "Well! I happen to have seen the dokder and Mary Yoder sitting very cozily on his porch just last week, sipping lemonade as if they had a right to be together. What do you say to that?"

Mary's jaw dropped at the woman's audacity, but before she could say anything, Lydia snorted as if Amelia were nothing but an old fool. "They were sitting outside on the porch, in full sight of the world, during the day, drinking lemonade and talking? I just don't see the scandal in that, Amelia. Maybe if you'd get a life of your own, you'd leave others to live theirs."

Ignoring Amelia's outraged gasp, Lydia stood. "Come, Mary, walk me into the house. It's time I headed home. The company has grown tiresome here."

"I wish you wouldn't rush off, Lydia. I wanted to talk to you about a new quilt pattern I'm considering," Charlene Byler said, frowning at Amelia. "I hope you know none of the rest of us believe anything improper is going on with you and the dokder, Mary," she added.

"Denki, Charlene. I'd love to look at your pattern. Why don't you come over to my haus tomorrow? I'll make kaffi."

Charlene smiled. "I will! Denki. Say, around ten in the morning?"

Lydia nodded, threw another glare at Amelia, and allowed Mary to take her arm and lead her toward the house, leaving Amelia and her gossip behind without another look.

Reuben was coming out of the house, having taken the empty lemonade container inside to be refilled in the kitchen, when he saw Lydia and Mary walking away from the picnic table where they'd been sitting. He thought they looked pretty grim. Glancing over at the volleyball game, he assured himself that Eliza was happily occupied. He carried the heavy container of lemonade over to the serving table and then turned to face Lydia and Mary, who had changed course to meet him.

"What's up? Is something wrong?"

Mary grimaced. "Oh, it's really nothing."

Reuben saw Lydia was holding two empty glasses, so he took them and refilled them while he listened.

"Nonsense!" Lydia interrupted, accepting her refilled glass from Reuben. "That Amelia just insinuated—no, plainly stated—in front of everyone seated at the table where we were, that there is something improper between you and Mary! I told her to mind her own business." Lydia took a sip of lemonade and frowned over at Amelia, who had remained behind at the table they'd vacated.

"You were pretty amazing," Mary said, smiling at the elderly woman.

"That may be, but my words won't stop that old bat."

"Lydia! That isn't very Christian of you," Mary chided her friend gently, although Reuben was sure he could see a gleam of amusement in her eyes.

"Maybe not, and I'll pray later for forgiveness, but she has tried my patience for many a year. And now she's spreading wrongful gossip about two lovely people. I won't have it. I'm going to talk to Abram Troyer. That's what I'm going to do."

Reuben could see that Mary wasn't amused anymore. She looked downright alarmed, in fact.

"Lydia, please don't bother the bishop with this silliness. If we ignore her, she'll find something else to talk about."

Reuben doubted that, not if Lydia had publicly humiliated her. She was more likely to make up something nasty about Lydia next in an attempt to compromise her credibility in the community, if that were even possible. But while he doubted Lydia could be hurt by the woman's sharp tongue, the same was obviously not true of Mary, who was clearly already suffering from it.

"Mary, I think Lydia should talk to the bishop. And I think you and I should go with her. That way we can air this out, and the bishop won't have to rely on hearsay."

Lydia beamed approvingly at him. "That is an excellent idea, Dokder! All that fancy schooling must have done you some gut! Come on, let's find him. If I know Abram, he won't be far from the desserts."

She turned and sailed off toward the dessert table and the people gathered at the nearby picnic tables.

"Oh dear. This is not gut!" Mary fretted.

Reuben wanted nothing more than to take her hand and squeeze it reassuringly, but in light of the gossip already circulating about them, he didn't think that would be the best plan of action. He had to content himself with words. "Mary, I think it'll be fine. We haven't done anything wrong. We'll simply tell him that, and he may want to go have a talk with Amelia Schwartz and set her straight."

"I just hate to be the subject of any kind of talk. This is so unfair!"

He smiled wryly. It was unfair, considering the gossip was about a nonexistent romance between the two of them—a romance he very much wished could become a reality. "Yes, gossip usually isn't about accuracy. It's often unfair."

She sighed. "I suppose there's no getting around it now. And look, Lydia has found the bishop, and she's dragging him our way. Great."

Sure enough, Lydia and Bishop Troyer were walking their direction, the bishop carrying a plate of pie and a cup of kaffi with him. He looked cross, but Lydia looked determined, and it was clear she was having her way.

When they drew near, Bishop Troyer frowned at Reuben and Mary. "Well now, what is this story Lydia is telling me? Didn't you heed my gut advice, Mary? I'm surprised at you. And you, Dokder—if you expect to find a place in our community, drawing respectable young Amish women off the path of righteousness is not the way to do so!"

Reuben slowly pulled in a deep, calming breath and reminded himself he was an adult, not a naughty boy being called on the carpet for bad behavior. For Mary's sake, as well as for the sake of his new business, he needed to convince this man that he wasn't a threat to Mary or to the community. "I understand, Bishop. And I have no plans to draw anyone from the path of righteousness. This is all a misunderstanding."

Bishop Troyer sighed, then looked around. Spotting an empty picnic table off by itself, he jerked his chin that direction. "Come, let us sit so I can enjoy my pie while we talk."

He walked off toward the table, and they all followed. Reuben glanced around and saw that their little clutch wasn't going unremarked by the good people of the community. Though nobody was overtly staring, he could feel eyes on him as he followed the bishop, Mary, and Lydia across the lawn to the table.

They all sat down, and Reuben realized he still held Mary's lemonade. He handed it to her, and she nodded her thanks.

"Okay, tell me your side of this story," the bishop said before forking a large bite of pie into his mouth. "Mmm. Germaine's pies never disappoint."

"Abram," Lydia said, "please pay attention. I want this straightened out. And then I'll expect you to have a private chat with Amelia Schwartz."

Reuben cleared his throat and looked at Mary for permission to tell the story. She shrugged and nodded. "I've been working with Mary and her parents to determine whether she might benefit from another surgery on her back."

"I know this. Please get to the part where the two of you were *schmunzla* on the dokder's front porch in front of Gott and everyone."

Reuben and Mary both spoke at once, tripping over each other's words in their efforts to correct the bishop's incorrect information.

"One at a time, please. Reuben, please continue."

"We were not kissing and cuddling on my porch, Bishop Troyer. We were sitting in separate rocking chairs, separated by a table, drinking glasses of lemonade, which I brought outside. Mary did not go into my house with me. It was entirely innocent. We were discussing the surgery."

"There, you see? I told you Amelia was blowing this all out of proportion," Lydia said smugly.

The bishop held up a hand, asking for silence. "Mary, what do you have to say for yourself?"

"Just that what Reuben said is correct, Bishop. Amelia pulled up to the curb in front of his house and made a suggestive comment before driving away. I was worried she might spread gossip. But I didn't think you'd believe her. Haven't I always been trustworthy?"

"Well, yes, you have, Mary." He glanced uneasily at Reuben. "But temptation can be a strong motivator. This is why I warned you not to be seen alone with the dokder. People will talk."

At that moment, Edie and Joe hurried up to the table. "What is going on? Elizabeth Miller just told me there was trouble of some kind involving you and Amelia Schwartz?" Edie wrung her hands together, looking back and forth between Mary, Reuben, and Bishop Troyer.

"Now, Maem, everything is fine," Mary began.

"Actually, there is a small issue, but we're sorting it out," Reuben said.

"I'm getting to the bottom of it, Edie." Abram Troyer nodded at Joe, who hadn't said anything so far. "Please, have a seat."

"Is this more nonsense like what you discussed with my daughter after services a couple weeks ago?"

"Now, Edie," the bishop began, but Edie interrupted.

"Abram, I respect you. You're a gut bishop. But sometimes I wonder if you're narrish! How can you even entertain the notion of my Mary misbehaving and doing something to shame herself and her family? She would never do that!"

"But temptation. . ." the bishop began.

"My daughter will not be drawn in by temptation. She has always been a gut girl. Is there a formal complaint, or just Amelia Schwartz causing trouble again?"

"I'm trying to find out! If everyone would let Reuben and Mary talk. Please."

Joe reached out and patted Edie's hand. "Edie, give them a minute to explain. It will all sort itself out."

Edie looked searchingly at Mary, then nodded with obvious reluctance.

"I actually think we've explained everything," Reuben said, feeling as if he were sinking into quicksand. "Bishop, is it improper for two people to sit on a porch and talk in full sight of the world?"

"Well, no, of course not."

"And will you accept my word that there's nothing improper going on between us?"

Reuben heard Mary's sharp intake of breath. The bishop looked at him searchingly.

"You are going to sit there and tell me you are not attracted to this woman, Dokder?"

Reuben swallowed and looked at Mary, who was looking back at him, her heart in her eyes. He glanced at Joe and Edie, who were staring at him, and he slowly shook his head.

Lydia cackled. Everyone turned to look at her in disbelief. "What? Anyone could see they're attracted to each other. Am I saying anything you all couldn't see for yourselves?"

Joe cleared his throat, and everyone turned to look at him. He blushed a little but said his piece. "It seems to me that the question isn't whether these young people are attracted to each other but, rather, what they plan to do about it."

The bishop nodded slowly. "Ja, that is a gut point, Joe."

Joe looked at Reuben, who wished the ground would open up and swallow him. "Well, Dokder, what do you plan to do about it?"

All eyes were on him. He looked at Mary, sadness in his eyes.

Mary couldn't take any more. "Excuse me. I'm here too. Please don't talk about me as if I can't understand you."

"I don't think anyone meant to do that, lieb," her mother began, but Reuben broke in.

"Excuse me, Edie, if you don't mind?"

Edie nodded reluctantly and cast a worried glance at her daughter.

Reuben cleared his throat self-consciously. "Um, well, I just want to say that while I won't attempt to deny that I find you very attractive, Mary, I also understand all the obstacles that stand between us and any hope of a relationship."

Mary swallowed against a sudden lump in her throat and nodded for him to continue. She knew that she couldn't possibly speak at that moment without bursting into tears.

"Well, the fact that I'm Mennonite, and you're Amish. And that I was never baptized, and you were. And the fact that I have to use far more technology in my daily life than you'd be permitted to have in your life. What I'm trying to say is, I know there is no hope for us. But the last thing I want to have happen is for you, or your family, or Bishop Troyer, to decide I'm a bad influence on you. I won't be your dokder, but I am happy to continue as your consultant and friend, to help ensure you get the medical care you need." He fell silent and looked at the faces around him, as if unsure of his welcome.

Mary bit her lip and realized it was up to her to make sure her parents and the bishop were comfortable having Reuben around. His very career could depend on what she said next. "Denki, Reuben," she began. "I really appreciate that you're willing to keep on working with my parents and me to explore whether this surgery is the right thing for me." Her voice broke, and she stopped speaking, taking a moment to gather herself. When her mother put a hand on her arm and started to speak, Mary held up a hand. "Maem, please, give me a moment. I'm not finished."

Edie bit her lip and nodded, clearly at a loss as to what to think or say. Mary stole a glance at Joe and found him gazing back at her compassionately. It was nearly her undoing, so she quickly looked away. The bishop was easier to look at, as he was clearly skeptical.

"Bishop Troyer, please believe me when I say that I'm mature enough to acknowledge that I feel an attraction that cannot be acted upon, and to safely avoid falling prey to temptation. Reuben is a gut friend. He's trying to help me get a surgery that could make my life so much better. And we're both adults. We both understand that there can be no romance between us. Won't you please give your blessing for me to continue looking into this, and for the dokder to continue helping me?"

It seemed that everyone was holding their breath, looking at Bishop Troyer to see what he'd say. He frowned and looked down at his shoes. Then he looked sternly at Reuben.

"Young man, while Mary isn't a child who needs my protection, she is a beloved member of my community. You grew up Amish. You know what's at stake here. Do I have your word that you won't encourage her to abandon her faith? She would lose everything."

"Oh, for goodness' sake, Abram, you heard them. They both understand, and they've both promised to avoid temptation. I, for one, am not convinced there's no way forward for them."

"Lydia! Don't encourage them to hold false hope!" Bishop Troyer spoke sternly to the elder woman, who shrugged.

"I'm not encouraging any such thing. I'm only saying that if Gott wants them to be a couple, He'll find a way, and that is no sin."

"There's no way that I can see, so leave it be," the bishop commanded.

Lydia heaved a sigh and nodded. "Very well. But I still say we should all pray for whatever outcome the Father wills, in both the surgery and the possible relationship, because you never know."

Bishop Troyer shook his head. "You always did have to have the last word, Lydia Coblentz."

She mimed zipping her lips, and he shook his head again, but Mary caught a faint smile playing about his lips. When he looked back at her, however, the smile was gone, replaced by a serious expression.

"I have your word then, both of you? You'll behave with the utmost propriety? Many eyes will be on you. You'll have to be careful not to do anything to cause speculation."

Reuben met the bishop's eyes. "Yes, Bishop. You have my word." He glanced at Mary, who nodded firmly.

"Ja, mine too."

"Very well then. It would be best if the two of you were never alone together. Why borrow trouble?"

Mary nodded. "Of course, you're right. We'll be careful to avoid that." With a glance at Reuben, she turned to her parents. "If you don't mind, I'm ready to go home now. I'm tired. If you're not ready, though, I understand. I'll find somewhere quiet to sit and wait."

"No, I think we're all ready. We've got to feed the stock after all, and it looks as if a storm may be coming in." Joe shaded his eyes with a hand and squinted to the southwest, where dark clouds were indeed shadowing the horizon.

"Oh dear, I hope we aren't in for any bad weather! I'd better let Ruth and Jonas know. They drove me today." Lydia stepped forward and pulled Mary into a fierce hug. "Don't you worry, child," she whispered so that only Mary could hear. "Everything will turn out fine, you just wait and see. Gott works miracles! Remember what I always say, difficulty is a miracle in its first stage!" She turned and hurried away, and the bishop watched her go, a look of fond amusement on his face.

"She always did speak her mind. My Amelia loved that about her. Well, all that's settled. Gut, gut. I wonder if there's any pie left."

He wandered off toward the pie table to see if there was anything interesting left.

"Well, I'm going to gather up our dishes," Edie said. "Joe, would you go get the boys? I wonder if Elizabeth would drive you back to the buggy, Mary."

"I'll ask. She's just over there." Mary started toward the table, where some of her friends were sitting. Reuben fell into step beside her.

"I'm really sorry about all that. I feel as if I somehow caused you a lot of trouble, and honestly, I never intended to. I'm not sure exactly what happened."

She grimaced. "Amelia Schwartz happened, Reuben. It wasn't your fault."

"Well, even though she got the details wrong, the woman's instincts are pretty good. Mary, I have to confess that I'm feeling pretty upset at the thought that there isn't anything we can do about how we feel. Um, if you feel it too, that is. Maybe it's just me."

She stopped walking and looked at him. "I feel it too. But it doesn't matter. You heard the bishop. And we both promised. So that's that. Done." She mimed brushing her hands off, started to walk again, and then stopped once more and looked at him sideways, a little smile playing about her mouth. "But I will admit, Reuben, I hadn't really thought about the possibility of us somehow finding a way to explore a relationship either, until Amelia started up this gossip and caused the bishop to speak to me, and then my mudder and finally Lydia all found it necessary to give me their opinions." She bit her lip. "The thing is, Maem and Lydia both seem to think maybe there could be a way, if we just pray enough. And if Gott wants it, it'll happen. I think that's where we should leave this for now, ja? And just concentrate on the surgery. We'll be friends and that's all. For now."

He stared at her, and she wondered if he'd agree to her terms. Then he slowly nodded. "Yes, I can agree to that. Not like we have a lot of choice. And your health comes first in my book, anyway, ahead of any other considerations."

"Well then." She started walking again. "That says a lot." She smiled at him, and he smiled back.

"Plus, this leaves room for a bit of hope." He grinned and continued toward the table.

"You're incorrigible. Oh, there's Elizabeth. Elizabeth! My folks are ready to go. Do you mind giving me a lift back to our buggy?"

"Sure, just let me get my cart," Elizabeth said.

But Reuben waved at her. "I'll go get it. And the little Haflinger mare, right?"

Elizabeth smiled. "Ja, that's right. Goldie. Denki!"

He walked off to get the horse and cart, and Mary sat down next to Elizabeth to wait. There were several other young people at the table, so her friend didn't say anything, although Mary was sure that, although their conversation couldn't have been overheard, everyone would have seen her and her parents with the bishop, obviously engaged in what was a serious conversation. Elizabeth reached out casually and gripped her hand, and Mary looked at her, surprised. "I won't say anything, because I figure if you want to talk about it, you will in your own time," Elizabeth whispered. "But whatever that was about, you've got my support."

Mary blinked back tears. "Just like that? Without even knowing what's up?"

"Of course. I know you. We've been friends a long time." Elizabeth smiled, and Mary returned the smile and squeezed her friend's hand.

"Denki. That means a lot."

"Just don't let small-minded people like Amelia get you down. You're too gut for that. And know that whatever the problem is, I'm certain that with Gott's help, it will all work out. You just have to have faith, ja?"

Mary nodded, feeling better. "Ja, you're right. I'll pray. Denki for being such a gut friend, Elizabeth."

"Of course! And why wouldn't I be? You're just reaping what you've always sown!"

"Here you go, ladies," Reuben said, leading the little mare up to the table, hitched to the pony cart. "What a sweetheart she is, Elizabeth!"

Elizabeth dimpled at the doctor. "Ja, she is, and doesn't she know it!" She laughed and fished around in her apron pocket until she found a carrot, which she fed to the eager mare, who bumped her with her velvety nose, hoping for another.

"That's all for now, greedy," Elizabeth said. She climbed up into the cart, and Reuben assisted Mary into the other seat, then handed her the crutches, which she laid in the back.

"Tomorrow I'll call the doctor I think would be your best bet, up at Akron General Hospital. I'll let you know when she can see you."

"A woman surgeon?" Mary asked, surprised.

"Sure. Any objections?"

"No, of course not. I don't know why that surprised me. Let me know when she can see me, and we'll hire a driver to take us up."

"Oh, I thought since I really want to be there to make sure she's right for you, I might as well drive you and your folks up to Akron. Is that okay?"

"Oh. Well, sure. Denki."

He nodded. "Good. Okay, talk to you later. Have a good rest of your day, Mary."

She smiled tremulously at him. "You too, Dokder. Goodbye."

She nodded to Elizabeth, who clucked at Goldie, and they trotted down the road to the line of buggies parked in the nearby field.

She saw her parents walking through the field, her brieder running along ahead of them. The sky to the southwest looked even more threatening than a little while ago.

"Whoa, look at those clouds," Elizabeth said. "I don't like the look of them."

"Me either. Good thing people are starting to head home. Wouldn't want to get caught in a storm."

Elizabeth drew up next to the Yoders' buggy, and Joe came over and lifted Mary down. "There you go! Here are your crutches, daughter. Let's get moving to beat that rain."

Mary laughed. Joe hadn't lifted her out of a buggy or wagon for years. "Dat, I'm too heavy for you to be lifting now. You'll pull your back."

Joe raised an eyebrow and tried to look insulted. "I'll have you know, you weigh little more than a feather. And I'm a strong man. Come on, boys, into the buggy!"

Elizabeth waved, and Mary turned to climb into the buggy when Reuben pulled up near them in the drive.

"Joe, I just heard a weather report, and it's alarming. Tornado watch until 10 p.m. Some nasty stuff headed our way."

Joe paused in the act of climbing into the buggy. "How long until it hits?"

Reuben scratched his head. "Maybe an hour or so. I wouldn't dawdle. I'm going back to tell everyone, and then I'm headed home to batten down the hatches."

Joe nodded. "Denki." He looked at his family and saw that everyone was securely inside the buggy. "Let's go. We need to get the stock secured and make sure we have what we need in the cellar, just in case. See you later, Dokder!"

He clucked to Sebastian, who trotted nicely down the driveway. Mary craned her neck to watch Reuben turn his truck around and head back to the farmyard to let everyone else know about the incoming storms. Then she turned back around and faced forward resolutely.

Forward was the way she needed to go.

CHAPTER THIRTEEN

The wind started to pick up as Joe pulled the buggy into the farmyard. "Daniel, go open the big doors. I want to put the buggy inside."

The boy jumped down and ran to open the big double barn doors. Joe pulled the rig right inside, and then his son pulled the doors closed and latched them. Everyone climbed down from the buggy, and Joe walked Sebastian to a stall.

"I'll put him inside. Boys, get the other horses and bring them inside. Unless a tornado comes right here, they'll be safer inside than out."

"Dat, is a tornado going to come here and blow down our house and barn?" Simon asked fearfully.

Joe ruffled the boy's hair. "Probably not, Simon, but it's always gut to be prepared. That's why I want you boys to gather up the weather radio and extra batteries, a battery lantern and a couple flashlights, and the Bible, and take them all downstairs to the basement. Go on now. Oh, and grab a few wool blankets too."

"Are we gonna have a sleepover in the basement, Dat?" Isaac asked eagerly. "That would be fun!"

"I hope not. We'd all get a stiff neck. Go on, get the things I said and put them on the benches down there, not on the floor, mind."

"Yes, Dat!" The boys all ran to gather up supplies. Edie watched Joe fork some feed into the horse stalls and make sure the water was full. "I guess I'll go inside and start supper. And I'll put some water and snacks at the top of the cellar steps for the boys to carry down. If we end up staying down there, we'll get hungry and thirsty."

"I'll come help you, Maem," Mary said.

"I'm getting the rest of the horses inside, and the milk cows. The beef cattle can take shelter in the open barns in the field if they need to." Joe headed outside through the main door, followed by the women.

"My, the wind has kicked up!" Edie exclaimed. "Mary, you'd better get your chickens into the coop."

"Send Nathan out to help me please, Maem. He's gut with the birds."

Edie nodded, and Mary hurried over to open the door to the coop she kept her layers and fryers in. Unsurprisingly, most of the chickens hurried inside, not being stupid. But a couple always wanted to run this way and that. Nathan came running out of the house and soon had all the strays shut safely into the sturdy coop.

"That'll have to do it. Let's get inside out of this wind, Nate. It's blowing grit into my eyes."

"Mine too!" They hurried inside, and Nathan held the door for his sister as she propelled herself up the steps on her crutches.

"Denki!" She grinned at the boy.

"No problem!" He grinned impishly back. "Let's make sure we have cookies for the basement, just in case."

She nodded. "Smart. I'll make sure."

After all was prepared in case of really bad weather, the family ate a supper of sandwiches made with cold meatloaf and cheese and washed them down with icy lemonade. They sat in the living room, and after dinner Joe read from the Bible while Edie kept a weather eye on the sky.

Following family prayer time, they broke out the board games and played Parcheesi. The sky continued to darken, and the wind picked up even more.

"Nathan, please get the weather radio and bring it in here," Joe said. The boy hurried to get the battery-operated device, which Joe turned on and set on the table. They all listened to the reports as rain began to fall.

"It's so dark outside, you'd think it was night!" Daniel observed.

"Ja, but the sky looks natural. It doesn't have that eerie green cast you expect when there are tornados in the area," Edie said.

"It sounds like the worst of it passed to the south of us," Joe said. "I hope everyone is okay."

"Let's say a prayer for everyone's safety tonight," Edie suggested. They all bowed their heads, and Joe asked God to watch over His children in the path of the storms.

Outside, the rain let up a bit, and the darkness became more natural for the time of day.

"Looks like it passed us by this time," Joe said.

"Gott was watching out for us," Edie pointed out.

"Ja, He was." Joe nodded. "Okay, boys, looks like we won't need to head for the basement after all. Why don't you go get the cookies you took down there, and we can have a little snack before bed, ja?"

"Yea!" they cried, hurrying downstairs to put away the storm supplies and retrieve the snacks they'd carried down earlier.

"That was close," Joe said once the boys were out of the room. "Storms passed only about thirty miles to the south. I expect there was some significant damage."

"It's been a pretty mild storm season so far. Hopefully we won't get any worse this summer," Edie said.

"I wonder if they'll be asking for volunteers to help tomorrow. We've got some things saved in case anyone needs help," Mary said.

Edie frowned. "Not enough to help multiple families, I'm afraid. But if people from all around the area pitch in, we should be able to offer help to many people."

Mary nodded. "I guess we'll have to wait and see if anyone needs help. I hate to think of people's homes and farms being damaged or destroyed by a tornado!"

Edie shivered. "Ja, it's terrifying. Once when I was a girl, a tornado passed by only a few miles from my home. Several farms were flattened. They lost everything, including livestock and hundred-year-old barns, and one family lost a child. It was terrible."

Mary took her hand. "Hopefully nothing like that happened tonight."

"We'll hear soon enough. You know how fast bad news spreads," Joe said.

The boys rushed back into the room, having stowed the supplies, and the conversation turned to more pleasant things.

About an hour later Daniel's eyes snapped up from the game he was playing with his brothers. "What's that? Someone's coming!" He jumped up and ran to the living room window, followed by his three brothers.

"There's a truck coming up the driveway!" Isaac cried. The boys turned in unison and raced for the kitchen, but Joe called out, stopping them in their tracks.

"Boys! Wait for me. Do not go outside until I see who is coming."

Obediently, albeit reluctantly, the boys halted their dash for the door. Joe walked past them and opened the kitchen door just as a figure came up the steps in the dark. "Who is there?" Joe called.

"It's just me, Joe, sorry to come after dark, but I figured you'd all want to hear about the storm damage."

"Dokder! Ja, ja, denki. That we would. Come in." Joe opened the door, casting a glance at the boys, who murmured hellos and then, upon their father's raised eyebrow, trooped back into the living room. Edie and Mary, meanwhile, had entered the kitchen.

"Dokder, how considerate of you to bring us news," Edie said. "Sit, sit. I'll make kaffi."

"That would be welcome. Denki."

Reuben sat at the table and was joined by Mary and Joe. Edie puttered with the coffeepot and soon had it heating on the stove. She set mugs on the counter and then pulled a plate out of the cupboard, opened the rooster cookie jar, and loaded the plate with brownies she'd made the day before. She placed the plate on the table.

"So, what have you heard? Was anyone hurt?" Joe took a brownie and bit into it. Crumbs fell into his long brown beard, and he brushed at them. "One of the problems with a beard," he murmured.

Edie poured coffee into the mugs, which she set on the table along with cream and sugar. Everyone doctored their cups and sat back to listen to Reuben while enjoying the coffee and brownies.

"I went out to the hospital to see if they needed any help," Reuben said. "Amazingly, nobody in the area was injured by the wind. One man had a tree fall onto the bed of his pickup truck, but it missed the cab, and he was fine."

"Praise Gott!" Edie breathed.

Reuben nodded. "Yes. I heard the storm was more intense farther south. But though a couple of tornadoes reportedly touched down, no serious damage or injuries have been reported yet. And the worst of it has passed to the west, and it's dwindling as it goes. So, looks like we dodged a bullet this time."

Joe nodded. "That is very gut news! I've seen tornado damage, and it can be terrible."

They finished their coffee and snack, and then Reuben stood. "Well, I'd best get back to Eliza. I left her at my place when I went to the hospital, and she'll be eager to hear how things are going. By the way, Joe, do you have a phone on the property? I could have called if I'd known the number. . .not that I mind coming out. But maybe some time calling will be more convenient."

"Ja, we do. I'll jot the number down for you." He got up and found a notepad and a pencil, wrote down the number, and handed it to Reuben, who was waiting by the door. "But we probably wouldn't have heard it ringing from inside, with the wind."

"Thanks. I'm glad to have it anyway." He tucked the piece of paper into his pocket and looked over at Mary and Edie, who were still seated. "Well, good night, Edie, good night, Mary. I'll be in touch as soon as I have news."

They smiled and thanked him for coming. He caught Mary's eye and gave her a last smile before letting himself out.

"Thank Gott the storms didn't do any damage!" Edie said, bustling around clearing up the kitchen.

The boys appeared in the doorway. "Maem, may we have a bedtime snack?" Simon asked.

"Sure, sit down there, and I'll get you something."

They eagerly sat down, and Edie poured them all milk and gave them each a brownie and some apple slices. Mary thought about how kind it was of Reuben to come out to the farm to tell them all was well while her brieder munched their snacks. When they finished, she stood. "Come, you lot. I'll read you all a story if you can get upstairs and into your pajamas and brush your teeth before I make it up the stairs!"

"We're going!" Isaac yelled, and the four boys pelted up the stairs.

"They forgot their milk glasses," Mary said. "Sorry, Maem."

Edie laughed. "No problem. Go read them a story, and I'll clear up."

"I'll go make sure all the stock is okay and bed them down," Joe said, putting on his hat and heading out the door.

Edie hesitated. "Mary."

Mary turned from the stairs. "Ja?"

"I understand how attraction works. And I like Dr. Reuben very much. But. . .please, be careful. Guard your heart, because I just don't see how this could work out. And I don't want you hurt."

Mary blinked a couple of times against moisture in her eyes and nodded. "Don't worry, Maem. I don't want to be hurt either. But I am going to take Lydia's advice and pray about it. If there's a way, then Gott will find it."

"Nothing wrong with that," Edie said. She turned and started running water in the sink to wash up the dishes, and Mary started up the stairs. She could hear the boys rushing around upstairs, hurrying to get ready for bed and bickering about which story they would listen to that night.

"This is gut," she murmured as she climbed. "This is normal. I want this for myself. Gott, please, if there's a way, let it be. But Your will be done."

"Mary, we're ready! Come on!" one of her brieder cried. And she smiled through the mist in her eyes.

"Coming!" She determined to forget her worries and just enjoy her family. And that's what she did for the rest of the evening.

CHAPTER FOURTEEN

About a week later, Mary was seated in her work shed concentrating on a new lure she was making. The battery-operated lantern cast a bright light, and she had the shutters thrown back and the windows opened to let in the summer day.

She squinted closely at the lure, held tight in a clamp, as she tied off a knot that would hold a small bundle of slim green feathers together, mimicking the tail on a dragonfly. She examined the work and smiled, satisfied. "That looks gut. Now for the wings, I'll use the striped silver and white feathers." She rummaged in a couple of small baskets that she'd made at work. They were seconds, and she'd brought them home to hold supplies in her shed. She found what she needed and began the painstaking task of fashioning the feathers to span the back of the "dragonfly" to give the appearance of shimmering silver wings. Satisfied, she wound thread over and under and around, fixing the feather wings in place. When she was finished, she had what looked very much like a dragonfly. For the head, she took a small hook, fixed it underneath the fake bug, and fixed it in place with more thread. The end of the hook with the little ring looked like an insect's head. The business end curved underneath, looking a bit like dangling legs. "At least fish seem to think so," she said, holding the finished lure up and admiring it in the light coming in through the window. "That's gut!"

"It is! Is it for sale?"

She jumped at the unexpected voice and turned to see who was there. Reuben grinned at her through the window. "Sorry to startle you. Nice work."

"Oh, denki! And you did startle me, goodness!" Mary put a hand on her heart. "But I'll live. Probably."

He chuckled. "That looks like a dragonfly."

"That's what it's supposed to be. So thanks."

"So, is it for sale?"

"Ja. I have them on a specialty website a Mennonite friend operates. Also on Etsy."

"Would you sell it to me?"

She looked at him. "Really? I didn't know you fished."

"Of course I do! What self-respecting Amish kid doesn't fish? My dat taught me when I was little. But we never had fancy lures like that!"

"Did you fly-fish?"

"No, we mostly bobber fished in the pond on our farm. I always wanted to learn to fly-fish though. Would you teach me?"

She bit her lip. "Um, I'm not sure that's a great idea, what with our promise not to be alone together and all."

"Right. Well, we could take the boys!"

"Are you a masochist? That would be a crazy expedition."

"How bad could it be?"

"Remember having to fish two of them out of the pond the other day? That would probably happen again."

"We could plan on swimming too. I think it sounds fun. Invite your folks too. We can take a picnic! How about Saturday afternoon?"

"You're serious?"

"I really am. But where can we go where we can fly-fish and also swim? Don't you mostly fly-fish in a creek or river?"

She looked at him thoughtfully. "I know a gut place, actually, if you're serious."

He grinned. "Great! Ask your folks if Saturday is convenient and let me know."

She looked at the lure she still held and impulsively offered it to him. "Here, take this as a small token of my thanks for all the help you're giving me."

"Really? Wow, thank you." Reverently, he took the little lure in his big hand and stood looking at it, clearly delighted.

"It's just a fly lure, not that big of a deal."

"No, I love it. I've never had anything like this. Can I use it Saturday?"

She shrugged. "Sure. But you might lose it."

He frowned. "I wouldn't want to do that. Maybe I'll get some cheap ones at Walmart to learn on before risking this beauty."

She grinned. "That sounds smart. Hey, bring your schwester along Saturday. It wouldn't be very nice to leave her home alone, and her not knowing anyone in the area yet."

"I will ask her. But don't worry about Eliza's social life. She's already managed to get hired at the bakery, and she made several friends at services last week. She'll be fine!"

"That's great about the job! And I can see her making friends easily. She's very friendly."

"That she is! Well, I did have a reason for stopping by, other than to admire your lures. I heard back from the spine surgeon in Akron I'd like you to meet. She can see you in a couple weeks."

He handed her a sheet of paper, on which was written the doctor's name and address and the date of her appointment. Mary reached out hesitantly, as if afraid the paper might burn her hand. She looked at it and then folded it up and placed it in her pocket. "Denki, Reuben." She took a deep breath. "I guess this makes it real."

He reached through the window and touched her arm. "It's real. And this doctor is very good. And I'll be there for you, don't forget. I'll plan to pick you and your folks up about two hours before the appointment. So, around eight."

"I don't think my dat can come. But Maem is coming. Okay! I'm ready."

"It's a little scary, I know. But complications from this surgery are rare. It's surprisingly straightforward. But Dr. Pavlik will explain all that to you. Well, I have to go. I've got office hours in a bit. See you soon!"

"See you."

Grinning, he tossed the little lure into the air and caught it. "Thanks again for this lure! I love it."

She nodded and watched him cross the farmyard to his truck. Her mother opened the kitchen door as he was climbing inside.

"Hello, Dokder! *Wie gets?*"

"Going fine, denki, and you, Mrs. Yoder?"

"I'm gut. Mary is in the shed, working on her fishing tackle."

"I spoke with her. She'll tell you! I have to go. . .have a gut day!"

"You too!"

He drove off, and Edie frowned after the truck. Mary wondered what she was thinking. She didn't have to wait long to find out, as her mother descended the steps and crossed the yard to lean into the window. "Mary!"

"Right here, Maem."

"Oh! I didn't see you at first, with the sun bright out here, and the shed darker. I just saw the dokder."

"Ja, he came to tell me he heard back from the spine specialist. We have an appointment in a couple weeks." She reached into her pocket and retrieved the paper, which she handed through the window to her mudder. Edie opened it and studied it a moment.

"Okay. I trust Dokder King to find someone gut."

"So do I."

"Well, then! In a couple weeks we'll know more. For now, we'll trust in Gott. He has a plan!"

Mary smiled. "He does. Maem, Reuben also wants to go on a picnic Saturday afternoon, and fishing."

Edie frowned. "I don't think that's wise, Mary. Remember what the bishop said."

"He wants all of us to come. You, Dat, the boys. He's asking his sister too."

Edie looked surprised. "Well! That's a horse of a different color, isn't it? I suppose that might be fine."

Mary smiled. "I said I'd teach him to fly-cast. But Dat is really better at it than I am. I wonder if he'll teach Reuben?"

Edie shrugged. "You can only ask. So, a picnic, hmm? I'll make deviled eggs, and I have some nice ham that would make gut ham salad. You can bake a cake. And if we catch fish, we could cook them up back here for dinner!"

"Or maybe build a fire and do it there?"

"That sounds delicious. I like the way you think!"

"We'd better make sure Dat is free. Will you ask him? We didn't set a time, but around lunch."

"Sure and certain. Where are you thinking we should go?"

"I thought Plum Creek, where the water runs by the shore so nice, but there's that wonderful gut swimming hole too? The one with the shallow entry?"

"Are you thinking about swimming?"

"I thought the boys might like to. Reuben said he'd swim."

"I guess we'll see what the day is like. Well! I'd better go talk to your dat. I'll see you inside in a bit?"

"Ja. I'm going to work here a while longer. I need to deliver more lures to Frieda. She'll photograph them and get them up on Etsy and our website."

"Gut, gut. See you in a bit."

Edie walked briskly to the house, and Mary could tell she was pleased with the notion of a picnic expedition on Saturday. It had been a while since they'd all done something like that, and Mary thought it sounded like wunderbar fun too.

"And Reuben will be there, which is a definite bonus," she whispered to herself before turning back to her workbench and starting a new lure to replace the one she'd given Reuben.

She'd think about the surgery later. For now, she was just going to enjoy a little simple peace.

CHAPTER FIFTEEN

The following Saturday dawned clear and warm. Reuben stepped out his back door and stood on the little deck overlooking his tiny, fenced-in backyard. He tilted his head back and closed his eyes, letting the morning sun warm his face. It was good to be alive.

"It's the perfect day for fishing and a picnic!" a pleased voice chirped from behind him. He stepped aside to allow his sister to come out onto the deck.

"This is such a nice little yard! You even have a garden. What are you growing?"

"Whatever Dr. Smith and his wife planted this spring. There are some pole beans and some cucumbers. Tomatoes, and a few rows of corn." He shrugged. "I've been picking veggies and keeping it weeded, but that's about all."

"What else is there to do?" She skipped down the steps into the backyard, and Reuben noticed the grass was getting a bit high. Another item for his to-do list.

"This is laid out so nicely! And look! There's a little herb bed in the back, and some raised containers of potatoes. Isn't that clever! You don't have to bend over to dig them out! I'll have to tell Maem about this. She'll want Dat to build her some raised beds so she can try."

She examined the tomatoes and chose three fat ripe ones and then bent down to look at the cucumbers. She picked two before heading back toward Reuben. "These will be nice to take to the picnic!" Her attention was grabbed by something over to the side of the yard, and she veered that direction. Reuben glanced over and saw that she was studying the long bed of watermelons and pumpkins that ran along the fence. He'd seen a couple of days before that some of the watermelons were getting close to being ripe.

"Look! You've got those neat little round watermelons! And I think they're the yellow kind. Those are extra sweet."

"Ja, they put in a nice garden before I came along. It must have been hard to leave it behind. I think Mrs. Smith was the gardener."

"Well, that's our good luck!"

She trotted back up the steps, her arms full of produce. "Get the door please, bruder. I'll put these in a basket. Then it'll be about time to go."

"Ja, you're right. Are you planning to swim?"

She grimaced. "Nee, probably not in front of strangers, with no place to change clothes. I think I'll just fish and maybe wade a bit if there's a shallow place."

"Suit yourself, but it's going to be a scorcher!"

"Just don't splash me! Remember, I'll get revenge when you least expect it." She went inside to find a basket, and he laughed to himself, remembering the times she'd done just that. She was a sneaky little thing!

"I'll grab the stuff from the front hall and put it in the truck. Meet you outside!"

"We're driving over, and then what?"

"Not sure. We'll play it by ear. If they have two buggies, maybe we'll all ride in buggies. If not, we'll have to take the truck. Mary can ride with us and show us the way."

She wiggled her eyebrows. "Sounds romantic."

"Good grief. What it sounds like is practical. Now let's get going before we're late."

She smiled knowingly but said no more, and they loaded his truck and headed for the Yoder farm.

"Reuben King! You promised!" Eliza's high-pitched shriek of protest rang out across the small clearing where they'd set up their picnic after arriving earlier. They'd ended up taking a buggy and the truck and had enjoyed a tasty lunch shortly after arriving. Then the boys wanted to fish, and Joe had obliged them while Mary sat at the picnic table with Reuben, Eliza, and Edie, enjoying kaffi and conversation. They'd watched Joe help each boy thread a worm on his hook and toss the line out. Then they all proceeded to sit on the shady bank watching their bobbers like it was their job.

Sadly, nothing was biting, and before long the boys became restless and begged for a swim.

Reuben had told Joe he'd help supervise, and the men had rolled up their pants and stripped off their socks and shoes to wade while the little boys splashed around in the shallow pool in the bathing suits Edie had packed for the outing.

Before long, Eliza decided to wade in the pond as well and, after removing her socks and sneakers, tied her skirts up between her legs and gingerly stepped into the water.

She'd shivered dramatically and said, "How can the boys stand this cold?"

"They just jumped right in," Reuben said. "You get used to it."

"Well, my feet are getting numb, so I suppose you could call that 'getting used to it.'"

"You just need to get a little wetter, and you'll see what I mean," Reuben said. Mary, sitting on the bank in a bag chair crocheting, watched the siblings with amusement.

But Eliza knew her big brother too well to take his statement lightly. "Never mind that, you just stay over there with the little boys and remember your promise."

Reuben grinned at his sister in a way Mary could only think looked wicked. "Promise? I don't recall making a promise."

"You did too! In the garden!"

He scratched his head, moving slowly through the water toward his sister. "I remember you asking me to promise not to splash you, but I don't recall doing so. Do you?"

Joe and the boys, playing a game of keep-away with a ball Edie had produced from her beach bag, were oblivious. But Mary and Edie watched with interest as Reuben prowled toward his younger sister, who was backpedaling into deeper water.

"Reuben! You stop right there! The promise was understood! It was implied!" She was giggling now as she backed away.

"You'd better stop running, or you're going to do the job for me," he teased, stopping his advance lest he drive his sister even deeper.

But she didn't notice, just kept backing up until the water reached the hem of her tied up skirt. "Reuben! Go back over there to the boys right now. I don't trust you."

He looked hurt. "Well, that's a fine thing to say to your brother whom you love."

She laughed. "Sure, I love you, but I don't trust you! Remember that time when we went on vacation to Lake Erie and you pushed me right over into the water? You earned your reputation that day! Mary, this man is not to be trusted around water, mark my words."

Mary chuckled. "Reuben, did you do that? How unkind of you!"

"What she left out is that first she dumped a bucket of water over my head while I was napping on the beach."

"Did you really do that, Eliza?" Edie asked, looking scandalized.

Eliza giggled some more. "Well, maybe."

"See? She had it coming." Reuben reached down and scooped up a handful of water, tossing it on his sister, who shrieked, "Reuben King! You promised!"

"Nee, I didn't!" His laughter rang out, and Mary smiled. He hadn't really splashed much on Eliza after all. The young girl was just being a little dramatic. "You're hardly even wet. But next time, bring a bathing suit and you'll be able to enjoy the water."

Eliza rolled her eyes and moved back toward shore when Reuben sloshed off toward Joe and the boys. "I didn't bring a bathing suit with me from home," she confided to the women. "Now I wish I had."

"Well, we can get you one in town. There's a store that sells plain clothes and modest swimwear," Mary said. "I actually need a new suit too. Mine is several years old and getting a little threadbare."

"I'll go with you girls," Edie said. "There are a few things I need. When shall we go?"

They talked about their schedules for the next few days and agreed on Tuesday afternoon. "We'll pick you up in the buggy. It's not too far from the dokder's place," Edie said.

Pleased with their plan, the women sat together on the bank, watching the men and boys splash around in the pond and watching the men teach the boys how to back float.

"If you can float, you can save yourself if you fall into deep water," Joe reminded his sons.

After a while, Edie noticed the boys were turning a bit blue. "Time to get out and dry off!" she called. With protests, they complied. Soon they were dry and dressed, and Joe and Edie took them over to the field to play a game of kickball while Mary, Eliza, and Reuben walked farther downstream to where the current ran faster and the water was deeper.

"This is a very gut spot for catching trout," Mary said. "Put the basket down there on the grass, Reuben. I'll show you both how to cast once we bait the lines."

They took the three fly rods she'd brought along, and she showed them how to put the lightweight artificial flies on them. She explained the action of casting, which was quite different from tossing a line with a hook and bobber into still water, and different from casting a heavy lure far out and reeling it in.

"Fly-fishing involves moving your lure across the water in a way that imitates a bug that is either skimming along the top, swimming below the surface, or falling in from a tree and struggling. Reuben, if you'll please place the stool I brought over on that nice flat place, I'll demonstrate."

He opened the sturdy, four-legged camping stool and placed it on an even piece of ground a couple of feet from the water. Mary maneuvered over to it, sat down, and dropped her crutches into the grass. She situated herself, accepted her rod from Eliza, and turned to look at the rapidly moving stream, gauging the best places to cast her lure. With a nod, she made her decision. "Watch me for a minute."

With a deceptively simple flick of her wrist, she cast her fly out into the stream and watched it float downstream with the current. "Now, watch how I move it." She jigged the line a bit, and the fly danced on the water, as if it were a water bug or some such creature, skittering along on the surface. Nothing took the lure, and she reeled it back in. "See? That's all there is to it!"

She offered him the pole, which he took gingerly, as if handling something a bit dangerous.

Eliza giggled. "It's not going to bite you, bruder. Go on, give it a try!"

He made a face at his sister before turning to the water. Taking a deep breath, he tried to imitate the practiced way Mary had cast the line. He grunted in disgust when it landed in the tall grass of the riverbank a few feet away instead of sailing out over the water like Mary's had.

Eliza crowed her amusement. "You might catch a hungry groundhog if you get lucky, bruder!"

"Ha ha. Let me try again." He gathered up the line, which was tangled in the weeds, and again attempted to cast it over the river. This time it went a respectable distance, but he became overexcited at his success and reeled it back much too quickly. Nothing took the lure.

"Too fast, Reuben," Eliza said knowingly. "Mary said slow and kinda bumpy."

He rolled his eyes at his sister. "If it's so easy, why don't you show me how it's done, then?"

"Denki! I will!" Eliza took the rod and walked down the bank a few feet and prepared to cast. Reuben grinned at Mary in anticipation of Eliza doing no better than he had. She smiled sympathetically back. "Don't feel bad, Reuben. Fly-fishing takes practice. Nobody gets it the first time."

They watched as Eliza scrunched her face in concentration, gauged the breeze, and drew back her arm before casting the line. And then they gasped as Eliza's line flew in a perfect, graceful arc, landing quite a ways downstream.

"Hey, did you see that?"

"Well, I'll be," Reuben muttered. "Beginner's luck, sis."

"Now reel it back but not smooth or fast. Make it kind of irregular and a bit jerky, like I showed you," Mary said.

Eliza nodded and began pulling the line back in, but not all at once and not in a smooth line. She bumped and jerked it, causing the lure to dance and jibe like a bug in the water.

"Gut! Gut! You're a natural," Mary said. "Let it rest a moment, and then pull it in some more."

Eliza nodded and stopped reeling the line in for a few seconds, and then she jerked it and began drawing it in again, when suddenly, a large, colorful fish exploded out of the water, Eliza's lure firmly seated in its jaw.

"Look! Look! I caught a fish!" Eliza yelled.

"You sure did! Now, gently reel it in, don't jerk or tug now, or it might escape," Mary directed calmly from her seat.

"Wow, that's a beaut!" Reuben said, grabbing the net and sliding down the embankment to scoop the fish out of the water. "Talk about beginner's luck!"

"Wow, that fish will just about feed us all," Mary said. "But it seems a shame to stop now. Reuben, why don't you try again?"

He shook his head and grinned at his sister. "Nope, I'm stopping while I still have a shred of dignity left. Eliza cast and fished like a pro. From now on, she can catch all our meals!"

They laughed as they made their way back to their picnic area, where everyone made a fuss over Eliza's lovely trout.

Joe showed the boys how to clean the fish, and they grilled it over the fire and enjoyed a nice meal together before clearing everything up and getting ready to head home.

"This was so much fun! When can we come again?" Nathan asked as he helped load their gear into the back of Reuben's truck.

"Yes, I'd like to fish again soon," Eliza put in.

"You caught the best rainbow trout I've seen come out of this stream in years," Joe said. "You might not have as much luck next time."

"That's okay! It was such fun, I just want to try again."

"Another convert hooked by fly-fishing!" Mary laughed.

"We can come again soon. Next time, I'm wearing my bathing suit under my dress," Edie said.

"Me too—assuming I find a suit I like," Eliza said.

Mary smiled and kept silent. Reuben looked at her and recalled her saying she couldn't swim.

If this surgery gives her the relief I hope it will, I'm going to teach her how. Everyone should be able to swim, and I know it's a sore point for her that she can't.

His thoughts were interrupted by the boys clamoring to ride in the bed of his pickup truck.

"Nee, sorry, boys. That's not safe, especially on the road. But if your maem and dat say it's okay, you can ride inside the truck with me." Cries of "Please, Dat! Please, Maem!" were heard, and Edie and Joe allowed the boys to climb into Reuben's truck.

"Wear your seat belts, boys!" Edie called.

"Don't worry, everybody in my truck buckles up," Reuben assured her. The boys did so, and Reuben waved as he pulled away, leaving Mary, Eliza, Edie, and Joe to come along behind them in the buggy.

"What a gut day!" Eliza sighed, squeezing Mary's arm as they walked behind Joe and Edie to the buggy. "I'd like to spend every day like this, except that I'd have a bathing suit so I could actually swim! It's hot!"

"We'll take care of that soon," Edie promised. The girls climbed into the back of the buggy, with Mary's parents riding in the front, and soon they were on their way home.

Mary agreed with Eliza that it had been a very gut day indeed! *The only thing that would have made it better would be if Reuben and I had been there as sweethearts. But I need to get that sort of idea out of my head.*

"What are you thinking about?" Eliza asked Mary, who pulled her attention back to Reuben's sister.

She smiled. "Just about how much I enjoyed today. And that delicious fish you caught!"

Eliza shifted in her seat to face Mary. "It was delicious! I can't wait to do it again. And Mary, I'm so grateful to you for being my friend."

She leaned in close and whispered, "The only thing better would be if you could be my schwester!"

"Oh, Eliza, there's no way that can happen, so best not speak of it!" Mary whispered back, glancing nervously at her parents, who were holding their own conversation and didn't appear to have heard Eliza's comment.

Eliza smiled and patted Mary's arm. "I know, it doesn't look promising, and I won't speak of it again, as it's none of my business and obviously makes you uncomfortable. But you just never know, with Gott—that's all I'm saying!" Then she mimed zipping her lips, grinned at Mary, and turned to look out the window.

Mary sat back in her seat, a little bit shocked that Eliza would voice such a thought out loud. Still, it was nice to know she'd like to have Mary for a schwester. Even if it was very unlikely.

CHAPTER SIXTEEN

"It was very kind of you to drive us up here, Dokder. You really didn't have to do that." Edie told Reuben as he maneuvered the car he'd borrowed from his nurse through traffic in downtown Akron. They were on their way to Akron General Medical Center, now part of the Cleveland Clinic, so Mary could be seen by a spinal specialist there for assessment.

"It's really no problem, Mrs. Yoder. I'd like to meet Dr. Pavlic and hear her opinion anyway."

"It'll be helpful having a dokder there to translate all those muddlesome medical terms—ach! Watch out for that truck!"

Mary, in the back seat, glanced over to the right at a truck that had just switched lanes and was moving past their car. It was staying politely in its own lane, from what she could see. Her maem was a nervous passenger.

"Maem, let Reuben drive in peace. We'll be fine."

"I'll just close my eyes and say a little prayer."

Reuben met Mary's eyes in the rearview mirror, and she saw a smile in them. Really, he'd been very patient with her mother, who had been making little comments and suggestions and not-so-little squeaks of fear throughout the drive.

"Maybe on the way back you'd prefer the back seat, Maem," she said. "You can't see anything from back here."

"Maybe that would be a gut idea," Edie said.

"Almost there, ladies," Reuben said, signaling for a left turn, which brought the big medical center into view. "We'll park in the garage."

A few minutes later, they were entering the lobby of the building they'd been instructed to visit and checking in with a receptionist who directed them to the correct floor.

As they rode up in the elevator, Mary felt herself growing nervous, something she had to admit her mother's constant fussing on the drive from Willow Creek had prevented until now. She closed her eyes and asked God for grace and courage. Her eyes popped open when she felt Reuben take her hand in his and give it a little squeeze for reassurance. She turned and met his eyes, and he smiled.

"It's going to be fine, Mary."

"Of course it is!" Edie said, turning to look at her daughter. Reuben had dropped Mary's hand, and her mother hadn't caught the slight impropriety. But the bishop's words came back to tease her, and she frowned. Was it improper for Reuben to accompany them to Akron like this? They could have hired a driver, after all.

"Stop thinking so hard," Reuben advised. "Soon enough you'll have answers."

Not to everything, Mary thought. But then they arrived at the floor where the surgeon's office was located, and the doors swished open, letting them out. They turned and walked a short way down a hall painted a soothing shade of gray, with soft lighting and beautiful photos of Akron hanging on the walls. They came to a big glass door with the surgeon's name on it: Dr. Veronica Pavlic.

"Here we are!" Edie chirped. Reuben opened the door and held it while the women walked through. Mary looked around and saw a number of people seated in the waiting area. A few stared curiously, but she was used to that. At least here, where several people had crutches, canes, and even a wheelchair with them, the curiosity wasn't because of her disability but rather because of her style of dressing.

Her lips quirked. Wasn't life funny?

"Can I help you?" asked a young woman seated behind a counter. She was wearing teal cat-eye glasses.

"Ja, denki," Edie said. "Mary Yoder to see Dr. Pavlic."

The woman smiled at Mary. "Right on time. If you'll please fill out this paperwork, the doctor will see you in just a bit."

Mary took the clipboard and handed it to her mother, and they walked over to an empty seating group and sat down. Reuben remained at the counter.

"I'm Dr. King," Reuben told the receptionist. "After Dr. Pavlic consults with Miss Yoder, I'd like to speak with her, if she has a few minutes."

"Are you Miss Yoder's doctor?"

He hesitated, then nodded. "I'm the one who referred her. I promised to come with her and her mother and talk to the doctor to be sure they understand all their options, and any procedure she recommends."

The woman nodded. "I'll tell the doctor, Dr. King."

He smiled at her, and Mary, watching from her chair, saw the young woman blush. Reuben tended to have that effect on women, she thought before sighing and going back to her paperwork.

The door to the examination area opened, and a plump woman wearing lavender scrubs and purple Crocs looked at a chart before calling, "Mary Yoder?"

Edie popped up as if stuck with a pin, and Mary pushed to her feet. She looked at Reuben, who nodded encouragingly. "I'll be here when you're done, and I told them I want to see Dr. Pavlic when she's finished examining you."

"Okay, thanks, Reuben." Mary and Edie followed the woman in scrubs through the door.

About forty-five minutes later, the door to the waiting room opened, and the same woman who had led Mary and her mother back scanned the room until her eyes landed on him.

"Dr. King?"

Reuben stood. "Yes, I'm Dr. King."

She smiled. "Would you please come with me? Dr. Pavlic is ready to see you."

Surprised at how quickly the exam had gone, Reuben frowned. "Is everything all right?"

"Oh yes. The doctor will fill you in. Right this way, please." She stood aside, and Reuben went through the doorway into a long hallway lined with exam rooms, which they passed, taking a couple of turns before stopping at an open door. The woman poked her head inside.

"Dr. Pavlic? Dr. King is here to talk with you."

"Great, send him in," a cheerful voice responded. The nurse stepped aside so Reuben could enter the office, and he glanced around the sunny space which contained the usual assortment of furniture and diplomas, plus two large windows looking out at the Akron cityscape.

"Hello, Dr. King, please, have a seat." The young woman, who Reuben knew to be one of the leading spinal surgeons in the state, gestured to a pair of comfy-looking armchairs arrayed before her desk.

"Thanks. Please, call me Reuben."

"Great. And I'm Ronnie. But. . .you know that." She studied him with intense blue eyes for a few moments. "Your name sounded familiar, but I wasn't sure until now. We went to OSU together, right?"

He nodded and smiled. "That's right. I don't blame you for not recognizing me right away. You were several years ahead of me, and it's been—what?—seven years since we saw each other?"

"At least that long. It's good to see you again, Reuben. So, what's your interest in Mary Yoder, if you don't mind me asking? Most patients aren't personally accompanied by their physicians."

He squirmed a bit in his seat before smiling sheepishly. "I'm not precisely her physician. That is, I recently took over the practice of her childhood doctor, Dr. Smith, in Willow Creek. But I'm not her physician. My interest in her is more. . .personal."

Was he blushing? He sincerely hoped not, but his face felt hot. Her knowing smile didn't help.

"Ah, I see. Well, she and her mother have given me permission to speak with you. I wanted a word first, and then we'll have them join us, okay?"

He nodded. "Is she a good candidate for the latest procedures I've read about?"

She looked thoughtful, pursing her lips and steepling her hands in front of herself, tapping herself on the lips with her index fingers. She nodded slowly. "I'm going to say yes, but guardedly."

Reuben felt a surge of relief sweep over him, but then he registered her final word. "Guardedly? May I ask why the caveat?"

She shrugged. "It's simply that she's in her late twenties and has had a number of previous surgeries, as you're aware. There's bound to be scar tissue, which can inhibit the success of the procedure I'm considering. I'm not saying it won't work, but I can't guarantee it will. And honestly, the Yoders both seem a bit gun-shy about proceeding. I won't try and talk them into this."

He shook his head. "No, neither will I. The risk of a bad outcome is real, and they need to make up their own minds. But I want them to have all the information possible to enable them to make an educated decision."

She nodded. "If this were me or a member of my family, I'd say go for it. But I can't do that with Mary Yoder. I will give her all the information and the odds of success, plus the risks involved. The usual. . .no change, or worse, a lessening of mobility or even paralysis is a possibility. Then she'll need to make up her own mind."

He took a deep breath. This was no more than he'd expected, and he'd even told Mary and her mother to expect to hear this. "But you do feel there's a real possibility that Mary could see a marked improvement in mobility? And even more importantly, a significant lessening of her day-to-day pain?"

Slowly, the other doctor nodded. "Yes, I do. In fact, I think it is likely. But there are always risks, and you'd be surprised how many patients choose to live with the evil they know, so to speak, rather than risk the evil they don't."

"Pretty much what I expected to hear, to be honest. And what I told them to expect."

"Okay, do you have any questions?"

They went over a few points until Reuben was satisfied he fully understood the procedure and the risks it would involve. He nodded. "Shall we call them in, then?"

With a smile she picked up the phone on her desk and asked the nurse to bring the Yoders into her office.

"So," the doctor began, once they had all settled comfortably into seats around her desk, "first, I want you to know I think you're a very good candidate for this surgery. I think it could definitely improve your life, Mary."

Edie inhaled sharply and raised her hand to her mouth, her eyes filling with tears. Mary reached over and took her mother's hand to offer comfort, but her own mind was swirling with so many thoughts and emotions that she couldn't immediately speak.

Reuben seemed to understand. He smiled and squeezed Mary's hand in reassurance. "That's what I thought too."

"That being said, the procedure is not without risks, and I want you both to fully understand the pros and cons before making a decision."

Edie waved her hand in front of her face as if fanning herself. "Sorry, sorry, it's just that I so hoped. . .but I almost didn't dare. . . and now you say she's a gut candidate. . .oh! Gott is so gut!"

"Your emotions are completely understandable, Mrs. Yoder. I'm a mother too."

Edie nodded and pulled herself together. "Please, Dokder, tell us what we need to know."

For the next twenty minutes, Dr. Pavlic explained exactly what the proposed surgery would involve, including all the risks inherent in the procedure and the possible outcomes, both good and, possibly, bad that could result. When she finished, Mary felt as if her head was spinning, as though she'd come untethered from reality and was in danger of being flung into some other state. There was so much to absorb!

But then she felt the reassuring squeeze of her mother's hand on one side and the warm strength of Reuben's on her other side, and she felt herself settle down. She took several deep breaths, and a calm settled over her. She looked over at her mother, who looked concerned, and managed a smile. "I'm okay, Maem. It was just a lot for a minute."

Edie nodded. "Ja, a lot to think about! We'll have to talk to your dat and see what he thinks."

But Mary shook her head. "Nee. I don't need to talk to Dat." She looked over at Reuben, who was gazing steadily back at her with compassionate, caring eyes.

"Nee?" he asked.

"Nee. I'm an adult, and I can make my own decision."

"But Mary. . ." Edie started, but Mary shook her head firmly.

"Maem, I know you are only looking out for me, but remember, Gott has a plan for me. I think He has put this opportunity before me, and I feel drawn to seize it. I think it is the right decision."

Her mother's worried blue eyes searched her face for a few moments, and then she slowly nodded. "Okay, I trust your judgment. You must do what you feel is right."

Mary smiled. "Denki, Maem." She looked at Reuben, who smiled back at her, looking as if he were proud of her for being brave. But the truth was, she was just tired. Tired of pain. Tired of crutches. Tired of not being like everyone else. And while she understood that this surgery might not result in full mobility, and she might still have pain and still need the crutches, Reuben and Doctor Pavlic both thought she would be at least somewhat better. That was enough for her to take the leap of faith necessary to move forward, knowing it would be a hard, painful process.

She smiled at Reuben, turned and gave her mother a hug, and then sat back and faced the doctor. "Okay, Dokder. Where do I sign up?"

CHAPTER SEVENTEEN

Three weeks from today, I'll be in surgery, Mary thought, looking at the large red circle boldly drawn around the big day in the engagement calendar she kept on her desk. She carried a smaller calendar in her bag, but pretty much her whole schedule was mapped out in the larger one on her desk. She loved the beautiful book, bound in brown leather with rings that could be refilled each year. It had been a gift from her maem and dat a few years ago for Christmas. In the back was a separate address section with contact information for family, friends, and business connections. She paged to the address section and flipped through the pages, perusing the names of people she hadn't seen or thought of in a while.

"I ought to send her a letter," she murmured over the name and address of a woman she'd met when they were both teens recovering from spinal surgeries in Nationwide Children's Hospital in Columbus. Her friend hadn't been as fortunate as she was, remaining confined to a wheelchair despite multiple surgeries aimed at restoring some use of her legs. Mary recalled that the girl, an Englisher, had been bitter and angry. And who could blame her? Even though Mary firmly believed in the Amish tenets stating that whatever happened was God's will, and was therefore for the best, as humans God's reasons could be hard to understand.

Mary had struggled herself more than once with anger—even anger against God. She was ashamed to admit it, even to herself, but during the darkest times when it wasn't clear whether she'd ever walk again, and when the pain had been so bad she'd spent much of her time drowsing in drug-induced stupors, she'd wondered what God could have been thinking.

Why hadn't He just taken her to heaven along with her Dat? It would have been easier on everyone. Once, she'd tearfully confessed these feelings to her maem, who had done her best to take care of a daughter who needed almost constant care for several years following the buggy accident that had killed her father and left her severely injured. Things had gotten better, and she'd been able to use crutches to get around. She'd been able to bathe herself and take care of other personal needs, much to her own relief—and no doubt her mother's too!

But after a certain point, the surgeries had diminishing returns. The final one, when she'd been seventeen, had left her no better off than before as far as she could tell, yet it had involved weeks of recovery and months of physical therapy, in addition to costing a fortune and inconveniencing her family and church community.

She had called a halt to further attempts at "fixing her problems" at that time and had not been willing to hear anyone's opinions to the contrary. . .until now.

"I hope this isn't a mistake," she whispered.

Closing her engagement calendar, she sat back and closed her eyes, rubbing the bridge of her nose with a thumb and forefinger to relieve a stress headache she felt coming on.

"Heavenly Father," she prayed, "please help my uncertainty and relieve my fear. I believe You sent Reuben to me for a reason. I've prayed and I'm confident—well, pretty confident—that this is the path You intend for me.

"Everyone is very supportive. Maem, Dat, the bishop, my friends. Even my boss, Jonas! Yet I can't help second-guessing the decision to have another surgery. How can I be sure this time will be any different? How can I be sure this won't be a waste of time and money, again! How can I stop being afraid?"

"You can't be sure of anything, child; you can only have faith. As for being afraid, refer to what I said about having faith. It's the only way people can get through things like this."

Startled, Mary sat up and opened her eyes to see Lydia standing in the doorway to the room.

"Lydia! I didn't hear you knock. I'm sorry, *kumma* in!"

"You were lost in prayer, is what you were lost in, and I apologize for interrupting. But you were lost in despair and fear too, and I won't apologize for interrupting that. Come sit with an old woman and talk this through."

Lydia made her way over to the chairs in front of Mary's fireplace and lowered herself carefully into one of the comfy old armchairs left over from when Mary's grandparents had lived there. The coffee table was a cedar hope chest that had first belonged to a grandmother a few generations back. It was old but had been lovingly cared for. Mary used it to hold her winter quilts and bedding. Another, newer, cedar chest stood at the foot of her bed and held her winter sweaters and linens.

"I'll get us some iced tea." Mary went into her tiny kitchen and got the pitcher of tea out of the fridge and carried it into the living room and set it on the coffee table in front of Lydia.

"Mary, sit. You don't need to fuss."

"I already got the tea, might as well get the glasses!" A minute later she put a basket containing two tea glasses, napkins, and four cookies on the table.

"Well, since this deal includes cookies, I guess I'm glad you insisted." Lydia poured the tea into the glasses and set them on coasters. She took a bite out of a cookie and closed her eyes momentarily in pleasure. "Mmm. This is gut! I love lemon."

Mary smiled. "Maem baked them yesterday and brought me two dozen. I'm glad to have someone to keep me from eating them all, like a total glutton."

They smiled at each other for a moment, and then Mary's face grew serious. "Lydia, I don't mean to seem as if I haven't enough faith. It's just really scary. You were there last time. Remember? It didn't do any good, and it was so hard recovering from it. I can't help being afraid that this is a mistake. And worse, what if something goes wrong and I actually end up worse off than I am now? Should I just be grateful for what I have instead of tempting fate?"

"Ah, but child, we Christians don't believe in fate, remember? We believe in faith. And I believe you have enough of that to get you through. You just have to dig a little to find it again." She took another bite of cookie and washed it down with iced tea while Mary contemplated what she'd said.

"You aren't shocked to learn that I'm questioning Gott's will in this?"

"Of course not. You're an intelligent woman. You know this is a risky venture. You're not questioning Gott's will so much as your own wisdom. But I firmly believe that Gott sent Dokder Reuben to you to show you the path to this final procedure and that it will be successful and you'll be ever so much better after you recover."

"You really do?"

"I really do, child. And so do your parents or they wouldn't have encouraged you. And so does Bishop Troyer. All the *Deiner* voted to approve the surgery. You know that. The church officials wouldn't have done that unless they were convinced this was going to help you."

Mary nodded. "It's true, the Deiner don't like to waste money. So you think I should stop worrying and just trust Gott to keep me safe and let the dokders do their job?"

"Pretty much. Pass those cookies, child. I want another. They're gut!"

Mary smiled and passed the plate of cookies to Lydia, who took two. "Denki, Lydia."

"For what? I'm only reminding you of what you already know."

Mary let out a surprised little laugh. "You know what? You're right. I'm having cold feet, I guess."

"Perfectly normal. I'll talk you out of them again next week, and the week after, right up until the surgery if necessary."

"Oh, I hope that won't be necessary!"

A little squeak caused both women to look toward the kitchen, where Hope was stretching luxuriously, having obviously just woken from a catnap.

"Ah! There's my little love," Lydia crooned. "Come here, Hope, and let your grossmammi see how you've grown!"

Hope strolled over and jumped up into Lydia's lap. "My, you've gotten to be such a big girl! Mary, she's about fully grown. And I can see what a hard life she leads here with you!" She scratched the cat in just the right spot behind her ears, causing her to let out a loud, rumbling purr that made the women chuckle.

"Oh ja, she has it real hard!" Mary said. "If she's not here ruling the roost, she's over at Maem's snoozing in front of her stove or lying in one of the boy's beds. They all argue about who gets to sleep with her if she's over there at their bedtime. Of course, she always comes back here to sleep for the night, but sometimes she starts in one of their beds. I wouldn't be surprised to see Maem and Dat get a kitten of their own one of these days. Too bad you're out of the kitten business, Lydia."

"Hephzibah is not sorry to be out of the kitten business, believe me. She's very content to spend her days relaxing and lording it over her mate."

"I'll bet. To be fair, Hope does catch an occasional mouse or bug, and since I'd rather not have to, I'm happy to take that in payment for her room and board."

Lydia held the cat up and rubbed noses with her. "You pay your way with love and snuggles, don't you, sweetie? I know you do!"

"Okay, that too," Mary said, grinning at the older woman. "She's a might spoiled, but then, she's spoiled me too. If she doesn't jump up and snuggle me to sleep, I feel cold and lonely."

Lydia smiled gently at Mary and put the cat down. "As to that, I have some ideas regarding a more satisfactory situation, but we'll discuss that when the time is right."

"What do you mean?"

"Never you mind." Pushing to her feet, Lydia groaned. "Ooo. I'm feeling my years. I'm thinking about heading south a bit earlier this year, maybe after Ruth and Jonas' wedding."

"What, and miss Christmas?"

Lydia shrugged. "I'd spend it with my son's family in Florida. He's been asking me to come for the holidays for years, but I always spend Thanksgiving and Christmas with Lisle's family."

"And Easter with your son, right?"

"Ja, but Lisle gets two holidays."

Mary thought a second, then grinned mischievously. "Well, your son actually gets three—no, four!"

"How do you figure that?"

"He gets New Year's, Groundhog Day, Valentine's Day, and Easter!"

Lydia chuckled. "I don't much care for any of those but Easter."

"What? But Groundhog Day is the first day of spring!"

"Now you're just being silly."

"Okay, not really, but it feels like it to me. After all, it's the day we start looking for spring—almost the same thing, right?"

"I'll think about it. Now I have to go. Ruth and I are baking pies tonight. I'll see you soon."

She took a step, and her hip gave out with an audible crack, and she cried out and fell to the floor.

Mary was horrified, and she pushed to her feet. "Lydia! What happened?" She hurried over to where the older woman lay on the floor, her complexion ashen, obviously in pain.

"Oh, nothing, I just tripped. I'm fine. Just help me up, would you?"

Mary bit her lip. Lydia did not look fine. Perspiration was beading on her upper lip, and her pupils were dilated. "Are you sure you should move? Maybe I should go get Maem or Dat?"

"No! No! Just help me up, and I'll be fine."

Hope slid over and touched her nose to Lydia's hand, and Lydia turned her head to look at the cat. "Oh, Hope, get out of the way so I don't squish you," Lydia said weakly. "Here, take my hand, that's a gut girl."

Taking a deep breath, Mary reached her hand down to Lydia, who took it, but when she tried to pull herself up, she cried out again and fell back, a look of shock on her face.

"Oh no. I think I've broken my hip! I can't move! And it hurts dreadfully!"

"I'm going for help. Just. . .stay right there, Lydia." Mary grabbed her crutches and hurried to the door leading to her parents' house, already calling out for help.

CHAPTER EIGHTEEN

An hour later, Mary and Edie were seated in the waiting room in the emergency department of the hospital in Millersburg. They'd been there about fifteen minutes and, since they weren't family, hadn't been allowed inside with Lydia. Lisle had arrived a couple of minutes ago and, after checking with them to find out what had happened, had been led back to her mother's bedside by a harried-looking nurse dressed in blue scrubs and white sneakers.

"Oh, Maem, I'm so worried. If only Lydia had agreed to the hip replacement when Dr. Smith recommended it several years ago!"

"Try not to worry so, Mary. Lydia is in gut hands. Remember, Gott is by her side. He'll make sure everything works out all right."

But Mary knew that sometimes when an older person broke a hip, they never got back to normal. Some stopped trying to recover and stopped moving at all, until they died of a blood clot or other issue.

Stop borrowing trouble! There's enough to go around already! Mary reminded herself. The outside doors whooshed open, and Ruth and Jonas hurried in. They looked around and, spotting Mary and Edie, crossed the room and took seats opposite them in a small seating group. There weren't many others in the waiting room.

"How's she doing?" Ruth asked anxiously. Lydia lived in Ruth's dawdi haus, behind the house Ruth had shared with her late husband, Levi. She and Jonas were engaged, and their wedding would take place that fall following the harvest.

"We haven't heard anything, but we've only been here about twenty minutes now," Edie said, looking at the wall clock for about the tenth time.

"What happened?" Ruth asked.

Mary explained how Lydia had fallen. "Ruth, it was bad. I think I heard the bone break before she fell. I think she fell because her hip was broken, not the other way around."

Ruth shuddered. "Oh, that's awful." She reached out and took Jonas' hand. "Is Lisle here? She's the one who called us. We'd have been here sooner, but we had to drop Abby off at Sally's."

Abby was Jonas' daughter with his late wife and would soon become Ruth's daughter as well. Mary knew Ruth loved the child just as much as if she'd given birth to her. Sally was Jonas' sister and had been an enormous help in raising the little girl, since her maem had died in childbirth.

"I understand. We don't know much. Lisle is with her, though, so that's gut."

They all nodded and sat back to wait. After a few minutes, Jonas stood. "I'm going to go get us all some kaffi. This could be a long night."

A couple of hours later, Reuben came through the door from the examining area and walked over to where they all waited. They'd been joined by Bishop Troyer. Reuben shook hands with the bishop and Jonas and smiled at the women.

"Good evening, everyone. You're all here waiting for news about Lydia, I'm guessing?"

"Of course! What's going on? Is she going to be all right?" Edie asked, wringing her hands.

"Lydia is not a young woman. She broke her hip—actually, that is what caused her to fall."

"I knew it!" Mary gasped. "I heard it break when she turned."

He nodded. "We've consulted a surgeon in Akron. We can't handle this sort of injury here."

"What does that mean? Do you have to transfer Lydia to Akron?" Ruth asked, again clasping Jonas' hand tightly.

Mary knew the older woman was like a mother and grandmother rolled into one for Ruth, whose own mother and father lived all the way in Texas. Lydia had moved in with her in the spring, after her house, and everything in it, burned to the ground during a freak winter thunderstorm while Lydia was in Florida. Fortunately, her beloved cats had been with her.

"Yes, we've arranged for transportation. It'll be here soon—a private ambulance. Then she'll be moved to Akron General Hospital, where she'll have surgery." He shook his head. "She should have had that hip replaced years ago. But she's a strong, determined woman, and with physical therapy, she'll be better than new in a few months."

"Well, that's gut, anyway," Mary said, offering Ruth a smile. "Can we see her?"

Reuben pursed his lips. "Things have calmed down back there, so I guess it would be okay. But she's drugged pretty heavily now, because of the pain. She probably won't make much sense and may not even know you're here."

"I just need to see for myself that she's okay," Ruth said, standing. "Mary, would you come back with me?"

Mary looked up, surprised. "Me? Wouldn't you prefer for Jonas to accompany you?"

"I'll see her later. You go ahead," Jonas said. "I'll wait here with the bishop."

"Ja, you go ahead, I'll talk to her when she's awake," Bishop Troyer said.

Mary smiled at the two men and pushed to her feet. "Denki. I'd really like to see her too, but I didn't want to presume."

She and Ruth followed Reuben through the door leading to the treatment area. Reaching Lydia's room, they found the door was open and the lights were dimmed, and inside Mary could make out Lydia's form on a hospital bed, covered with several white cotton blankets.

"Where's Lisle?" Mary whispered, not wanting to wake Lydia if she was sleeping.

"Her mann, Joe, arrived a while ago, with overnight bags for Lydia and Lisle. She's going to ride to Akron with her mother. I sent them down to get something to eat. Lisle was starting to look translucent." Reuben stepped aside to allow the two women to enter the room. Ruth went first, going around to the far side of the bed, leaving the near side for Mary, as it had more open space and she was able to maneuver her crutches without too much trouble.

"Lydia?" Ruth whispered. "It's Ruth. Mary and I came to see you." Lydia opened her eyes a slit and peered at Ruth. A ghost of a smile flitted across her lips. "Ruth, I'm sorry to be so much trouble."

"Nonsense! You're no trouble! Your hip broke. You can't help that."

Lydia closed her eyes and smiled again. "I could have had the hip replacement when they told me to. Now I guess I have no choice."

"Don't worry about that now, lieb. Everything will be fine. You'll get your hip taken care of, and then you'll come home and stay with me, and plenty of people will stand in line to help you, the way you've helped so many others in this little town."

"She'll go to a rehab center for a while first but not for long, if I know Lydia," Reuben put in.

"They can't keep me down," she murmured, and Mary thought she looked old for the first time. Her skin was gray and translucent, and her eyelids looked delicate and fragile.

"Oh, Lydia, I'm so sorry you have to go through this," Mary whispered.

"Don't fret, child. I'll be fine."

"She'll actually be better off once she gets her brand-new hip," Reuben said.

"Yes, just think, Lydia, I won't be able to keep up with you!" Mary laughed softly.

"Not for long, though," Lydia said.

"Right! You two will be recuperating at about the same time," Ruth said.

"Can't wait," Mary mumbled, and Reuben chuckled.

"You'll be glad afterward too, just wait and see if you're not."

She smiled at him sideways. "So you say."

"Oh, stop. You'll be fine," Lydia muttered without opening her eyes. "Now go. I'm weary. Is Abram out there? I'd like to speak to him."

They all stood. Ruth bent down and kissed Lydia's forehead, causing the old woman to smile and reach up for Ruth's hand. "I'll be fine, child. I'll be walking into your wedding! See if I don't."

"I'll hold you to that," Ruth said. She stepped out of the room, and Mary leaned down and kissed Lydia's cheek. "You take care of yourself and do what they tell you. I know you, Lydia."

"Oh! Ask Ruth to take care of my cats, will you?"

"Of course she will. But I'll remind her."

"Denki."

"What's this I hear about a broken hip?" Bishop Troyer spoke from the doorway.

Lydia opened her eyes and smiled at the man, who was frowning sternly at her. "Sorry to inconvenience you, Abram. Thank you for coming."

"Of course I came." He smiled and took her hand.

"Abram, I'm a bit afraid."

"Then let's pray. God is here for you."

Mary realized they'd forgotten her presence, and she turned to head back to the waiting room. Reuben was standing a few paces down the hall, waiting for her. "Oh! You didn't have to wait for me. But. . .thank you. I'm not sure I'd find my way out of here on my own."

He fell into step with her, and they walked through the ER. He returned a couple of greetings and opened the door for her leading to the waiting area, where Ruth and Jonas were gathering their things.

"Can I give you a ride home?" Reuben asked the couple.

"Nee, denki, we have a driver," Jonas said. "So, is Lydia going to be oll recht?"

"Yes, will she make a full recovery?" Ruth added anxiously.

"I think so, as long as she takes her rehabilitation seriously. Hip replacements are commonplace nowadays. Her age makes things a bit more complicated, but she's healthy and fit, so she shouldn't have any real problems."

"Oh, thank Gott!" Ruth said. "I love her like my own grandmother. I was so worried when I heard about her accident."

"You should have been there," Mary said. "It was terrifying. The sound when her hip broke!" She shuddered. "And then she fell, and I couldn't get down to her. I had to leave her there on the floor while I went for help. It was terrible. If my surgery will allow me to be more helpful in such situations, it'll be worth it for that alone!"

"Let's all say a prayer for Lydia and for Mary," Ruth suggested. She looked around, and everyone nodded. "Jonas, will you please lead? Your prayers are always so heartfelt."

She smiled at him, and he smiled back, and their feelings for one another couldn't be clearer. Mary felt a tiny bit envious, and she chided herself. She wanted nothing but happiness for her friends.

"Dear Heavenly Father, thank You for holding Lydia in Your hands today when she was injured. Please keep her in the palm of Your hand during the trials ahead, and please hold our sister Mary in Your hands as well during her upcoming surgery, bringing both her and Lydia through whole and well. In Jesus' name, amen."

"Amen," they all repeated. Then, smiling at each other, they gathered their things and headed outside to go home.

"Mary, where are your parents?" Reuben asked, suddenly realizing they had disappeared while they were in visiting Lydia.

Mary looked around as if they would suddenly appear. "I don't know. I forgot they were here!"

"Oh, they went home to tend the animals and the boys," Ruth said. "I almost forgot. I said we'd drop Mary off on our way home."

Mary frowned. "But you live in the opposite direction. It's quite a bit out of your way. I hate to be such a bother."

"I could drive you," Reuben offered.

"Well, there you go!" Ruth said. "It really wouldn't be a bother for us, but if Dokder Reuben wants to take you, that sounds fine to me."

"But it's out of your way too, Reuben," Mary began. "And remember what the bishop said."

"You can trust me, Mary," Reuben said. "I promise to be a complete gentleman."

"Well!" Ruth said brightly, "That's good enough for me! Come, Jonas, let's not keep the driver waiting."

Jonas shook Reuben's hand and gave Mary a little shrug, as if saying, "Hey, don't look at me!" and he followed Ruth from the room.

Mary didn't know what to think. On the one hand, the bishop had been very clear about the two of them not being alone in potentially compromising situations. On the other hand, they were both trustworthy adults who had given their word.

Which meant there was nothing to worry about.

Except...they were attracted to each other—of that she had no doubt. What to do?

Reuben stood and watched all of this pass over Mary's face, and he chuckled. "Your face is like a book, Mary Yoder. Stop worrying. I'm only driving you home. Tomorrow, I'll likely drive your family to Akron to see Lydia again. Now, it's getting late. What do you say we go home?"

"Not like I have much choice now," she muttered, pushing past him and out through the waiting room into the hallway which led outside to the parking area.

"You always have choices," he said, hurrying to catch up. "You could call a cab."

She rolled her eyes and started into the lot. "Where is your truck parked?"

"Over there, under the trees." He pointed, and she could see his truck under a big maple.

They made their way across the lot in companionable silence, and she realized she prized the comfortable silences she could share with this man as well as the stimulating conversations she'd had with him. She smiled, thinking about the day she'd shown him how to fish. Now he wanted to learn how to tie his own flies. He'd suggested she teach a class at the community center, but she couldn't see herself standing—or sitting—in front of a room full of strangers, many of them no doubt men, teaching them anything.

He opened the passenger door and assisted her up onto the high seat by taking hold of her waist and lifting her up into the cab. Then he stowed her crutches in the back seat.

She tried not to think how his hands felt spanning her waist as he walked around the front of the truck and climbed in the driver's side.

"It's a beautiful night," he commented, and she had to agree.

"Ja, very mild, and the breeze feels very gut."

He fastened his seat belt, started the engine, and then turned to look at her, his hands on the steering wheel. "You know, I didn't get any dinner. How about you?"

She frowned, realizing that she hadn't eaten. "I guess I didn't think of it. Lydia came over while Maem was making dinner, and then she broke her hip when she got up to leave. I hadn't thought of it, but of course, now that you've said something, I realize I'm famished."

"So am I. I got the call that one of my patients had fallen, and I headed straight to the hospital. I've been busy consulting with the orthopedic surgeons in Akron and making sure that ER doc took good care of her. But now that all the excitement has died down, I'm starved." He glanced at his watch. "It's actually not that late. Not yet nine. The Frosty Treat will still be open, and it's on the way home. Want to stop?"

She frowned. "I don't know. . . . What will people think, seeing me in a truck with the English dokder, getting supper this late in the evening?"

He shrugged. "Who cares? If anyone asks, we'll tell them what happened. Goodness, we were just with the bishop."

"Hmm. I suppose it will be all right."

"Great. A cheeseburger and some onion rings sound really good right now."

She felt her mouth water. "They really do."

A few minutes later they pulled into the parking lot of the Frosty Treat, a roadside place that was only open in the summer months because there was no indoor seating.

"Look! There are Maem and Dat!" Mary pointed to a picnic table on the patio. "And there's their buggy. We can sit with them, and that will take care of any possible conjecture. And I can ride home from here with them! This is really perfect!"

Reuben twisted his mouth wryly. "Yeah, perfect, except I'd been looking forward to spending half an hour in your company without a bunch of people around."

She looked at him and frowned. "Oh, Reuben, I'm sorry. But we probably shouldn't anyway. I mean, I'd like to spend time with you, but to what end? You know what the bishop said."

"I know, I know."

Joe looked up from his plate of food and caught sight of them. He must have said something to Edie, because she turned and smiled when she saw them.

"Mary! Reuben! Come sit with us over here."

Mary pasted a smile on her face, though she was not feeling cheerful. "Hi, Maem. Hi, Dat. We saw you and decided to stop. Well, actually, we stopped to get something to eat, and saw you. Why did you leave without me? Reuben had to drive me home, and that's out of his way."

Joe gave a wry smile. "Somehow I doubt that bothered him much." He gave Reuben a stern look. "Right, Dokder?"

Reuben had the grace to look embarrassed. "Um, right, Mr. Yoder. I'm sorry. I know what the bishop said about us being alone together."

"Call me Joe. Mary's mother and I trust you both. But I would appreciate you considering that others may not and respecting my daughter's reputation."

He looked pointedly at Reuben, who shifted a bit, obviously uncomfortable. "Yes, sir. Again, I am sorry."

Joe nodded. "You two go order your food, and we can all sit together. Then when you're done, Mary will ride home with us. We will not risk exposing her to impertinent remarks and conjectures."

Edie fretted. "Mary, we thought you would ride home with Ruth and Jonas. I'm sorry to put you in a difficult spot, and dokder, I apologize for troubling you."

"It was no trouble at all, Mrs. Yoder."

"Call me Edie. Nevertheless, we weren't thinking. I got worried about the boys and just pulled Joe on out of there. I am sorry."

"It wasn't Ruth and Jonas' fault," Mary said. "They did offer, but it is so far out of their way, and the dokder offered to drive me, and I accepted. Actually, Ruth and Jonas seemed quite happy that he offered, as they needed to get home to Abby."

They went to place their orders, then returned to eat with the older couple. Other than exchanging a few glances, they couldn't have any meaningful interaction. After dinner, they went their separate ways.

As their buggy pulled out of the lot, Mary craned her neck to watch Reuben's truck driving off in the other direction on the highway. She sighed and returned her eyes to the front and caught her mother's worried look.

She mustered a smile. "It's okay, Maem. I'm fine. He's just a friend."

Her mother nodded and turned around to face the front again, and Mary sighed. Now all she had to do was make herself believe it.

CHAPTER NINETEEN

The next week was a busy one, as the apples in the orchard were ready to pick, making it difficult for Mary's parents to get away to see Lydia. She, Ruth, and Abby hired a driver and managed to get to Akron two days after Lydia was transferred. She was stable, and her hip replacement surgery was scheduled for the following day. Since she was in considerable pain due to the broken hip, she was on strong medications, so she wasn't in the mood to chat anyway. She was obviously pleased to see them, and her daughter and her family were there as well and said they'd be there for the surgery the next day.

Although she wasn't really family, Mary hated that she couldn't be there daily. She knew Ruth was also anxious about the procedure, and wished she could go.

The morning of the surgery, Mary was seated in her mother's kitchen supervising breakfast for her brieder when a knock came at the door.

"I'll get it!" Simon cried, jumping up and hurrying to the door. He flung it open, and there stood Reuben.

"Come in, Dokder!" Simon said, stepping aside and holding the door open. Reuben looked past the boy and met Mary's eyes. "Guder mariye. May I come in?"

She nodded. "Guder mariye, Reuben. Have you eaten?"

"Nothing this good," he said, eyeing the platters of bacon, eggs, and toast sitting on the counter.

She smiled. "Well, if you have time, sit and eat. There's plenty."

"Don't mind if I do, denki." He filled a plate and took an empty seat at the table. He helped himself to apple butter for his toast. "Mmm, this is *appenditlich*!"

"Mary made it!" Isaac said. "From last fall's apples. Now we're picking new apples, and Mary will make more, which is gut, since we are almost out of last year's supply."

Reuben smiled at Mary. "Glad to hear it. Wouldn't want to run out."

She took a sip of kaffi. "What brings you here this morning?"

He wiped apple butter off his lip with a napkin. "I wanted to offer you a ride to Akron. I'm picking Ruth and Abby up in a while, so they can be there when Lydia comes out of recovery. I thought you might like to go too?"

"Oh! I would!" She bit her lip. "But I'll need to ask Maem if she can spare me for the day."

"You should go. We're all going to be picking apples all day, and you can't do that, so why not go?" Nathan pointed out reasonably. "Then tomorrow you can start making applesauce and apple butter and apple pie!"

Mary laughed. "Well, at least I'm useful for something."

Nathan looked stricken. "I didn't mean it like that, Mary."

Her face softened. "Of course, I know that, Nathan." She pushed up from the table and grabbed her crutches from where they leaned against the counter behind her. "I'll just go make sure Maem doesn't need me for anything."

She left Reuben enjoying his impromptu breakfast and her brothers' company, and went looking for her mother. She found her making her bed, fluffing up the pretty pillows she'd covered in blue and white quilted wedding ring shams she'd made herself when she was engaged to Joe.

"Finished with breakfast already?" she asked Mary with a smile. She gave a pillow a final fluff, then turned to face her daughter.

"I am. The boys aren't. They have to eat their third helpings. Reuben stopped by, and he's having his first helping," she added casually. But her mother, not having been born yesterday, wasn't fooled.

"Dokder Reuben is here? What does he want?"

Mary took a calming breath. "He has come to invite me to ride to Akron with him, Ruth, and Abby so we can be there when Lydia awakens from her surgery. Her daughter, Lisle, will also be there with her family, but Ruth and I would really like to go. May I ride along?"

Edie considered her daughter. Mary fidgeted a bit, afraid her mother would say no, for her own good of course.

But Edie surprised her by nodding firmly. "Ja. Of course you may go. I only wish I could join you, but those apples won't pick themselves, and the boys won't pick them right unless I'm there supervising."

Mary kissed her mother on the cheek. "Denki, Maem. We'll be back this afternoon. Perhaps we'll all stop somewhere to eat."

"Do you have money?"

"Ja, I'm good."

"Okay, give Lydia my love. I'll see you later. And Mary?"

Mary, who had already turned toward the stairs, turned back. "Ja?"

"It would be smart if Reuben dropped you off before returning Ruth and Abby home. *Fashtay?*"

Mary nodded. "Yes, I understand. I'll ask him to do that."

She went carefully down the steps, Edie watching her with love and worry in her eyes.

Fifteen minutes later, they'd collected Ruth and Abby and were headed east toward Akron. Reuben glanced at Mary, who was seated in the front passenger seat. Ruth and Abby were in the back. He tried to think of something to say, but his mind was blank.

"How long will it take for us to get there?" Abby piped up from the back seat.

"About an hour, depending on traffic," Reuben replied, his eyes on the road. They were traveling two-lane highways until they were almost in Akron. They passed two buggies traveling in the buggy lane, and Abby strained to see them out her window. "It's funny being in the truck looking at the buggies instead of being in the buggy looking at the truck going by!" Abby giggled.

"I always give them plenty of room," Reuben commented. "I remember what it's like being passed by a big truck going sixty miles per hour. It rocks those light buggies!"

"The rain is the worst," Ruth said. "I absolutely hate driving in the rain, especially if it's dark out. In fact, I pretty much avoid it."

Mary nodded. "Ja, it's dangerous, even with the new flashing lights and all the reflective tape. All it takes is for one driver to be looking at their phone for a moment, and bam!"

Abby looked alarmed, and Ruth said, "But Gott watches over us to keep us safe."

"Most of the time," Mary murmured too quietly for Ruth and Abby to hear. But Reuben heard, and he glanced at her sympathetically.

"Won't be long now," he said.

Soon they were pulling into the multilevel parking garage at the hospital. A few minutes later they'd asked directions to the orthopedic surgery waiting room and were riding up in an elevator.

"This is fun!" Abby said.

"Haven't you been in an elevator before?" Reuben asked as the doors swished open on their floor. They stepped out, Abby jumping over the crack between the elevator and the floor in an exaggerated manner.

"Maybe?" She looked at Ruth, who shrugged. "I'm not sure. You'll have to ask your dat tonight."

Ruth held Abby's hand. The child was full of pent-up energy from their ride and wanted to skip. They found the waiting room, and when they stepped inside and looked around, they saw Lydia's daughter and her mann sitting over to one side. There were other people as well, but fortunately the area was quite large, and there was plenty of room for them to join their friends.

"Ruth! Mary! How nice of you to come. And little Abby, I believe you've grown an inch since I saw you last!" Lydia's daughter, Lisle, patted the seat beside her. Abby looked at Ruth for permission, then walked over and hopped up onto the seat.

"Where are your kinner?" Abby asked, looking around hopefully for Lydia's grandchildren, with whom she'd been friends as long as she could remember.

"I left them home with their other grossmammi today. I'll bring them later this week to see their Grossmammi Lydia."

"Oh." Abby was obviously disappointed.

"We'll have to have you over to play soon, Abby," Lisle said. "My girls would really like that. They've been asking for me to invite you for a while now."

"Oh! I'd love that. Would that be all right, Ruth?"

"I think so. We'll need to check with your dat, but I don't see why not." Ruth took the seat beside Abigail and placed her knitting bag on the floor in front of her chair. She greeted Lisle and her husband, Joseph. "Here's Mary Yoder, and I'm not sure you've met Dokder Reuben King?"

"Ja, the night Maem fell," Lisle said. "Denki for your help that night."

"You're welcome. Have you heard anything yet?" he asked, looking around the large room.

"Just that she went into surgery at eight as scheduled," Joseph said. "We were able to spend a little time with her this morning. They said it would take about an hour, and then maybe we could see her in recovery."

"Although, probably not all of us," Lisle cautioned.

"Of course you must go," Ruth said. "She's your maem, after all."

"I hope she'll be all right." Lisle wrung her hands together.

"Now, Lisle, remember, this is all part of Gott's plan," her husband said. "He is holding her in His hands and He will bring her safely through."

"And she'll have the new hip she's been putting off for years!" Mary said. "This could make a real difference for her."

There were nods all around. Reuben stood back up. "I'm going to go see if I can get a status on her. Might as well be some use being a doctor, right?"

"I have to say it is handy having our own personal dokder to check on Maem!" Lisle giggled.

Reuben smiled at her. "I'll see what I can find out."

He wandered out of the room, and they all sat quietly, waiting. Mary had also brought along knitting. She pulled out her current project, a sweater for one of her brieder. It was a deep forest green with a mock turtleneck and would be very warm when finished as it was a fine merino wool. She planned to give it to him for Christmas, so being able to work on it away from home where he wouldn't pop into the room unexpectedly was too good to be missed.

"I really like that color, Mary," Ruth said. "Who is that for?"

"My brother Daniel. He's twelve. I'm making it a bit big so it'll last a couple years."

"Smart," Lisle said. "Where did you find that green yarn? It's pretty, yet masculine and practical at the same time."

"The Plaid Sheep Company in Berlin," Mary said. "They have a nice selection of hand-dyed wool."

"I haven't been there in a while. Time to go back!" Lisle said.

"What are you working on, Ruth?" Mary asked as Ruth picked up her own bag and pulled out a pair of what appeared to be socks in a soft black wool.

"Socks for Jonas for Christmas. I want to complete five pairs for him, to keep his feet warm this winter."

"What a thoughtful gift! I'm sure he'll love them," Lisle said. "Right, Joseph?"

"Hmm? Oh, socks. Ja, you can't have too many pairs of gut black wool socks in the winter, that's for sure and certain."

"Good save, Joseph," Ruth murmured.

He grinned. "I'm just reading this book. Sorry if I'm not tuned in to your conversation."

"What are you reading?" Abby asked curiously. "Is it Tom and Pippo? That's my favorite."

They all chuckled. "Nee, it's a Louis L'Amour novel. One of the Sackett series."

Lisle rolled her eyes. "He's read all those books multiple times! Doesn't want to try anything new."

"Well, they're really gut! Have you read them?"

"I read a couple of them. I prefer a nice romance novel."

It was Joseph's turn to roll his eyes. "Drivel. I'll take Louis any day."

"When you read one, you can criticize it. I have a nice collection of Christian romance at home. Feel free to check them out," Ruth said sweetly.

"I think I'll stick with the Sacketts, for now at least," Joseph said.

"Well, maybe I'll borrow one of your Louis L'Amour books one of these days. I do like a good adventure too!"

"Anytime. Just come on over."

"Yes, we have about a hundred novels. Not only L'Amour but Zane Gray too, plus a few Christian mysteries. You honestly would be very welcome to borrow anything you like," Lisle said.

"As long as you return it," Joe said, glancing at Ruth over his book. Then he returned to his reading.

The women smiled at each other. Abby noticed some children's books in a bookcase across the room. "May I go see what they have for kids to read?" she asked, pointing at the books.

Ruth glanced across the room. "Sure, go ahead. But don't go anywhere else, okay?"

"I won't!" The child hopped down and hurried across the room to look at the books. Ruth saw another little girl, about the same age, shyly wander up to the bookcase and say hello to Abby, who smiled at her and held out a book for her to look at.

"Childhood is such a simple time," Lisle sighed, watching the children. "They make friends so easily, with no worries about all the complications that await them as they grow up."

"Oh, I don't know," Ruth said, looking at the two girls who were chatting like old friends as they compared books. "I think children are aware of complications. They just seem to be less bothered by them and more likely to just dive on in to a new adventure. More accepting, you know?"

"I guess I see your point. But I couldn't just go up to a strange woman and start talking to her."

"That's more about who you are, than about your age, I think,

Lisle," Ruth said thoughtfully. "You're a little shy with strangers. But when you get to know someone, look out!"

Lisle chuckled. "You may be right."

"She is," Joe muttered from behind his book.

"That's enough, you," Lisle said.

The two little girls came over, each carrying several picture books. "Ruth, this is Suzie. Her daddy is having surgery this morning on his shoulder."

"Hello, Suzie," Ruth said with a smile for the English child, who was about four, just about Abby's age.

"Hi. My mommy said I could come over and say hello, but I shouldn't bother you if you don't want. Do you want?"

They laughed. "You're not bothering us, Suzie," Lisle said. "What books have you got there?"

Abby and Suzie showed Ruth and Mary their selections. Then Abby asked Ruth to read aloud to the girls. She agreed, and they both sat cross-legged on the carpeted floor in front of Mary and Ruth.

"Ah, I see you found a Tom and Pippo book," Ruth said, opening up the book about a little boy named Tom and his stuffed monkey, Pippo.

"Yes! He's my favorite!" Suzie said.

"Mine too!" Abby agreed.

"Well, then, let's see what they do at the zoo," Ruth said, and began reading, stopping after each page to show the girls the pictures.

After a couple of minutes, a young English woman wearing blue jeans and a red sweater came over to stand nearby. When Ruth finished reading the book to the girls, she stepped forward.

"Um, hello. I'm Cynthia Stevens, Suzie's mother. I hope she's not bothering you?"

The three Amish women smiled at Suzie's mother, who smiled tentatively back.

"Nee, she's no bother. She's giving Abby something to think about other than our friend Lydia's surgery."

"That's exactly what I thought when your little girl invited her over here. Suzie can use something to think about other than her father's surgery. He's having his rotator cuff repaired. He's a power lineman and was injured after the big storm a couple weeks ago when a branch fell and hit him on the shoulder."

"Oh! That was quite a storm!" Mary said. "I'm glad he wasn't hurt more seriously!"

The other woman's eyes misted up, and she smiled. "Oh, I'm watering up again. Yes, we were very lucky, and God was watching out for him that day, that's for sure."

Mary smiled at her. "Yes, and now He will hold your husband in His hands safely while his shoulder is mended."

"I know," Cynthia said. "And your friend? Is her surgery serious?"

"My maem. She's quite elderly, and she broke her hip," Lisle said. "She's been putting off a hip replacement, because she's so stubborn! So she's getting it now, the hard way."

Ruth patted Lisle on the arm. "She'll be fine. Reuben should be back soon with word of her condition. It's been over an hour since they took her to surgery."

Mary looked at the doorway leading out of the waiting room. Periodically a nurse or doctor would enter the room and call the name of a family waiting for news. They would all get up and hurry over to hear about their loved ones. But so far, no news of Lydia.

Father, she prayed silently, *please keep Lydia safe. Let her wake up following the surgery with a new hip that will make her life easier in the days and weeks to come. And also, please let this woman's husband come through just fine. Your will be done. Amen.*

She felt a tug on her sleeve. She opened her eyes and looked at Abby. "Are you praying, Mary?" the child asked.

She nodded. "Ja, for safe outcomes for Lydia, and for Suzie's dat."

"Thank you so much!" Cynthia said. "I'm sure he'll be fine. I just hate the waiting!"

"Mrs. Braun?"

Mary raised her head from her knitting when a sober-faced doctor opened the door and scanned the room. There was something in his face—a hint of dread mixed with exhaustion—that made her uneasy.

A middle-aged English woman stood and faced the doctor. "Yes, here I am. Is my husband out of surgery, Dr. Brinker?"

The doctor swallowed and glanced around the room. "Would you please come with me, Mrs. Braun? I need to speak with you."

She didn't move, and Mary felt her anxiety level climbing.

"Of course, but first, please tell me my husband is all right, Doctor." She started across the room, followed by a younger couple Mary hadn't noticed before. The woman looked a lot like Mrs. Braun, and Mary guessed her to be her daughter and possibly her son-in-law. Mary noticed the other occupants of the waiting area were casting nervous glances at the doctor and at Mrs. Braun, and she realized she wasn't the only one sensing something wasn't quite right.

"I would rather speak to you all privately," the doctor said, holding the door open. Mary noticed a second man stepping up behind the doctor in the hallway—a hospital chaplain she guessed by the man's clerical collar. He also wore a serious expression. Mary clasped her hands together in her lap as she watched the trio follow the doctor and the cleric into the hallway, and the door swung partly closed, remaining slightly ajar.

There was a silence in the waiting area, broken suddenly by a terrible cry from the hallway. "Nooooo! Nooooo! I don't believe you! It was just a simple procedure!" And then a terrible sobbing.

And then someone reached in and pulled the door closed.

There was silence in the room, and then people started whispering to each other in worried, upset tones. Mary looked at Ruth, who was holding Abby's hand. Abby's new friend, Suzie, had climbed up into her mother's lap and was sucking her thumb.

"Maem? Why was the English lady yelling? Why is she crying?" Abby asked quietly. Mary noticed that the child had called Ruth "maem," and her heart swelled for Ruth while at the same time it broke for the stranger in the hallway.

"I don't know, Abby." Ruth looked at Lisle and Joseph. "We should pray for them, ja?"

They nodded, and they all closed their eyes to offer silent prayers. They didn't know the details, but based on what they'd heard, they couldn't be good.

The door to the hallway opened again, and there was no sound or sign of the bereft family. Reuben stepped into the room, looking worried.

"Dr. King, did you hear anything about Lydia?" Lisle asked, standing up and taking a step toward Reuben.

Reuben looked around at all the anxious faces, then looked at Lisle and gave her a tight smile. "She is out of surgery and doing well in recovery. They'll be in to get you in a bit."

"Thank Gott!" Lisle said. "I was worried, after what just happened."

Reuben stepped closer to them and spoke quietly. "Yes, I was just coming down the hallway when the doctor gave the news to the family in the hallway. I think he tried to get them to go with him somewhere more private, but the woman appeared very insistent, so he had to tell her. They're with the hospital chaplain in a private family room right now." He shook his head. "Even with all the advances in medicine, sometimes things go wrong. And there's nothing the medical team can do, in spite of all their training."

"If it is Gott's will, there is nothing to be done," Joseph said quietly.

Cynthia Stevens looked at the door with a worried expression on her face. "I wish they would come tell me my husband is safely through his surgery. I know it's not typically a difficult procedure, but after what we all just heard, well."

"Mommy, is Daddy going to be okay?" Suzie asked in a tiny voice. Cynthia rallied a reassuring smile for her child. "Of course he is, Suzie. We just need to have faith. The doctors and nurses know what they're doing. And God is watching out for your daddy."

"Would you like me to see if I can find anything out?" Reuben offered.

"Oh, I don't want to be a problem," Cynthia began, but just then the door opened again, and a stressed-out looking nurse poked her head into the room. She looked around and said, "Mrs. Stevens?"

Holding Suzie in her arms, Cynthia stood. "That's us!" she cried, grabbing her purse and hurrying toward the nurse. "Is my husband...?"

The nurse smiled reassuringly. "He's just fine, Mrs. Stevens. Came through like a champ. Come with me, and I'll take you to see him in recovery."

Cynthia turned toward Mary's group and beamed a happy smile at them. "Thank you all for your support! God bless you all! I hope your friend does well!"

"Bye, Abby!" Suzie called. "I'm going to see my daddy!"

Abby waved goodbye, and the door closed behind them.

"You see, Abby? Gott brought Suzie's dat through his surgery just fine. And Lydia too! We'll see her soon."

Mary let the relief flow through her friends and swirl around her. But she didn't feel it in her heart. She couldn't get the anguished cries of the bereaved woman out of her head. Her husband's surgery was supposed to be minor...routine. And he was, most likely, gone to be with Gott.

Was it worth the risk? Was the ability to walk better and have less pain worth the risk of dying?

She stood and thrust her knitting back into the bag. "I'm going to find a restroom."

Ruth glanced up at her. "Do you want company?"

"Nee, denki. I'll be fine." She picked up her crutches and headed for the door. Reuben stood and followed her, reaching the door first and opening it for her. She didn't look at him, but passed through the door. "Denki," she muttered, and started off down the hall.

"Mary?"

She paused, squeezing her eyes shut. She didn't want to talk right now. She needed to be alone to think. Maybe talk to Gott and try to get her head right. "I'm fine, Reuben," she said, not looking back. "I'll be back in a bit, okay?" She resumed walking down the long corridor, and Reuben fell into step beside her. After a couple minutes, he touched her sleeve, and she stopped walking and turned to him.

"Are you sure? Do you want me to go with you?"

He knew she wasn't going to find a bathroom. He understood her better than she'd realized.

And that fact, which could have brought her joy in other circumstances, brought only despair. Because he understood her, and he cared for her anyway. And she couldn't have him.

She shook her head. "I'm sure. Go back to Ruth and Lisle. I'll see you in a while."

She turned and walked away, unsure of where to go but needing to be alone. Maybe there was a chapel she could go sit in, where she could think about things without everyone offering advice for her own good. Decide what she wanted before she lost her mind!

He stood and watched her until she turned a corner and disappeared from sight. Then he went back toward the waiting room.

On the way back to the waiting room, Reuben stopped by the nurses' station. A stern-looking young man with a stethoscope around his neck was writing in a chart. Reuben stopped and waited politely to be noticed. After a minute, the man looked at him, an eyebrow raised. "Can I help you?"

"Yes, thank you. I'm Dr. King. I'd like to check on the status of my patient, Lydia Coblentz. She's in surgery."

"Of course, Dr. King. Give me a minute. We've had a difficult half hour, and I'm catching up on a couple of things while we have a lull."

Reuben looked at the man's name tag, hanging from a lanyard around his neck and miraculously turned out the right way so his name was visible. GREG McKNIGHT RN.

"I was in the hallway when the doctor and chaplain told the family about the man who didn't make it."

The nurse winced. "Yeah. That's not SOP. Generally we try to get people somewhere private before wrecking their worlds. I understand she insisted, wouldn't budge." He shrugged. "Rough on everyone."

Reuben smiled sympathetically. "When does anything go by standard operating procedure? Never in my experience. More like it goes by Murphy's Law."

"You said it. Okay, I'll check on your patient. Thanks for your patience." He went over to a phone and made a call. Reuben saw him nod, make a note on a pad, and hang up. He turned around, and when Reuben saw the smile on the other man's face, he relaxed.

"Mrs. Coblentz is doing just fine. She's out of surgery and in recovery. They'll be moving her to her room in about an hour. You're welcome to go back and see her. But because of what. . .happened, we aren't allowing family back there right now. I hope you understand."

Reuben nodded. "No problem, Greg. Point the way, and I'll go see her and report to her family."

A few minutes later, he was standing at the foot of the bed of a still-sleeping Lydia, reading her chart.

"Looks like everything was textbook for you, at least, Lydia, my friend." He returned the chart to the hook on the end of the bed and went around to stand beside the bed. He picked up Lydia's wrist and took her pulse. Normal. He noted her color. Good. Her breathing sounded fine, and she was resting comfortably. She wasn't showing signs of waking up yet, so Reuben decided to head back to the waiting room to relieve everyone's minds.

Reuben entered the waiting room, which had cleared out considerably since he'd been gone. Lisle stood when she saw him. "Is Maem okay? Did you see her?"

"Yes, I just came from her recovery room. She's still asleep, but everything went just fine. They'll take her up to her room in an hour and then we can go see her there."

"We can't see her in recovery?" Lisle looked disappointed.

"No, because of losing the patient a while ago. They're trying to keep things calm."

"Of course," Joseph said. "Lisle, it won't be long. Let's go down to the cafeteria and get something to eat. I'm famished. I'll bet Abby could use a bite, right, Abby?"

"I could eat a horse!" she squealed.

"Put away the books you and Suzie looked at first, please," Ruth said. While Abby did that, she looked at Reuben. "Where's Mary?"

He shook his head. "She needed privacy. She didn't want to talk. We'll find her in a while. I felt I needed to respect her wishes."

Ruth sighed. "She's so brave, but what happened would make anyone think twice about having surgery that wasn't absolutely necessary, I suppose."

Reuben went over to the sign-in desk and told the woman stationed there where they were going, in case Mary came looking for them. Then they all headed to the hospital cafeteria for a bite to eat.

When the elevator doors opened, there was Mary, looking surprised to see them. She smiled wanly. "Where are you all off to?"

"We're going to get lunch!" Abby said. "Come with us, Mary."

Mary shrugged. "I guess I could eat something. It's been a long time since breakfast."

They piled into the elevator and went down to the first floor. The cafeteria was crowded, but they found a table big enough for all of them, and Mary said she'd sit with Abby if Ruth would grab her a sandwich.

"What do you want?" Ruth asked.

"Egg salad, ham salad, whatever. And a Coke. And chips." Mary smiled. "And maybe some Jell-O."

"Me too, Maem!" Abby said.

"I know what you like, lieb, don't worry."

Abby bounced in her seat a bit when the others went to get into line. Mary sat and thought about how families could be built. You could have your own biological children, but that wasn't the only way. Maybe, if she ever married and it turned out she couldn't bear a child, she would be as blessed as Ruth and adopt a child as wonderful as Abigail.

"Are you sad about something, Mary?" the child asked innocently.

Mary made an effort to pull her attention back to the present. "Oh, I'm just full of thoughts, I guess."

"Are you worrying about things?"

Mary gave a one-shouldered shrug. "Maybe, a little."

"Maem says we shouldn't worry about stuff because Gott is taking care of us," Abby pointed out seriously. "But sometimes it's hard. I won't tell if you're worrying about something." The child reached over and took Mary's hand and held it, smiling sweetly at her.

Mary's eyes flooded, and she blinked rapidly. Impatient with herself, she smiled at the little girl. "Denki, Abby. I appreciate that."

"You're welcome, Mary. Here comes Ruth with my food!" And just like that, the child's world refocused to something really important, like the red Jell-O Ruth placed on the table along with some macaroni and cheese and a small bowl of peas.

They enjoyed their lunch, and then they headed to the visitor's desk to find out whether Lydia had been moved to a room yet.

"Let's see." A tiny woman in her eighties or nineties was manning the desk. She peered myopically at her computer screen, frowning. Then her expression lit up with satisfaction. "Lydia Coblentz. . .ah! Yes, here she is. Room 409. Just take those elevators down there at the end of the hall."

"Denki," Lisle said, and they all trooped off toward the elevators and rode up to four.

Emerging onto the unit, they stepped up to the nurses' desk and asked where Lydia's room was. The duty nurse pointed the way, then said, "But only two of you can go in there at a time. There's a waiting area just over there where the rest of you can wait your turn. Please don't stay long. Mrs. Coblentz needs her rest. Oh, and I'm sorry, but the little girl won't be permitted in the room. She can wait with you in the waiting room. Hospital policy."

Lisle turned to the group. "Ruth, would you like to go in with me first? Abby can stay out here with Mary?"

Ruth frowned, doubtful. "Is that okay, Abby?"

"I can't see Lydia?" Her lip poked out in a pout, and Mary was afraid she was going to cry.

"I know that's hard, but I'll be glad to have your company," Mary said. "I have an UNO deck in my bag. I don't suppose you play?"

Abby sniffed and shook her head. "I want to see Lydia."

Reuben stepped forward, shaking his head. "UNO is pretty hard for a little kid, isn't it, Mary? I don't think Abby could really understand it. I'll stay out here and play with you, though. Look, there's a perfect table in the waiting area, with four chairs."

Catching on, Mary nodded sagely. "Right. I forgot how young Abby is. I guess we only need two chairs. There's probably something for little kids in there. Let's go see."

"Hey, I'll play UNO with you guys!" Joseph said, hurrying to catch up with them. "I should warn you I'm pretty good."

Abby stood staring suspiciously after them. "Are they joking me?"

Ruth shrugged. "Well, I'm not sure. It's possible. But UNO is a hard game for someone as young as you, Abby. Why don't you see if there's a nice picture book?"

Abby crossed her arms. "I'm going to play UNO. Denki. Please tell Lydia I love her." She turned and walked to the table and climbed up on a chair.

"Deal me in."

The three adults looked at her.

"Deal me in? Where did she hear that?" Reuben asked. "She's a card sharp. I feel as if I've been misled."

Abby laughed. "I heard the older kids say it after worship last week. They were playing cards, and one of them said, 'Deal me in!' "

"That explains it," Mary said, suppressing a smile. "A couple of the teenagers are on rumspringa. They probably learned the phrase from some Englisher friends."

Joseph frowned. "Abby, it would be best if you didn't repeat phrases you hear from older kids, especially if you don't understand them."

"But Uncle Joseph, I understand. It means give me some cards so I can play too. Right?" She looked around innocently.

"Um, right. But I still wouldn't repeat everything you hear. Okay?" Joseph winked at her, and she smiled as she picked up her cards.

"Okay! I'm first, right?" She slapped a card down on top of the discard pile. "It's a Skip card. You miss a turn, Uncle Joseph!" She giggled. "This is fun!"

"It's going to be a long afternoon," Reuben said, looking toward the door through which Ruth and Lisle had disappeared.

"Your turn, Dr. Reuben!" Abby said cheerfully. "Oh, if you don't have a blue card, you have to pick up cards until you get one. Don't forget to say UNO when you only have one card left, or you'll lose!"

"I thought you said you hadn't played this game before?" Joseph growled teasingly.

Abby shook her head. "Nee, I didn't say I hadn't played. I just said I wanted to see Lydia. I play with my cousins all the time!"

"Your cousins? You mean my kids?" Joseph asked in disbelief.

"Ja! I usually win. UNO!"

The adults all laughed and collected the cards to deal a second hand. Reuben looked at Mary, who was intently studying her cards. "Do you want to go in next?"

Mary looked around the table. "I just want a moment with her, to see for myself she's all right. Joseph, do you mind if I just run in for a minute? I'll come right back out and you can go in."

Joseph shook his head. "No, it's fine, Mary. I don't need to see her today. Lisle will give her my love. You and Dr. Reuben can go in next, and then we can all head home and let her get some rest, ja?"

"If you're sure?"

"I am. I'll see her tomorrow. She's going to be here a few days due to her age and the fact that she broke her hip. They want to be sure there are no complications."

"Are complications likely, do you think?"

Reuben patted her hand. "No. Lydia is doing very well. But her age puts her at high risk. It's routine to keep her a few days. Then she'll have to go to a rehab facility for a couple weeks to learn how to use that brand-new hip. When she comes home, she should be walking pretty well. She'll probably have to use a cane for a while."

Abby had laid her card down and was watching the adults impatiently. But she was too polite to interrupt their conversation. Reuben noticed and nudged Mary, who glanced at the discard pile and laid a card down.

"UNO," she said. The others played their cards, and Mary went out on her turn. She sat back while the other three finished the hand, which she'd won. It gave her time to think.

A few minutes later, Ruth and Lisle walked into the waiting area. They were smiling, much to Mary's relief. Lydia must be fine.

She stood, and Reuben moved her chair and handed her the crutches she'd laid on the floor under the table.

"Oh, denki," she said. They listened to a quick report from Lisle and Ruth, who said Lydia was well, but tired.

"We won't stay long," Reuben promised. He and Mary started toward the door, and Lisle and Ruth sat down to play cards.

As they made their slow way down the hall toward Lydia's room, Mary kept her eyes on the floor, not speaking to Reuben. She didn't want him to try and talk to her about what had happened earlier. She would tell him she was having second—and third—thoughts about her own surgery another day. Today was about Lydia, and she didn't want to turn the focus to herself. Besides, Reuben would just nag her to death if he knew what she was thinking.

"Here's her room," Reuben said, pulling her from her depressing thoughts. They entered and found Lydia snoozing in her bed, propped up slightly, her feet straight out in front of her, covered by a white hospital blanket. Lisle or Ruth had removed her stretchy blue surgical cap and replaced it with her prayer kapp. She looked tired but neat.

They pulled up chairs beside her bed, and Lydia pried her eyes open to peer at them.

"Oh, I thought it was Lisle. Hello, Mary. Hello, Reuben. "Wie bischt?" she whispered, reaching out her hand to Mary.

Mary blinked back tears. "I'm fine! How are you doing?"

"I'm fine for an old woman with broken parts."

"I don't see an old woman," Mary sniffed. "I see a dear, brave friend."

Lydia made an impatient noise. "A stubborn woman, too prideful to do what my dokders told me, and see where that got me? They tell me I'll have to have the other hip done in a few months, because apparently I wore it out favoring the one that was already in need of replacement."

"Oh dear, I'm sorry, Lydia."

Lydia somehow managed to shrug while lying down. "Eh. *Sis Gottes wille.* I'll be fine."

"It may be Gott's will, but I can still be sorry you have to go through it," Mary said, holding Lydia's hand.

"Well, it'll be your turn soon enough. We can recover together when you have your surgery. It'll be fun. I'm going to sleep now." She closed her eyes, and soon a gentle snore issued from her parted lips, and Mary sat back.

Reuben stood and put his hand on Mary's shoulder. "Will it be your turn soon?"

She didn't answer, didn't look at him, just shrugged a bit. "I'm...not sure. After today, I...need to pray and think some more."

"All right."

She did look at him then. "All right? You're not going to argue with me?"

He gave her a small smile. "What would be the point? You're a grown woman. You'll make up your own mind."

She turned back to stare at Lydia. She'd made it through her surgery. Granted, it was a simpler surgery from what she understood. But at Lydia's age, it was still higher risk than Mary's surgery would be. And Lydia would be so disappointed in her if she chickened out. But she wasn't sure she could go through with it. "I have to pray and think."

"Right. Got it. Well, let's go join the others, and we can head back to Willow Creek. I've got to catch up on my patient charts this afternoon. Just..." He paused and ran a hand through his hair, obviously frustrated but trying not to say anything he'd regret.

"Just...what?"

He turned and made eye contact with her. "Just don't take too long about it, okay? There are other people waiting for this surgeon to do this procedure on them. Your surgical date is valuable. If you don't want it, others will."

"Wait, what do you mean by that?"

"This is a new procedure. But it's showing a lot of promise. So far, the success rate is impressive. Naturally, there's a waiting list for people trying to get it done."

"But it must not be too long, right? I didn't have to wait very long to get scheduled."

He didn't answer, but he looked everywhere other than at her.

"You look. . .guilty. Reuben, what did you do?"

"Well, it turns out Dr. Pavlik and I were at OSU together. She was a resident when I was in med school. So you got bumped up the waiting list a bit."

She stood and placed her hands on her hips. "Reuben King! Are you telling me you used unfair influence to put me ahead of someone who's been waiting longer than I have?"

"No! Maybe. Not ahead of people who have been waiting longer, necessarily. But an opening came up, and I said you'd take it. They called to ask. It would be narrish to say no when an opportunity falls in your lap. But if you're going to change your mind, we'll need to let them know so they can give the spot to someone else, that's all."

She wasn't sure how to feel about that. "You're sure you didn't cause someone else to lose their spot?"

"No, she wouldn't do that, and I wouldn't ask her to. But of the people waiting, you were offered a spot. Partly because of my old friendship with the doctor, sure. But also because you are an ideal candidate for the surgery, and others may not be. You're young, strong, fit, and motivated. She knows you'll work hard to recover after the procedure, so her work won't have been wasted. There are a lot of things that go into deciding who is eligible for surgery and who is a better fit for any given surgery at any given time."

"Hmm. Well, I'm sorry, but I still need to think and pray more before I can give you a final answer, Reuben. Please don't rush me. If I can't have a few days, just go ahead and call it off now. I've done fine this long."

"It can wait a few days."

"Oll recht, then." She cast one more look at Lydia, who slumbered on, oblivious.

Reuben waited for her to precede him out of the room. He looked back at Lydia and was surprised to see her eyes open, watching him.

She winked. "You'll have to convince her all over again. Lisle told me what happened. Good luck, Dokder." She closed her eyes again, and he followed Mary into the hall.

Somehow he didn't think it was going to be easy to convince her. But he'd try.

CHAPTER TWENTY

Mary pulled her buggy into a parking space at the hitching rail on the north side of the courthouse square in downtown Willow Creek. The town was built around a town square, surrounded on all four sides by quaint shops and businesses located in lovingly renovated historic buildings, many of them dating to the 1800s.

Parking on the square was usually a challenge, and today was no different. Mary's goal was the Hot Crossed Bun bakery a few doors down from the hitching rail.

Another customer was coming out when Mary approached the door, and the woman politely stepped aside and held the door for Mary, who smiled her thanks and went inside. It was a bit dim inside compared to the bright daylight she'd just left behind, so her eyes took a moment to adjust.

"Mary Yoder! What brings you here?"

Mary looked for the source of the cheerful greeting and smiled to see Reuben's sister, Eliza, smiling at her from behind the counter.

"Eliza! Guder middag! I'd forgotten you were working here."

"Good afternoon to you too, Mary! How can I help you?"

"Well, Lydia Coblentz is coming home from the hospital today, and she just loves the cream sticks you make here. I thought I'd get her several of the small ones as a welcome home gift."

"Gut choice! Our cream sticks are very popular. How about half a dozen?"

Mary nodded. "Sure. That sounds perfect. Well, maybe add one more, for me."

Eliza giggled. "A baker's half dozen?"

"There you go." Mary pulled out her little crocheted change purse and counted out the amount for the pastries. Eliza handed her a bag.

"So, Reuben tells me you aren't sure you'll go ahead with the surgery?"

Mary frowned, surprised that Reuben had been discussing her business with his younger sister. But then, he really wasn't her doctor, and she supposed he had to talk to someone. Still, it made her feel uncomfortable.

"Um, I'm thinking about it. And praying. I'll let him know soon."

Eliza peered at her curiously. "What happened to make you doubt your decision, if you don't mind me asking?"

Mary shifted her weight and wondered how much to say. She looked around. They were alone in the store. She wished someone would come in so Eliza would have to help them and she could escape. She sighed. No such luck. "Did your bruder tell you what happened while we were waiting for Lydia to come out of surgery?"

Eliza frowned. "Ja. That poor woman, her mann died in surgery."

Mary nodded. "It got me thinking. He was just having some routine procedure. And my surgery is relatively new, not exactly routine. And I don't really need to have it in order to survive or anything. So why would I risk my life just to get around a little easier? Doesn't that seem a bit like *hochmut*?"

"Prideful? To want to walk better without crutches and have less daily pain? I don't think so. Seems reasonable to me."

"I can't explain how I feel. I'm just not sure."

"I think I can explain it. No offense, Mary, but you're afraid is what you are."

Mary was surprised at the younger woman's frank speech. After all, they barely knew each other.

"Well, maybe."

Eliza nodded firmly. "I can't really blame you, I guess. But my brother is very smart and very gut at what he does. If he says the procedure is safe—as safe as any surgery can be—then it is. Also, didn't you pray about this?"

Mary nodded mutely.

"I assumed so. I believe Gott leads us to where we need to be. If you prayed, and this procedure became available to you, then it seems to me Gott led you to it. If you turn away, aren't you afraid you're turning away from Gott's plan for you?"

"Well, yes, when you put it that way. But what if I fooled myself into thinking Gott wanted me to have the surgery, and I pushed and made it happen? Maybe what happened and my fear are Gott's way of talking to me and leading me away from what He actually doesn't want me to do."

Eliza stared at her. "Mary, you're overthinking this, and you're making me dizzy." She reached into the display case and took out a gooey-looking brownie. She placed it onto a small square of wax paper and handed it to Mary. "Here, you need chocolate. It'll help you think straight. Tell Lydia I said hello, and I'm praying for her recovery."

The bell above the door jingled, and several tourists came inside. *Well,* Mary thought, *I wasn't exactly saved by the bell.* But Eliza had given her something more to think about.

"Denki for the brownie. I'll let you get to work."

"I'll probably see you Sunday at services, ja?"

Mary nodded and went to the door. One of the tourists jumped to open it for her, and she smiled her thanks and walked back to her buggy. She unhitched the horse and then sat eating her brownie and thinking.

"Heavenly Father, have I got things all mixed up? Please help me understand what I should do. I'm afraid. I'm afraid of the pain and of the hard work I know recovery will bring. And I'm afraid of dying. I know I shouldn't be, because if I died I'd be with you. But I'm still afraid. I still have things I want to do. And…dreams I'm not ready to give up on." She sighed and gazed out the front window of the buggy for a few seconds, struggling with herself. "Your will be done."

She finished the brownie, licked the chocolate from her fingers, and then backed her horse out carefully, watching for oncoming traffic. Tourists didn't always remember to watch for horses and buggies, and she didn't want to run anyone over either. Then she pointed the horse toward home and decided she had to have an answer for Reuben by the next day.

If only she could make up her mind!

How can I convince her to go through with it? Should I even try? If something goes wrong and I pushed her into going forward, she'd never forgive me. I'd never forgive me. Reuben pulled a weed viciously from his tomato bed and tossed it into his garden bucket. Another joined it.

He reached blindly down and grabbed another plant, yanking it out by the roots, and tossed it into the bucket.

"If you're going to sit out here and talk to yourself, it's no wonder you're pulling marigolds. Maybe you should give it a rest until you can weed undistracted, big brother."

"What?"

Eliza smiled from a couple of feet away and pointed at the bucket. He looked down and groaned. Then he studied the denuded patch of ground where a line of marigolds formerly bloomed.

"I'm sorry. You're right, I am distracted." He sat back on the grass and set the bucket off to the side, removed his gardening gloves, and stuck them in his pocket. "I'm no fit company, I'm afraid."

Eliza sank gracefully down to sit in the grass with her legs folded to the side. She leaned forward and propped her elbows on her thigh, and her chin on her hands. "Want to talk about it?"

He sighed and scratched his chin. "It's Mary. She's probably going to decide not to go through with her surgery. And I'm debating whether it's my place to try and talk her into having it, or just let it go and mind my own business."

Eliza plucked a piece of grass and slipped it between her lips. She sucked on it for a bit before glancing sideways at her brother. "I saw her in town today. She came into the bakery while I was working and bought some cream sticks for Lydia's homecoming." They sat together in silence for a couple of minutes, each with their own thoughts. "Do you want my opinion?"

"No. Maybe." He looked at her. "Okay, ja."

"Go see her. State your case. Ask her to talk about her worries. Then let her make her own decision. She will anyway. And if you hope to have a relationship with her—and don't bother saying you don't, or can't, or whatever. I know you do, and I believe Gott will find a way—you have to trust Mary to know her own mind. If she decides against it now, that doesn't mean she won't decide to do it next year, or in five years."

"But it would make such a difference for her!"

"Maybe. Maybe not. Is it that you don't want her unless she can walk better?"

Shock raced through him. His immediate thought was to defend himself. He wasn't like that! Was he? He tilted his head, considering. No. No, his attraction to Mary had nothing to do with how well she could get around, and everything to do with who she was. Her kindness. Her sense of humor. Her generous nature. Her courage and strength. His desire for her to have the surgery was entirely due to his hope that she would be more comfortable if she did.

"No. That's not it at all. I just want her to be able to live more easily. She told me she wished she could move faster. And she wants to learn to swim. And she admitted she's in pain much of the time, walking or sitting. That has to be exhausting. I want it for her, not for me."

Eliza nodded. "I know."

He blinked at her. "You do?"

"Of course. I wanted to make sure you knew that yourself. So, go do what I said. It can't hurt."

She climbed to her feet and brushed off her lilac-colored dress. "Dinner is at six. Stuffed pork chops."

He smiled. "Denki. You know, you're pretty smart for a kid."

She turned and walked toward the house, then looked back at him over her shoulder. "I'm not a kid, Reuben, in case you hadn't noticed."

He watched her climb the outside steps to the apartment. "No, you're not. And I've noticed other men noticing too."

He looked at the murdered marigolds and wondered if he could put them back in the ground.

"Nope. Some things, once done, are irreversible." Climbing to his feet, he gathered his gardening things and headed inside. There was just enough time to go see Mary before supper if he hurried.

But when he knocked on the door of Mary's dawdi haus, no one answered. Thinking she might be in her mother's house, he walked around to the kitchen door and knocked there. He heard pounding feet and grinned when the four boys piled up to the door and peered out at him.

"Hi! Dr. Reuben, hi!"

"Maem! Dr. Reuben is here!"

"Well don't just stand there gawking out the door at him," Edie called from somewhere behind the boy pileup. "Step aside and let him in."

The boys stood out of the way, and Daniel opened the door, smiling sheepishly. "Sorry, Dr. Reuben. Come inside."

"No problem." He stepped into the kitchen and smiled at Edie. "Is Mary here? I came to talk to her if she has a few minutes. I knocked on her door, but she didn't answer."

"Nee, she went over to Lydia's to help Ruth settle her in. She got home from the hospital today, you know."

He nodded. "Of course. I knew she was coming home. My sister said Mary stopped in at the bakery to buy pastries for Lydia. I guess I didn't realize she'd be over there this late."

"Ja, she's staying for supper. It's not too far, after all, and it's still light out until after seven."

"Okay, well, if you wouldn't mind telling her I was here, I'd appreciate it. I guess I'll talk to her another day."

He nodded at Edie and waved at the boys, all of whom were standing in the kitchen listening to their conversation.

"Good night!" He let himself out and walked to his truck. He was nearly there when he felt a tug on his shirt and looked down to see Mary's youngest brother, Simon, tugging on his sleeve.

"Wait, Dr. Reuben. Are you okay?" The six-year-old smiled up at him with a grin that showed he was missing a couple of baby teeth. "Because you look kind of sad."

Reuben squatted down so he was eye level with the boy. "That's really kind of you to ask, Simon. I'm okay, denki."

Simon frowned. "Mary's been kind of sad the last few days too, ever since she went to the hospital to see Lydia. I don't know why, though. Lydia is home now, and she's going to be better than ever, Dat said." He looked puzzled by the incomprehensible behavior of adults.

Reuben considered how much to say. "Your sister is just a little worried about her own surgery, I think, Simon."

The boy frowned. "But why? Gott will take care of her and make sure the doctors do a gut job. Maem says Gott has a plan for us, and He holds us in the palm of His hand, and He watches over us. Mary knows that. She must, because she's all growed up now. Like you."

"Maybe...maybe you could remind her of that, Simon. Sometimes grown-ups need to hear a truth from someone else to help them remember it. I think she knows in her heart that Gott has a plan for her, but scary things like surgery can make a person forget stuff like that."

Simon considered that and then nodded seriously. "Ja, I can understand that. Like when I fell in the pond, and my bruder jumped in, and the other boys ran to get help. I knew Gott had a plan for me, but while we were trying to get out of the water, I was real scared. I forgot to ask Gott for help. But He sent it anyway! You all came. Gott sent a lot of help for us!"

"But He worked through your brieder to get you that help, didn't He?"

"Ja! They thought of getting help, and they ran real fast."

"So maybe you're the one to get help for Mary, by telling her to listen to Gott's plan."

The boy grinned at Reuben. "I can do that! I want to be like my brieder and get help for my sister. Thanks, Dr. Reuben. Come back soon!" The child threw his arms around Reuben, and then he pelted back to the house and inside, banging the screen door behind him. Reuben heard Edie call out a reminder not to bang the door, and he smiled, remembering his own childhood and what he and his siblings had always done to help each other in times of need.

He stood and looked at the house and then at the dawdi haus. He saw Mary's pretty calico cat—what was its name?—sitting inside a window, looking out at him.

Oh yes, Hope. He waved at the cat and then felt like a fool. He looked around, but nobody had seen. Shaking his head at his own silliness, he climbed into the cab of his truck.

Hope.

Listening to God's Word would give Mary hope.

Learning how to put aside worry and self-doubt was not easy. He reflected that, over recent years, he'd done his share of worrying about his studies and then his work.

"Huh. I haven't really trusted in You, have I, Father? And I didn't even realize it. I've been going to church every Sunday, at least recently, but I've been allowing my worldly concerns to crowd out what's most important—my relationship with You."

Reuben sat in his truck, astonished by this realization. How had he let this happen? It was pretty much what his parents had been worried about when he left the community to pursue his dream of becoming a doctor.

"But I don't have to continue in that vein! Now that I've realized the danger, I can renew my relationship with you, Father. And I can be a better man."

Reuben felt tears sting his eyes. He wiped them away, embarrassed for anyone to see him sitting in his truck cab crying. But he knew his heavenly Father saw him and knew him and loved him in spite of his weaknesses. "Thank You for Your patience with me, Father," he whispered. "I don't know how I expected Mary to trust You fully, when I was offering her that advice with a false heart."

After a few moments, he started the truck and drove home. He had to get his head on straight before he could talk to Mary. And that wasn't going to happen tonight.

But driving home, he realized he felt lighter than he had in a while. As if burdens had been lifted from his shoulders. Or maybe, as if someone was helping him carry his burdens. Someone.

CHAPTER TWENTY-ONE

Mary was sitting in a comfy chair in the yard, soaking up some sun. She'd done all her chores and helped her maem with breakfast. Now she was reading a new book she'd gotten at the library. She sipped from a glass of lemonade and felt glad to be alive on such a day.

Her maem bustled outside, a basket over her arm. "Mary, I'm taking some eggs and bread over to the widow down the road. She's been lonely since her mann passed, and we ladies have sort of been taking turns making sure someone goes over to see her a few days a week. Will you be all right here?"

Mary rolled her eyes. "Maem! I'm going to be thirty in a couple weeks. Of course I'll be all right. Where are Dat and the boys?"

"They're tedding the hay over in the north field this morning. I made up another big pitcher of iced tea and put it in the refrigerator. Your dat may send one of the boys back to get it if they run out before lunch."

"Okay, Maem. I'm going to read a bit, and then I have some mending to do. Do you have anything that needs mending? I can add it to my pile."

"Oh! Ja, now you mention it. Isaac tore the knee out of his jeans again. If you'd put a patch on those, that would be a help. And one of your dat's work shirts is in the mending basket. I believe a seam gave out in the shoulder. That's it. I'm pretty caught up."

Mary nodded. "Gut. I'll get those and take care of them this afternoon. Drive safe, Maem."

"Denki! I'll see you later. Ah! Your dat has the buggy all hitched up for me." She climbed into the buggy, skillfully turned it around, and, with a last wave for Mary, headed out the long gravel drive and down the road.

Mary looked around and heaved a sigh of contentment. It wasn't often she had the place to herself. Not that she'd want to be alone too much, but occasionally, it was very nice.

Half an hour later Mary closed her book with a snap. She wasn't sure she liked this one. The heroine was behaving like a ninny, and Mary preferred the characters in books to act as if they had an iota of intelligence. "I'll read it anyway, because here it is," she muttered. She was about to push to her feet and go start the mending when she heard the hay wagon pulling into the yard. "Gut timing. Here come Dat and the boys!"

"Mary! Mary! We found a bee tree!" The boys were beside themselves with excitement. "Honeybees!" Isaac explained, jumping down from the wagon and running over to her, followed by his two younger brothers. Daniel, Mary noticed, stayed to help their Dat with the horses.

"A bee tree? Truly? How exciting." Mary smiled at the boys. "What will we do about it?"

"We'll get the queen and move the hive into one of our hive boxes!" Isaac said. "Then the bees will make honey for us instead of just for themselves!"

Joe and Daniel walked over to them, grinning. "It's a nice big hive, and from the look of them, ready to swarm," Joe said. "We'll take a box over with us, and we'll be ready when the swarm gathers. Then we'll box them up and bring them home."

"The tree they're in looks like it's about ready to fall over," Daniel added. "It's been dead a long time. Looks like an old lightning strike."

"I know the tree you mean, over in the woods to the east side of the field, ja?" Mary asked.

They all nodded. "So we'll have extra honey to sell and use for ourselves! I love honey!" Simon said.

"Okay, boys, let's go inside and eat lunch, then we'll head back out there. Mary, I see your mudder has gone out. How long ago did she leave?"

"About half an hour, maybe a bit longer."

"Gut. Will you join us for lunch?"

"Ja, I was just going inside when you arrived."

He picked up her book and glass, and she smiled her thanks as she pushed to her feet and grabbed her crutches, and they headed inside.

Later that afternoon, Mary sat in her living room working on the basket of mending. She'd patched her bruder's jeans and fixed her dat's shirt. Now she was darning a sock she'd been meaning to fix for months. It was at the bottom of the basket, and she'd all but forgotten it. Earlier in the day she'd come across its mate in her dresser and remembered the one with the hole in the heel.

She'd just tied off her yarn and snipped it from the darning needle when she heard footsteps running through the breezeway between the dawdi haus and the main haus.

"Here comes one of my brieder!" she chuckled. Hope, who had been curled on the sofa, stood and stretched luxuriously before beginning a vigorous bath.

The door from the breezeway burst open and Simon rushed inside. He clutched a jar of dark amber honey in one sticky-looking fist. "Mary, look! Look what I brought you! It's honey!"

"I see! My, that looks delicious. But why don't you put it on the kitchen counter and then wash your hands with hot water and soap, okay? Then you can tell me how you got the honey."

He grinned and hurried into the kitchen. She heard the sink running and her brother washing his hands. Then he was back. "Do you have any lemonade? I sure worked up a thirst getting this honey for you." He twinkled at her, showing his adorable dimples, and she nodded. "I happen to have some fresh made this morning. Go help yourself."

"Denki!" He rushed back into the kitchen, and she heard him getting a glass from her cupboard and pouring lemonade. Then he came back, carefully carrying the glass, sipping as he walked because he'd overfilled it. He placed it on a coaster and sat down on the sofa next to the cat.

"Hi, Hope! How are you, girl?" He scratched the cat right where she loved it, on the chin, and earned a loud purr in return. "She likes me!"

"Of course she does. So tell me how you got the honey? I didn't think you'd get the bees today."

He bounced on the edge of the couch. "Neither did we! But when we got back with the bee box, the bees were swarming! They'd made a great big ball of bees on the outside of the tree. Dat just walked up and sort of pried them off and tipped them into the box! Then we had to send Daniel back because there was another queen in the tree, and more workers, so we got her too! So we have two new hives! And the tree is full of honey. Gallons of it! We're going to take it apart carefully to keep from wasting any."

"My goodness! Did anyone get stung?"

Simon's face grew serious. "Dat got stung twice! But he didn't cry, and it barely swelled up. We boys stayed back. Dat told us to." He gulped some lemonade.

"Well, I love honey, so thank you for bringing me some."

"I know! Dat sent me over with it."

Mary picked up her mending and decided to fix the strings on an old prayer kapp that she used while doing housework. They sat there together companionably. Simon told Mary about tedding the hay, and more about the bee tree. After a while he realized he was hungry, and she sent him back into the kitchen for cookies. He brought her two, and she ate them while he told her about something that had happened in school that week involving a game of softball.

After a few minutes, Simon's face grew serious.

"My goodness, it looks as if you have something heavy on your mind."

He peeked up at her through his eyelashes, then nibbled on his cookie, turning it in a circle as he nibbled around the edges. He took another drink of his lemonade, and then he popped the last bite of the cookie in his mouth and swallowed it.

"I was just wondering about Gott's plan."

She stopped her sewing and looked at him. "Gott's plan?"

He nodded earnestly. "Ja, Gott's plan and how it works."

"Well, I think He has a plan for each of us, and we have to listen carefully to Him so we don't miss it when He tells us what the plan is."

"What if you can't hear, like Mr. Petersheim? How does he know what Gott's plan for him is?"

Mary covered a chuckle with her hand. She didn't want to insult the boy when he was being so serious. "Um, I think Gott speaks to our hearts, not our ears. At least, that's how it has worked for me. It's like you hear Him in your mind, do you understand?"

Simon nodded. "Of course. I talk to Gott all the time."

"You do?"

"Ja. Don't you?"

"Well. . .ja, I guess I do. I hadn't thought of it, but I do."

"What do you talk about?"

"Whatever's on my mind, I guess." She gave a little shrug. "What about you?"

"Oh, me too. I tell Him if I'm worried about something, like the time I broke Daniel's special wooden box that Dat made him. And I sort of felt His answer." He tapped his chest. "Here. And I knew what to do, you know?"

Mary nodded. "I do know what you mean. That's how it is for me too."

"But you've never done anything like that." He looked at her with the adoring eyes only a much younger sibling could see his older sister through.

She laughed. "Oh, Simon, I was a little girl once, and sometimes I was naughty. I'm no different than you."

"Really?" His eyes grew big. "What did you do?"

"I honestly don't remember anything in particular. I didn't have siblings my age so I couldn't break their stuff." Then a memory surfaced. "Wait! I do remember one time. I was maybe six or seven. . ."

"Like me!"

"Right, like you. And Maem had asked me not to touch a

particular dried flower arrangement she kept in a vase on the sideboard in the living room."

"Why not?"

"It was special to her. I believe the flowers came from some special occasion. But that didn't matter. The fact that she'd asked me not to touch them should have been enough. But I wanted to look at them, so one day when she was outside hanging laundry, I used my crutch to move the vase over to the edge of the sideboard. I didn't mean for anything to happen, I only wanted to be able to see them better."

"Oh no. They fell off, didn't they?" he breathed in horror.

She nodded seriously. "Ja. And they were old and brittle, and they broke into a million pieces. And the vase broke too."

"Did you get in trouble?"

"Of course. But the worst thing was that it made her cry."

His eyes popped. "Maem cried?"

She nodded solemnly. "Ja, and it was because of me. So I learned my lesson and promised I'd never make her cry again."

He was silent for a minute, thinking. "I saw Maem crying the other day," he murmured thoughtfully. "I asked her what was wrong, but she just dried her eyes and told me it was something sad she'd heard and had nothing to do with me and everything would be all right. So I gave her a hug and she was okay then."

Mary looked at her brother. He'd seen their maem crying? Recently? But. . .why would she be crying?

"Simon, when was this?"

He thought a minute. "I think it was the day after Lydia's surgery, last week."

His answer made her heart stutter. Was her mother crying because she'd told her she might not go through with the surgery?

Had she made her mother cry again after all?

"Mary, I've been thinking."

She forced her attention back to her young brother. "About what?"

"About you." He bit his lip. "Do you believe Gott has a plan for you?"

"Of course I do. Didn't I just tell you that a few minutes ago?"

He nodded. "So if you know Gott has a plan, and you know He's taking care of you, why are you afraid to have the surgery to make your back better?"

She stared at him. "Did. . .did someone tell you this? That I'm afraid to have my surgery?"

"Nee. Well, I guess Dr. Reuben might have said something when I was talking with him the other day."

She looked at him sharply. "Dr. Reuben talked about my business with you?"

"Only a little, because I asked him why he looked sad. But I already noticed myself. I know you're afraid. I heard you talking to Gott one night. You were alone in the kitchen and I tiptoed downstairs because I was thirsty. But when I heard you talking to Gott, I decided I could get water from the bathroom. But I heard you first. I'm sorry."

He looked contrite. In spite of her embarrassment, she couldn't be angry. Besides, she'd been conducting a private conversation out loud in the family kitchen. What did she expect?

"So, are you afraid that if you have the surgery, you'll die?"

"Well, maybe, a little."

"But Mary, Gott won't let anything bad happen to you. He loves you. He knows we need you. He won't take you away. And even if He did, you'd be in heaven with Jesus, so that would be good for you, right? Even though we'd miss you something awful, you'd be happy. And we'd all be happy for you."

She smiled at his innocent take on the situation. And really, he wasn't wrong.

She looked at him, and it was as if a weight had been lifted from her shoulders. "You know, Simon, you're pretty smart for a little kid."

He grinned. "Smart enough for another cookie?"

"As long as you eat all your supper and don't get me in trouble."

He went and got another cookie and brought one for her. "Are you going to do it?" He asked around a mouthful of snickerdoodle.

"The surgery?"

"Ja. Because I was thinking, maybe if you can walk better and you don't need your crutches anymore, we could practice swimming together next summer. Don't you think that would be gut?"

Her eyes misted up. "I think that would be absolutely the best thing ever." She reached over and caught him up in a big hug.

"Don't squish me!" He hopped down and looked at her. "So, will you listen to Gott's plan for you? And if He tells you to get the operation, will you do it?"

"I'll listen really hard, Simon."

"Gut. Because Gott talks in your heart, not in your ears. So you have to pay attention. I'm going back home, see ya later!"

"Hey!"

He stopped and looked at her. "Ja?"

"Please don't talk about me with Dr. Reuben or anyone else, okay? I'm not mad, but some things are just private."

He looked a little puzzled but nodded. "Okay, I won't! See you later!"

He ran back out, and she heard his bare feet pounding across the breezeway.

She pulled a tissue from a box on the table. "I'm going to listen real hard, Gott. And You'll tell me what to do. I'm sorry I've been so afraid, and maybe resistant to hearing Your plan."

So she settled back in with her mending, and listened real hard.

CHAPTER TWENTY-TWO

Determined to talk with Mary, Reuben drove back over to her place early the next morning, before his office hours. He pulled into the driveway and there she was, feeding her chickens, which were running all around the farmyard competing for the grain she tossed out in graceful arcs.

He pulled in behind the buggy parked in the driveway and hopped out, closing the truck door behind him and standing there watching her. Strands of her sunny hair had escaped her kapp and floated around her heart-shaped little face. She glanced at him, then went back to feeding the chickens. When the bucket was empty, she dropped it on the picnic table and picked up her crutches and started over to him.

"Guder mariye," he called before walking over to her.

She poked him in the chest with her finger. "Don't talk about my business with my little brieder. Getting Simon to work on me to have the surgery is pretty low, Reuben. I thought better of you than that."

She turned and started back toward the house, and he fell into step with her. "Hey, wait. It wasn't like that."

She glanced at him, her expression cold, and he felt fear. Had he blown his chance with her?

"No? Then how was it, Reuben? He came to me yesterday and said you'd told him I was afraid to have the surgery. Did you do that, or not?"

He scratched the back of his neck. "Well, yes, I did. But it's taken out of context!"

"I don't see what context would make this okay! He's six, Reuben!

You used him to further your cause."

"No! I was walking back to my truck yesterday after I came to see you, but you weren't here. So I was going home, and Simon ran after me and asked me why. . ."

"Well?"

"He asked me why I looked sad," he muttered, embarrassed.

"He did?"

"Yes. And I told him something about having stuff on my mind, and he said he asked because you had been looking sad too."

"He. . .did?"

"Yes. He said you'd looked sad since coming back from Lydia's surgery. He asked me why, since Lydia was doing well. That's when I said you were worried about your own surgery. I'm sorry, I shouldn't have. It just came out." He shrugged helplessly. "And then he started talking about God's plan and how you shouldn't be afraid because God would watch out for you. And I suggested he should talk to you about it and tell you what he thought. It's not like I coached him or anything. More like, I let him know he should have been having the conversation with you instead of with me. But, I am sorry."

She searched his face, and she must have been satisfied with what she saw, because she blew out a breath and the fight went out of her. "Oh. I guess I could see how that could happen. He's a pretty smart kid."

"Don't forget persistent," Reuben said. "He's relentless."

She laughed. "He is that. So, he talked to me yesterday and he did remind me about Gott's plan, and I guess I'd forgotten about that. It took a six-year-old to remind me."

"That's where the expression 'out of the mouths of babes' came from, I guess."

"No doubt." She peeked up at him, looking a little shy. "Reuben, he said if I had the surgery, we could swim together next summer. We could learn how together so we'd both be safe in the water." Tears misted her blue eyes, and she wiped at them impatiently. "Remember I told you I wished I could swim better? You. . .didn't tell him that, did you?"

"No, I promise I didn't."

"He came up with it himself," she murmured. "So he must really mean it."

"Seems natural to me. He almost drowned, so he wants to learn to swim better. You're his big sister, and if you can get around better, he figures you might want the same thing. And as it happens, he's right."

"Ja. Maybe Gott spoke to me through Simon. I did promise him I'd listen hard to hear Gott's message. Maybe the message was coming through my little bruder all the time."

"That wouldn't surprise me. I had a little epiphany myself after talking with your bruder."

"You did?"

He nodded. "Yes. And with my little sister. Maybe Gott is working on a theme, here—reach the stubborn through their younger siblings."

She chuckled. "You could be right. So. Your sister talked to you about me too?"

He looked at her cautiously. "Will I be in trouble if she did?"

"That depends."

"On?"

"What she said. And what you said."

"She asked me a hard question. And made me accept a hard truth."

"Let's sit down. My legs are getting tired, and this conversation is going to take a while." She walked over to the picnic table and sat on the bench, facing out. He sat next to her, leaving a good foot of space between them. You never knew when Amelia Schwartz might drive by, after all.

"So, you and your sister were chatting about my life. . ."

"No, it wasn't like that. I was out in the garden, pulling weeds. At least, I thought I was pulling weeds. I was woolgathering and pulling marigolds."

She let out a horrified laugh. "You were not!"

"Afraid so. She asked me why I was murdering the flowers. Then she told me I'd been spending a lot of time brooding, and she thought it was about you. She was right, of course."

"So, what was the hard question, Reuben?"

He was afraid to tell her, but he knew he had to be completely honest with this precious woman. So he took a deep breath. "She asked me why I was so determined that you have the surgery. She asked if I only wanted you if you could walk better. My knee-jerk reaction was to lash out and tell her she was being ridiculous. But I stopped and thought about it. What if that was it? What if I was so selfish that I wanted you to undergo a dangerous procedure because I needed you to be more...normal. More perfect."

He chanced a glance at her face and found it to be uncharacteristically unreadable.

Gathering his courage, he continued. "I was afraid for a minute, Mary—afraid of my own motives. But I thought about it and realized that has nothing to do with it. I think you're wonderful just as you are. You're brave and kind and giving and hardworking. And you're beautiful." He reached out and took her hand, and she turned it over and laced her fingers through his and lifted her eyes to meet his.

"You think I'm beautiful?"

"That's all you heard? I also said some things about you being wonderful, etcetera." He smiled slowly at her. "But yeah, I think you're beautiful." He reached up and tucked a stray wisp of hair behind her ear. "But that's only a small part of your appeal to me, Mary. Do you understand what I'm saying?"

Her lips parted, and he saw a dawning understanding in her eyes. They'd spoken of their mutual attraction and their desire to get to know one another better. They'd lamented the seemingly insurmountable obstacles standing between them. They'd tried to figure out a way to circumvent those, and failed. But they'd never spoken of their true feelings. There hadn't seemed to be a point. And somehow, at least he had felt that saying the words out loud would make it hurt more, knowing they couldn't be together.

Nothing had changed. He knew that. But he was tired of hiding from his truth. So he decided to tell her how he felt and worry about the consequences later. Or not. If things couldn't work out, at least he'd have told her.

"I think I understand. But let's stop beating around the bush. Please, tell me straight out."

He smiled into her eyes. "Okay, but then you have to tell me how you feel too." She nodded.

"Mary, I was attracted to you the very first day I saw you in your mother's kitchen, the day I was looking for the Hostetler farm. Remember?"

She nodded. "I also thought you were very handsome. But I realized you weren't Amish. So you were off-limits. I tried to put you out of my mind."

"No harder than I did. But as hard as I tried, I couldn't seem to do it. Every time I saw you, or talked with you, you edged a little farther into my heart."

"Your heart? Reuben."

He smiled. "Yes, my heart. Mary, for a long time now, I've had deep feelings for you. Feelings I haven't dared confess. But now, I want to tell you, even if nothing can come of it. May I?"

Her eyes grew large and luminous, and she nodded. He turned farther toward her and caught her other hand and held them both captive between them for a moment. Then, releasing one of her hands so he could brush his knuckles gently over her soft cheek, he spoke from the heart.

"Mary," he said. "I lo. . . Oh! What was that?" He slapped at his neck, jumping up and looking wildly around.

Mary was startled. "What is it? What's wrong?"

His eyes fastened on something on the ground, and he squatted down and picked something up. "Uh-oh. I'm in trouble."

Mary tried to see what he was holding. "What is that?"

"It's a honeybee. It stung me, and I killed it when I swatted it. I'm allergic." He dropped the dead insect and put his hand on his neck. "Mary, I need your help."

He sat down again, took two deep breaths as if to calm himself, and pulled out his cell phone. "I'm going to call 911 first, and then I need you to help me get the stinger out." He pulled his wallet from his pocket and handed it to her. "Please get a credit card out of here." He dialed 911. A moment later, he said, "This is Dr. Reuben King. I'm at the Joseph Yoder farm on Briarpatch Road in Willow Creek, and I've been stung by a bee. I don't have an EpiPen with me. I need help fast. I'll go into anaphylactic shock pretty soon. Yes, I'm sitting still. We're getting the stinger out with a credit card. Okay, thanks. Tell them to hurry, please." He hung up.

Mary stared at him in horror as realization dawned on her. He was allergic to bees! "What can I do?"

"Take the card and flick the stinger out. Don't squeeze it. That'll just release more venom." He turned his back to her, and she saw a swelling on his neck with a small black stinger sticking out of it.

"I'm afraid I'll hurt you."

"If you don't get it out, I could die. Hurry."

"You'll die?"

"Mary. Please, hurry."

She nodded, taking a couple of calming breaths of her own. She noticed that his breathing was starting to sound a bit labored. She bent forward and placed the edge of the credit card against the stinger and gave a little flick. To her surprise, it came right out. "I got it!"

"Good. Now I need an antihistamine. Please go to my truck and open the glove box. There's a box of Benadryl there. Hurry, Mary."

She grabbed her crutches and hurried toward his truck. She opened the door and popped open the glove box. There was the box. She grabbed it and hurried back to him. She popped a pill out of the foil and gave it to him. He swallowed it dry.

"How are you feeling?"

"My throat is starting to swell. I only have a few minutes. Hopefully the Benadryl will help. Should have gotten it first. Stupid of me." He sounded hoarse, and she saw fear in his eyes.

Then a thought occurred to her. "Wait! I think we may have an EpiPen in the house!"

Hope bloomed in his eyes. He opened his mouth but couldn't find his voice. She saw the beginning of panic. "Wait here! I'll be right back!"

She grabbed the crutches and went faster than she'd ever gone before, pulling herself up the steps and staggering through the kitchen door. "Maem! Maem!" she screamed. "Help! Reuben is dying!"

Her mother clattered down the stairs. "What on earth, child! What's wrong?"

"Where's that EpiPen we have from a couple years ago when we thought Nathan was allergic to peanuts? Reuben's been stung! He's allergic!"

"Oh my. I think it's in the basket above the stove! I don't know if it's still any good!"

"Just get it for me! Hurry, please!"

Edie reached for the basket and rummaged in it. "Here it is!"

Mary grabbed it, turned, and tore back through the door, across the yard to Reuben, who was struggling visibly for each breath. "What do I do? I've never used one!"

Edie had followed her. "Oh, Gott, help us, please!" she prayed. "Mary, open the box, get the pen out." Mary did so, and she saw there was a safety cap on the end.

"My thigh," Reuben gasped. His face was pale as milk.

"Stick it through his pants leg," Edie said. "Hurry, Mary, seconds count."

Mary pulled the safety off and looked at the pen. There was a diagram on it showing what to do. She popped out the needle and, taking a deep breath, jammed it hard into Reuben's thigh through his pants. She pressed down and administered the dose of medicine. Then she looked at him and realized he wasn't breathing.

"Reuben! Breathe! Maem, he's not breathing. What should I do?"

"I don't know! His throat must have swelled shut. It can't be good, how he's folded up like that. Let's get him on the ground and stretch him out so his throat isn't folded up or bent."

They struggled with the big man, basically knocking him onto the ground from the bench, then stretching out his limbs. "Should I try mouth to mouth? We had training at work."

"I don't know!" Edie looked helpless. Mary tried to remember how it worked. Then she remembered—ABC: Airway, Breathing, Circulation.

"I have to make sure his airway is clear!" She tilted his head back to open his airway. She looked inside his mouth, which had fallen open. She saw nothing in the way. What next? What next? It had been years since the course.

She snapped her fingers. Breathing! "Now I have to give him a breath." She leaned down and placed her mouth over his, forming a seal, and blew her breath into his mouth. There was some resistance. Was there something there after all? Or was it the swelling? Would the EpiPen work, or was it too late? Tears flooded her eyes. "Oh, please, Gott, don't take him away now," she whispered. She seemed to hear a whisper in her heart—*Try again.*

She took a deep breath, leaned over, and tried again. This time, there was definitely less resistance, and the air got through. She saw his chest rise. "Maem! Look! I'm doing it!"

In the distance, she was aware of sirens getting closer. But still too far away. She breathed for Reuben again, watching his chest rise.

"Wait, ABC—the C stands for circulation. Does he have a pulse?" She felt for a pulse at his wrist and was very relieved to feel a faint but steady beat. "Oh, thank Gott! He's alive, Maem!" She saw Reuben's chest rise on its own. "He's breathing again! The EpiPen must still have been good!"

The siren was very close now, and Mary turned to see an ambulance coming down the long driveway, lights flashing red and blue. She looked down at Reuben, and his eyes blinked open. He looked confused. She put her palm on his cheek. "Don't try to talk yet, lieb," she told him in Deitch. "You're going to be all right. Help is here."

He raised one hand and covered hers, turning his face slightly to kiss her palm.

The paramedics hurried up to them. "What's happening here?"

"He was stung by a bee on the back of his neck. He's allergic. We flicked the stinger out, and he took a Benadryl, but he didn't have an EpiPen. He couldn't breathe. Then I remembered we had one for my bruder, and I got it. I administered it in his leg, and I gave him mouth to mouth. He had a pulse, so I didn't need to do CPR." She stopped and looked surprised that she'd said all of that.

The paramedic took Reuben's vitals. "Wow, Doc, you're a lucky man. If she hadn't kept her head and remembered the EpiPen, you probably wouldn't have made it. You look a little rough, to tell you the truth."

"I feel a little rough," he rasped. "But it's good to be able to feel anything. I thought I was a goner."

"We're going to take you in to Millersburg, get you checked out in the ER." He signaled to his partner, and they loaded Reuben up on a gurney and put him in the back of the ambulance.

"May I go with you?" Mary asked, moving toward the back of the ambulance.

"Sorry, ma'am, I don't think I can allow that." He eyed her crutches, obviously thinking she'd be uncomfortable or in the way.

"Let her come please, Gary," Reuben whispered. "After all, she saved my life."

Gary looked at Reuben, then at Mary. Then he shrugged. "Okay, you heard the doc. You can't tell those guys no. They always insist on having their own way." He assisted her into the ambulance and showed her a bench to sit on, next to Reuben. He sat on a stool on Reuben's other side, monitoring his vitals on the way to the hospital.

Reuben kept his eyes on Mary, and she held his hand.

"Reuben," she whispered while Gary was busy talking to the ER on his radio. "You were about to tell me something before the bee stung you."

A tiny smile tugged at his mouth, and he pretended to be confused. "I was? Can't imagine what that was."

She swatted his shoulder gently. "Reuben! Tell me. Please."

His face gentled as he looked at her. He squeezed her hand and said, "Come closer."

She leaned down and he said, "Closer."

She put her ear near his mouth, and he whispered, "I love you, Mary."

She covered her mouth with her hand as tears filled her eyes. "Oh, Reuben," she whispered. "I love you too!"

Then she burst into tears.

Reuben looked at Gary, who looked puzzled at Mary's sudden and seemingly random emotional outburst. "It's letdown stress. You know, after the danger is past. She'll be fine."

Gary nodded. "You'd know best, Doc. We're almost there. Hold tight."

Three hours later, Reuben and Mary were seated outside the hospital on a bench, warm evening breezes playing about them, waiting on a ride.

Reuben had been given a clean bill of health and roundly scolded by the ER doc on duty for failing to carry his EpiPen. "You're very fortunate the Yoders had one in their home. You know you'd most likely be dead if they hadn't, right?" She'd shaken her head in disgust. "Doctors are the worst patients."

Reuben couldn't exactly defend himself, so he'd taken it in stride and promised to keep one in his truck and one in his home from then on. The doctor had shaken her head again and left to care for another patient.

Sitting outside, Reuben stared up at the stars. The night was clear, and he could see the Big Dipper—the only constellation he'd ever learned to reliably identify. Mary sat beside him, hands folded in her lap, keeping her thoughts to herself.

"I'm really sorry I put you through that, Mary." He glanced sidelong at her to try and gauge her mood. After her confession and breakdown in the ambulance, she hadn't said much. She'd had to stay in the waiting room when they rolled him back to an examination room, as she wasn't family. That's where he'd found her several hours later, no longer alone, having been joined by her parents and his sister. They were all currently down in the cafeteria getting dinner, but Mary had elected to sit with him while he waited for a ride back to her place to get his truck. His sister would join them in a minute, and the three of them would ride over together. Her parents would drive their buggy back after they ate.

She shrugged. "I'm just glad we had the EpiPen and that it was still good. I have never been so afraid in my life. Not even when the boys were in the pond. That time, you and the other men got them out. This time, even though my mudder gave advice, it was me who had to save you. What if I'd failed?"

"But you didn't. I was an idiot for not carrying a pen in my truck. The old one expired, and I just didn't remember to replace it. Totally irresponsible. If one of my patients did that, I'd read them the riot act. Kind of like the ER doc did to me in there."

"You deserved it!" she said with feeling. "Oh, Reuben. You weren't breathing, even after we gave you the EpiPen. I was so afraid! Maem and I got you onto the ground, and I gave you mouth-to-mouth breathing."

He looked genuinely surprised. "You did? Nobody told me that. How did you know how to do that?"

"Jonas has us all do first aid training every five years at work. It's an OSHA thing."

"Fortunate for me. So, that got me breathing again?"

She nodded. "You had a pulse, so luckily I didn't have to test my memory of how to do CPR."

"That's as close as I ever want to come to dying until I'm a very old man. Thank you, Mary. I owe you my life."

She looked at him, her eyes filling again. "I'd give mine for you, Reuben."

He reached out to take her hand again, but she pulled away from him. "We can't."

"But you said you love me, Mary."

"And I do. But we still can't be together, so we can't sit in public holding hands like a pair of teenagers on rumspringa. That's just when Amelia Schwartz would drive by!"

Glumly he folded his arms across his chest. "You're right, of course. I apologize." He brooded for a couple of minutes but then chuckled.

She turned and glared at him. "What's so funny?"

"Oh, it just occurred to me that you gave me my first, and probably only, kiss, and I slept through it."

"Reuben! I did not kiss you! I gave you artificial respiration to save your life! My mudder was there for goodness' sake!"

His grin tipped her off to the fact that he'd been pulling her leg. She let out a disgruntled breath. "Very funny."

"Come on, Mary. We can laugh, or we can cry."

"I feel like crying at the moment."

His expression grew serious. "So do I. But please don't give up hope yet. After talking with Simon, I had this—well, I can only call it an epiphany—when I realized I've been ignoring Gott and not giving Him His due. Not for a long time. I've been so caught up in my worldly concerns, studying and then practicing medicine, that I let my relationship with Him fall into second place. I've been praying and I've promised Him to do better. And now I'm promising you that if I can find a way, we'll be together."

She turned to look at him, her eyes wide. "Reuben, it's wonderful that you're healing your relationship with Gott. But the one way I will not accept being with you is for you to give up practicing medicine. Do you understand?"

He smiled wryly. "Ja."

"Gut. And since I can't leave the church to be with you, that seems to be that."

The van Reuben had called for a ride pulled up just as Eliza hurried out through the front doors of the hospital. "There you two are!" Eliza said. "And here's the van. Good timing!"

Reuben and Mary shared one last look, speaking silently to one another of hope and determination, tempered with the understanding that you simply can't always get what your heart most desires.

The van pulled into the driveway at Mary's house. Eliza hopped out first, followed by Reuben. He turned to give Mary a hand down.

"Go on and get in the truck, Eliza. I'll be right there."

Eliza hurried over to Mary. "Denki again for saving my bruder!" She gave Mary an impulsive hug and then ran over to the truck and climbed inside.

Reuben turned to Mary and said in a quiet voice, meant for her ears alone, "If there's a way for us to be together, our heavenly Father will help us see it. Don't give up."

She nodded without smiling, and he smiled softly at her before closing the van door. They watched it drive off, and Reuben cleared his throat and looked as if he had something more to say.

"What is it, Reuben?"

"Mary! I just needed to make sure—before I was stung, when we were talking, did you indicate you'd decided to go ahead with the surgery? I'm not trying to talk you into it, or rush you. I just need to know."

"It's all right. And yes, I've decided I am going to have the surgery. I listened hard to hear Gott's plan, and I believe that is what He was telling me through both you and my little bruder."

"I'm so glad."

He drew her into a spontaneous hug, and her arms encircled him tightly. She didn't care that his sister could see them. This might be the only time she ever got to feel his arms around her, so she held on tight. Of course, that would be right when Amelia Schwartz, riding in the back of a hired van with a group of women returning from some outing, happened to be driving by on Briarpatch Road, looking out her window at just the right time to see them hugging. Her pale, oval face stared incredulously out of the van window, and Mary saw her turn and gab to the woman beside her. Mary knew this would be all over town before morning. She pulled away from Reuben, who hadn't seen the nasty woman, and smiled at him. "We have a problem."

"What?"

"That van that just went by? Amelia Schwartz was in it."

He stared at her for a moment, dumbfounded. Then he threw back his head and roared with laughter. Mary stared at him. "What's so funny about that? Our reputations will be in shreds! The bishop will feel it necessary to pay us another visit and talk to us as if we were kinner!"

He wiped at tears in the corners of his eyes and got himself under control. "It's just that it's really pretty funny that after all this time, when we finally do something that might be construed as slightly inappropriate, even if it was just a hug with my baby sister looking on, that woman would pick that moment to drive by!" He started chuckling again, and Mary couldn't help but join in.

"Ja, but it won't be funny when the bishop hears it from her. She won't make it sound innocent like it really was."

He smiled at her. "We'll worry about that when the time comes. Now, go inside and get a good night's sleep. You have surgery in a few days."

"Do you need to reschedule? Did you tell them I was thinking about canceling? Maybe they didn't hold my spot."

He smiled again and turned to walk to the truck.

Looking over his shoulder at her, he winked. "I never canceled it. You never actually told me you'd decided against the procedure. Good night!"

Through the open truck window, she heard Eliza chastising Reuben for not having an EpiPen with him in his truck earlier. "What were you thinking?" she demanded as Reuben turned the truck and, with a last wave, headed down the driveway. Mary couldn't hear his response as the truck drove away. But she thought the question pertained to a lot of different things, such as what had she been thinking when she admitted to a man she could not have that she loved him.

Denki for helping me to help Reuben today. And denki for letting me know of his love, even if it comes to nothing. But, if there's a way, I pray You'll help us. She laughed softly as she climbed the steps to the house. *Of course, star-crossed couples have been begging You for just this ever since You created us, I'll bet. Still, if there's a way, please help us see it. And Your will be done. Denki, Vader.*

CHAPTER TWENTY-THREE

Mary blinked a couple of times when she heard someone saying her name. She wanted to sleep.

"Mary, wake up. The surgery is over. You're in recovery now. You need to open your eyes and wake up."

She wished they'd go away. She was so tired.

"Mary Yoder, open your eyes."

The voice was familiar, and persistent, so she opened her eyes, hoping if she complied, they'd be satisfied and go away. She blinked again and recognized Reuben sitting in a chair beside her bed. He was smiling softly. "There you are. I was starting to wonder if you'd ever wake up."

"Reuben," she croaked. Oh! Her throat hurt, and she realized she was very thirsty.

"Here you go, nice and easy." He held a spoon to her mouth, and when she opened, he slipped some crushed ice chips between her parched lips.

"Mmm," she mumbled, grateful for the cool relief. He offered her another spoonful, and she nodded.

"How do you feel?" he asked, giving her yet another spoonful of ice.

She considered that. Her throat was a bit better. She remembered being told it would hurt when she awoke due to having been intubated during surgery. Other than that, and feeling tired, she was fine.

"Not bad," she whispered.

He smiled. "Excellent." Reaching down, he grabbed the toes of one foot. "Wiggle these for me."

She did, and he moved his hand to the other foot. She wiggled those toes too, and he looked satisfied. "Your parents are waiting to see you. They let me in first because I'm a doctor. I confess I abused my power."

She giggled a bit and he smiled. "I'll go get them now. I wanted to see for myself that you were fine. In an hour or two they'll move you up to your room. Tomorrow you'll feel better, and I'll come back and see you then, okay? I've offered to drive your folks back and forth each day while you're here."

She nodded and reached for his hand. He took hers, and she noticed she still had an IV tube running into her arm and a blood pulse oximeter on one finger. "How long until I know if the surgery worked?" she croaked.

"Well, they're going to keep you here for about a week because this surgery is pretty new. They'll be getting you up for PT starting later today, I imagine. But you'll be on pretty heavy pain meds for a few days, so it'll be hard to tell for sure right away. I'd say within the week you'll have a good idea."

She lifted his hand to her face and pressed it against her cheek. She closed her eyes and savored his nearness. They were quiet together for a minute.

"Pray with me?" she whispered.

"Of course I will."

"Out loud, please. My brain isn't working well enough to come up with anything."

He nodded, overcome that she trusted him to do this for her. She closed her eyes, and he followed suit. "Father, please watch over Your daughter, Mary, and help her to recover fully from her surgery. Please hold her in Your loving hands and bring her home soon. Watch over her medical team too and help them to help her. Glory to You, Lord. Your will be done."

Reuben added a silent request for Gott to find a way for them to be together if possible.

They opened their eyes at about the same time and smiled at each other. He bent and placed a chaste, comforting kiss on her forehead, and stood. "I'll go get your parents. I'll see you tomorrow, Mary. I love you."

She smiled. "I love you too, Reuben." She would have added that they were torturing themselves saying the words, but her throat was too sore. Besides, she liked saying them and hearing them. He squeezed her hand and left the room.

She closed her eyes and rested for a few minutes, until a nurse bustled into the curtained nook and took her vitals. "Well, you're doing just fine, Mary!" the perky woman chirped. "Pulse, blood oxygen level, respiration, blood pressure all look dandy! Helps you're young and fit. Okay, I think your folks are going to be here in a minute. Your young man went to fetch them. He's a cutie, I have to say!" She wiggled her eyebrows and winked at Mary, who smiled back, though she was a touch embarrassed. No point correcting the nurse's wrong impression of their relationship, she supposed.

She closed her eyes again and was awakened minutes later by her mother and stepfather entering the tiny room. She smiled at them. "Hi."

"Oh, Joe! Look, she's awake." Her mother kissed her forehead, right where Reuben had, and smoothed a hand over her cheek, probably assuring herself Mary wasn't running a fever. "How do you feel?"

"A little tired," she whispered, "and my throat hurts."

Edie sat down in the chair, and Joe stood behind his wife, a hand on her shoulder, smiling at Mary. "Well, you did it. I'm betting in a few days you'll be running all over the place!"

She smiled. "Probably not running. But I hope I'll be walking faster and without the crutches."

Edie frowned. "Remember, you'll most likely still need a cane, best-case scenario."

"Ja, I know. But that will seem amazing, believe me, Maem."

Edie nodded. "Well, they're going to move you to a room soon. We aren't allowed to stay too long. You need your rest. But Reuben is going to bring us back tomorrow morning. Isn't that nice?"

Joe grinned at that. "I think he'd come regardless, but we make a gut excuse."

Mary giggled a bit and then coughed. Edie looked for water and spotted the cup of ice. "Here, lieb, let me." She scooped some ice chips onto the spoon and fed them to Mary, who gratefully took them.

"I want to sit up."

"You're not allowed yet. Just rest. Here, have a bit more ice. Hopefully you'll be up to a light meal later."

"I want to sleep more than eat."

Edie nodded. "That's normal. Just do what they tell you, and you should recover quickly. You're young and strong."

"That's what the nurse said."

"What did I say?" The nurse popped back into the room. "Oh, you must be mom and dad! Hi, I'm Tina. I need to check Mary's vitals again. Then I'll leave you to visit for a few more minutes. Mary, we're waiting for your room to be ready. After your folks leave, you can rest here until then, okay?"

She efficiently checked Mary's vitals and left them to visit.

Mary dozed while her parents carried on a quiet conversation about everyday life. It seemed just moments later that the nurse returned with a man who introduced himself as Eugene, an orderly who would be moving her up to her room. The nurse took her vitals again and nodded at Eugene. "Mary, Eugene is one of our best drivers. He's going to take you on up to your room now. You're going to be just fine."

Joe and Edie gathered up Mary's belongings and stood back while Eugene raised the rails on her bed. Then he maneuvered her through the recovery room, into a hall, and onto an elevator. Mary watched the ceiling tiles flash past and heard her parents pattering along behind her. Soon he was rolling her through the doorway of a sunny, spacious hospital room with a view across a parking lot to a field and woods beyond.

"You got a nice view, Mary," he commented as he lined the surgical recovery bed up with her hospital bed. Another nurse bustled into the room, and the two of them helped Mary move seamlessly from one bed to the other. "See you later, Mary! Take care, now." Eugene grinned his sunny grin and rolled the bed out of the room. The new nurse wore pink scrubs and had her curly red hair bundled up in a messy bun atop her head. Her blue eyes sparkled at Mary, tiny lines radiating from the edges the only clue that she wasn't a teenager.

"Hey, Mary, I'm Melody. I'm your day nurse this week. Welcome to the surgical floor! These must be your folks?" She turned and shook hands with Edie and Joe. "We're going to take good care of your daughter, Mr. and Mrs. Yoder. That starts in a couple hours with her first physical therapy session. We'll get her up walking to the bathroom, and tomorrow she'll walk in the halls a bit. You're welcome any time. We have a couple comfy chairs, as you can see. Mary, the call button is right here if you need it." She held up a remote attached to the wall by a long white cord. "And the television control is on your table, should you want it."

"I'm just really sleepy right now." Mary yawned to prove it. "I'm sorry," she croaked. "Oh, my throat hurts."

Melody picked up the cup of ice chips that was sitting on the tray table next to the bed. "Here you go, sweetie. You can have as many of these as you like." She spooned some into Mary's mouth. "After PT we'll give you a light supper. Probably chicken broth and Jell-O. What's your favorite flavor?"

"Lemon."

"Mine too!" Melody smiled. "Well, I'm going to take care of a few things. I'll be back soon. Press the button if you need anything."

She left, and Joe and Edie walked close to Mary's bedside. "We need to leave soon, lieb," Edie said. "Reuben is taking us home. But we'll be back in the morning, okay?"

Mary nodded drowsily. "S'okay, Maem. I'm just going to sleep now."

Reuben came quietly into the room. "Here you all are."

Mary pried her eyes open a slit, smiled at him, and closed them again.

"She really just needs her rest now. Ready to go?"

Edie squeezed Mary's hand, and Joe nodded to Reuben. "Ja, we're ready. The boys will need supper. You and your sister are welcome to join us if you haven't got other plans."

Reuben smiled. "Thanks. I'll check with Eliza, but I think that would be fine."

The elder couple left the room, and Reuben walked quietly back to Mary's bedside. He drew the blanket up to her chin and brushed his knuckles over her soft cheek. She didn't stir. "I'll see you tomorrow, Mary," he whispered. Then he reluctantly left her to her rest. He'd see her tomorrow, and hopefully by then she'd be showing some signs that the surgery had been a success.

Following supper at the Yoders' that night, Reuben and Eliza were headed back to his place in his truck.

"That was very nice, Reuben. How kind of them to invite us when they must be so worried about Mary!"

Reuben nodded. "They're really nice people."

"I like Mary's little cat, Hope. She's pretty well behaved. Maybe I'll look into getting myself a cat one of these days."

"Don't bring one to my apartment, please. Once you head home, I don't want to have to take care of it."

She rolled her eyes. "Don't worry, I won't. Why would I get a cat I couldn't keep? Honestly."

He smiled. "Okay, then. Just so we understand each other." He drove in silence for a couple of minutes and then said, "So, have you been making new friends since you've been here? It's been about six weeks, right?"

She looked at him. "Are you asking about friend friends or boy-friends, Mr. Subtle?"

He chuckled. "You caught me. Maem put me up to it. She wonders if you've met anyone you're interested in."

She frowned and turned her eyes front. "I'm not really interested in finding anyone right now. I won't be eighteen for a couple months. What's Maem's hurry?"

"I suppose she just wants to see you settled. And she probably has the ulterior motive of wanting grandchildren."

She blew out an impatient breath. "I understand all that. But I'm not in a big hurry to settle down. I'm enjoying my job at the bakery and the friends I'm making in the community. And to put your mind at ease, I'm still planning on being baptized and settling down to a normal Amish lifestyle. Just...not yet, okay? I'm not in any hurry, like I said."

He pulled into their driveway and turned off the truck. He folded his arms across his chest. She looked at him warily. "Okay, you've got something to say, so just go ahead and say it."

"I just want you to be careful, Eliza. The world isn't as friendly and safe as we were raised to believe. There are people who would take advantage of a pretty young girl like you. I wouldn't want anything to happen to you."

She waited a few beats. "That's all?"

He turned to look at her in the light coming into the truck cab from an outside fixture set on the side of the house to illuminate the parking area of the clinic. "That's plenty. Can you promise to be careful? Don't take rides from people you don't know well, especially men. In fact, I'd rather you didn't take any rides from men at all."

"What about buggy rides after Sunday services with nice Amish boys?"

"Them either," Reuben muttered.

She laughed. "You get points for consistency, and honesty. Don't worry. I'm careful, and I'm not naive or gullible." He looked at her. "I'm not! I have a friend at home who was...imposed upon by a man she accepted a ride from during her rumspringa. Nothing happened in the end, but it was apparently a close call. It frightened me to hear her tell it. And it made an impression on me. I'm very careful. Mostly, I only take rides from you and a couple girls I'm getting to know."

He nodded. "I'm sorry it has to be like that. It's not fair."

She shrugged. "Nobody said life was fair. Come on, big brother. Let's go inside. I'm in the middle of a good book. And I have a couple letters to write to folks back home."

They went inside, and Eliza headed into her bedroom. Reuben got a Pepsi from the fridge and sat down to watch some HGTV. He concentrated on the home-fix-up program, and tried not to think about the woman he loved lying in a hospital bed possibly in pain.

Suddenly he sat up. "I could call her!" Would she mind? What if she was asleep? He thought about it for a couple minutes. "I'm doing it."

He looked up the number for the hospital, called, and asked to be connected to Mary's room. He gripped the phone tightly while he counted the rings. After four, he nearly gave up, but then a tired voice said a tentative, "Hello? This is Mary."

"Mary! It's Reuben! I hope you don't mind that I called, but I was sitting here thinking about you, and worrying. I just...wanted to hear your voice and be sure you're okay. Are you?"

He heard a stifled giggle. "Ja, Reuben, I'm fine. Just tired. I don't have any pain. They say the drugs are masking it, and I'll probably feel it tomorrow." There was a moment of silence. "So, you were thinking about me?"

"I was. Eliza and I had supper at your parents' home and got back a while ago. She's reading, and I tried watching television but couldn't concentrate. I just really needed to hear your voice."

"Well, this is about the one place you could hear it over a phone, I'll give you that," she said. "At first I wasn't sure what I was hearing. Then I figured it out and thought it must be a mistake, but I answered anyway, and there you were."

"I'm glad you answered."

She was quiet a moment. "Me too. I had physical therapy earlier. They helped me get out of bed and showed me how to walk to the restroom, hauling my IV pole along with me. Fun stuff."

"I'll bet." He smiled at the sarcasm. "Did you get lemon Jell-O?"

"Ja! It was gut. The soup was okay. And I have pop to drink. Plus I have a television, and I thought I might as well try it out. I've been watching a program where a couple has to decide whether to fix up their old home and keep it, or allow a Realtor to find them a new house. It's fun."

" 'Love It or List It'! I was watching it too."

"Well, it's nearly over, and then I'm going to sleep. But...we can watch the final ten minutes together if you like?"

He grinned. "That sounds perfect. Oh, the commercial is over.

They're going into the final house the Realtor found for them."

"I like their original house best. I think they should keep it."

"No way! It's a dump. They need to list it!"

They laughed their way through the end of the program, and when they hung up, promising to see each other the next day, Reuben felt ridiculously happy. Even though he knew they were flirting with probable heartbreak by getting closer to each other. For him, at least, it was worth it.

CHAPTER TWENTY-FOUR

Several days later, Reuben walked into Mary's hospital room alone. Edie and Joe were unable to make the drive with him that day, though they'd all gone together the last couple of days. He swung around the corner of her room, carrying a dozen salmon roses in an antique white hobnail vase, and stopped short at the sight of several people sitting around the room.

"Reuben! What have you got there?" It was Jonas Hershberger's sister, Sally, along with her husband. They were seated in the armchairs under the television, while Ruth Helmuth leaned against the wall by the windows. Seated in a straight-backed chair by the bed was Lydia Coblentz.

"Lydia! How are you doing?" Reuben asked. He'd seen her since she came home, but she hadn't been out and about yet.

"I'm feeling just fine, young man. I still have to use the cane for a couple more weeks, but my surgeon told me I could dump that dratted walker at my appointment this morning. That's what we're all doing here. Thought we might as well kill two birds with one stone!"

"I'm so glad you all came!" Mary said. She was sitting up in bed, and Reuben noticed a big box of Esther Price chocolates sitting on the bedside table, along with a stack of books. He knew she liked to read and thought what a nice gift the books were.

"You brought me roses!" she gasped. "I love them! What a lovely color. And that vase is just beautiful. Simple and lovely. Denki, Reuben!"

She smiled softly up at him, and he felt his chest swell with happiness.

"Well, I found the vase in my apartment, and I got the roses at Walmart. It's nothing, really."

"Nonsense!" Lydia said. "You had to go to quite a bit of trouble to make that come together. You'll do, Dokder, you'll do." She smiled smugly.

"We've been here about an hour, actually," Sally said, standing. "We really need to get going, don't we, Ruth?"

Ruth smiled and tucked a strand of red hair back behind her ear. Her hair was always escaping her prayer kapps. "Ja, we really do. Abby is having a playdate with Lisle's kinner, and we don't want to overstay our welcome."

"Nonsense!" Lydia scoffed. "Abby is a delightful child and no trouble at all. I know Lisle enjoys having her over, as do my granddaughters."

"She really is a gut girl, Ruth," Sally said.

"Ja, and in just a couple months, she'll be mine! I can hardly believe it."

"She's a very blessed little girl, that's what," Lydia said, using the cane to help herself stand. Reuben saw it was one of the sensible kind with four feet tipped with rubber.

"It was nice to see you all," he said as they filed from the room.

Calls of 'You too! See you soon!' floated back to him. He set his flowers on the table beside Mary and plopped into one of the comfy chairs.

"Well, here we are," he said.

"Ja, here we are."

They stared at each other for a minute, and then Mary settled back against her pillows and picked up her television remote. "Let's watch TV," she said. "I think 'Property Brothers' is on. I love that show."

"Have you ever seen it before this week?"

"Nee, but the way they interact is so real. Yes! It's just about to begin. Shhh."

He smiled. He could get used to just hanging out with the woman.

CHAPTER TWENTY-FIVE

Several evenings later, Reuben was sitting with Mary once again in her room; this time, "My Lottery Dream Home" was playing in the background. Mary's parents had just headed down to get dinner.

"Funny how fast you can get used to turning on this box and staring at people doing things we'd never, ever do," Mary mused, staring at the television with fascination while a Realtor showed a young couple who had won the lottery a ridiculously expensive house in Texas somewhere.

"I know." He smiled. "It's entertaining. I guess they know what people like."

"Mm-hmm," she hummed, her attention on the television. A commercial break came on after a few minutes, and Mary sat back and turned her attention to Reuben.

"Sorry. I find it riveting. It's probably a gut thing I can't watch this at home. I'd never get anything done!"

"I have a personal rule that I don't turn it on until the end of the day, after work and chores and everything are done. But I've noticed my sister is pretty fascinated as well. Not like she won't be able to give it up, but with that obsession you can temporarily feel for something you know won't be in your life for long."

She nodded. Then she took a sip of ice water and frowned.

"What are you thinking about?" he asked softly.

She looked at him, and he saw shadows in her eyes. "I saw Dr. Pavlic today. She told me I can go home tomorrow."

He looked arrested. "I didn't see her today. It's not in your chart. Are you certain?"

She nodded. "Ja. They told me tonight before you all got here. Dr. Pavlic told me I've done really well with my physical therapy, and she said I'm past the danger of a wound infection. So tomorrow, I get to go home."

She smiled sadly at him. He couldn't speak for a moment and had to look away so she wouldn't see his dismay. He took a deep breath and then looked at her again.

"Well, that's great, Mary! I'm impressed with your progress. It really shows your determination and strength of character. I'm truly happy for you."

She swallowed convulsively. "But—realistically, it means we can't see each other anymore, Reuben."

"I know."

"It's been so nice this week, spending time together and talking on the phone. But we both know it can't last, right?"

He stared at her, misery in his eyes, and nodded in a jerky motion. "Right, of course. This has been, like, a time out of time."

"Ja! But tomorrow we have to go back to our real lives, in which I'm an Amish spinster and you're a dokder. And we can't be more than casual acquaintances."

"Even though we love each other."

"Right," she said very softly. "Even though."

The program came back on, but neither of them noticed.

"I really thought. . ." Reuben started. Then he shook his head. "Never mind."

"No, what were you going to say?"

He turned haunted eyes to her. "I really thought God would find a way for us to be together."

She was silent, chewing her bottom lip, trying not to let the tears flow. "Maybe He still will," she offered, though she sounded like she didn't really believe it.

"Right, you never know." He stood. "Well, your parents will be back soon, and then we'll head home. I'll be here to pick you up tomorrow. What time did they say you'd be discharged?"

She stared at him. "You. . .still want to pick me up? I thought we'd probably hire a driver."

"You'd rather hire a driver?"

"No, of course not. I just thought you wouldn't want to. . .since it's. . .over."

He looked away and ran his hand through his hair, causing it to stand up crazily. "Don't be narrish. Of course I'll pick you up."

"I'm not crazy. I was trying to be thoughtful."

"Well, don't, okay?" They just looked at each other, and she thought she could see hope dying in his eyes, no doubt a reflection of her own.

"I hate this," she muttered.

"Me too. But there's nothing we can do about it. So we might as well accept it and move on."

She opened her mouth to say something else, but at that moment, her parents came through the door. "Well! We had a gut dinner, and now we're ready to head home," Edie said. "Did you two have a gut visit?" She looked from one to the other, and her smile slowly died. "Um, is everything oll recht?"

"Yes, everything is fine. Mary just told me that she gets to go home tomorrow. Isn't that great news?" He tried to smile but failed, and stood staring at the floor with his hands jammed into his pockets for a few moments before shaking his head. "Well, I'll go get the truck and meet you guys by the front door. Night, Mary. See you tomorrow."

He swung out the door, and they could hear his steps retreating down the long hallway. Nobody said anything for a few moments. Joe shuffled his feet, and Edie looked stricken. Mary let the tears roll silently down her cheeks.

"Oh, lieb, I'm sorry," Edie said, sitting on the bed by Mary and taking her into her arms.

"I thought Gott would find a way for us!" she cried. "My heart is breaking."

Joe walked over and patted her awkwardly on the shoulder. "Don't give up hope, lieb. We can't know our Vader's ways."

Mary sniffled. "I know. But we basically just told each other good-bye. Tomorrow will just be one friend giving another friend a ride."

"Your dat is right, Mary. Trust Gott. If it's right, He'll find a way. If not, well, another path will become clear to you, eventually."

"Eventually," Mary sniffled. "Right."

The older couple looked at each other helplessly. "Well, we'll be here tomorrow morning at ten. I know your brieder will be very excited to hear you're coming home, not to mention Lydia and Ruth!"

"Thanks, Maem. I'll be fine, and it will be very gut to be home."

Edie gave her one more hug, and she and Joe left the room. Edie stopped in the doorway and threw her a kiss, then hurried after Joe.

Mary lay back in her bed and sighed. "I should be so happy, Gott," she prayed. "But I'm so, so sad. Please either find a way for us to be together or help me move on. I know You know best, and I'll accept Your decision. But, oh! Vader, if there is a way. . .I love him so much." She lifted her head and smiled softly. "But, Your will be done, Vader. Amen."

CHAPTER TWENTY-SIX

Reuben was in the backyard puttering around in his garden, which he'd recently found himself taking a more active interest in, when he heard a buggy pulling into the parking area to the side of the house.

He pushed easily to his feet, leaving the basket of weeds he'd been pulling—no marigolds this time—in the grass beside the tomato bed, and walked to the gate leading into the side yard.

He opened the gate and stepped through, expecting to see a family with a sick child or maybe a farmer who had been injured at work.

So he was pretty surprised to see Bishop Troyer climbing down from his rig, his standardbred mare, Spot, reaching for the grass along the edge of the drive.

"Bishop! What brings you here? I hope you're not sick or injured? Here, let me help." Reuben hurried forward and secured the horse to the hitching rail before turning to regard the leader of Mary's church community.

"Nee, nee, I'm fine. I came to talk to you, Dokder Reuben."

"You did?"

"Ja." The bishop waited a few beats, but when Reuben seemed to be glued, speechless, in place, he ducked his head to hide a smile and then cleared his throat. "Well, are you going to leave an old man standing in the yard? Or will you invite me to sit on your nice porch and maybe give me something cold to drink?"

Reuben snapped out of his dazed reverie, led the way up to the shady front porch, and gestured to one of the rocking chairs. "Sit, please. I'll, uh, just go in and get some fresh lemonade. Mary taught me how to make it. It's very gut."

"I believe I will." The bishop sat, and Reuben hurried inside and upstairs to his kitchen. He retrieved the pitcher of cold lemonade he'd made that morning, carefully following Mary's recipe, and set it on a tray. He added ice and fresh mint and placed two glasses, a handful of paper napkins, and a plate of Oreos on the tray for good measure. Then he hurried back downstairs and outside to set the tray on the table in front of the rocking chairs.

"Oreos! I haven't had one of those in years!" The bishop picked one up, twisted it to separate the halves, and then scraped the white icing off each half with his teeth before eating the chocolate cookies. "Mmm. Just as good as I remember!"

Reuben poured them each a generous glass of lemonade and handed one to the bishop, who tasted it and sighed. "Ahhh, ja. You've learned well I see. Delicious! Mary is a gut teacher and a gut choice because she makes the best lemonade in town. Don't tell her mudder I said so. Denki, Reuben."

He drank deeply, and Reuben sipped his own and wondered what the man could possibly want.

Finally, the bishop sat back and sighed in contentment. "I love these late summer afternoons. It's not autumn yet, but you know it won't be long."

"Yes, sir. But it's still plenty hot."

"Which is why I'm grateful for this lemonade!"

Reuben took another sip and squirmed in his own chair, wondering if he'd somehow managed to get himself or maybe Mary in trouble—again!—with the community, and the bishop was here to chastise him. Or worse. Just when Reuben didn't think he could wait another minute, the bishop cleared his throat.

"You are probably wondering why I've stopped by today."

"Well, yes, as a matter of fact. I hope there isn't anything wrong?"

"Nee! Nee! Just the opposite, in fact. I've watched you these last months, young man. And I've been pleased with what I've seen."

"But. . .Mrs. Schwartz. . .Mary. . .that, um, embrace. . ."

The bishop waved a hand. "That was a misunderstanding. I know all about it."

"You do?"

He nodded. "Ja, ja, of course! Not to say I'm unaware that you and Mary Yoder are still interested in each other, and perhaps keeping a bit too much company for two people who were told they shouldn't encourage an impossible relationship, hmm?"

Reuben felt sweat breaking out on his upper lip.

"But not to worry, Dokder. I must tell you that the fact that you're still interested in each other, and yet have, from everything I've heard and personally observed, behaved with propriety and respect toward Mary and her parents, has not escaped my notice."

"It hasn't?"

"No! And I asked myself, Abram, can't you think of some way these two young people could be together without violating the Ordnung and ending with Mary under the bann?"

Reuben leaned toward the bishop a bit. "And what was your answer?"

The bishop chuckled. "Well, at first I had to tell myself, no. There is no way! You are a dokder. You drive a truck. You have a phone in your house. You have to have these things to do your job. Mary has been baptized. You left the community and became a Mennonite. Of course, you weren't baptized, which makes a difference.

"But the fact remains that Mary can't leave the Amish church, and you can't return to it and remain a dokder. And you're a gut dokder! It would be a shame, and a loss to the community, for you to give that up. Ironic, yes?"

He beamed at Reuben, who blinked back at him, at a loss. How could this good man seem so cheerful while discussing such a heart-breaking and hopeless situation?

"Yes, I'd hate to do that. But I've thought of it, I confess. If I may speak freely?"

"Of course!"

"Bishop Troyer, in case you have any doubt, I love Mary. She's everything I've ever wanted in a fraa. She's brave and strong and loyal. Look at how she's overcome enormous physical adversity! She's generous and devout. She's kind to everyone and a good sister, daughter, and friend. How could I help but love her? In addition to all of that, there's just something about Mary that I haven't encountered before. Something that resonates with me. She makes me feel. . . Well, she makes me *feel*."

The bishop smiled gently. "Ach. I remember those feelings. Now you're starting to sound like a man in love. I do understand. My late wife, Amelia, was such a woman! I miss her so."

Reuben blew out a breath. "Gut! I was afraid you thought I saw Mary as someone pleasant with whom I could spend my life. Which isn't untrue, but there's so much more!"

Bishop Troyer nodded his head. "I get that, young man. But consider that despite the excellent results Mary has reaped from the surgery, she still needs a cane to walk, and as I understand it, always will."

"That doesn't matter to me."

"Please hear me out." The bishop frowned sternly.

"Sorry."

"She is strong and a gut worker, this I know. But is she strong enough to run a household on her own? Can she carry heavy baskets of wet laundry outside and hang it on a line? Can she hitch a buggy horse up alone? Unhitch him and cool him down, groom him, pick out his hooves, all that? What if the horse gets rough? Can she move out of the way quickly enough?"

"I could hire help. It isn't important to me that she can't do all the heavy lifting most Amish women do. She isn't most Amish women. She's just Mary, and I love her."

"Yes, yes, but here's the clincher for many men. Can she bear kinner?"

Reuben felt his jaw drop. This man continued to surprise him with his straightforward speech. But he supposed that was the bishop's job, after all. Still, the Amish did not generally discuss such things, and Reuben, in spite of being a physician, had grown up Amish and still had the sensibilities he'd been raised with. He felt his cheeks flush.

"Aha! I see I've surprised you. I apologize if I've embarrassed you, although I'm a bit surprised a dokder would have such delicate sensibilities, I confess."

"Normally I don't. But this is about personal things important to me and someone I care about."

"Ja, it makes a difference. But I had to say it. Have you considered this?"

Reuben looked the bishop in the eye. "Yes, I have. In fact, Mary and I have discussed this matter."

"Really? Interesting."

"Surely you're not surprised?"

The bishop shook his head slowly, his long gray beard brushing his round belly. "Nee. Not really. I knew you two were growing close but hadn't realized you'd talked about the hard stuff. So, what do you think?"

"I think that, while I would love to be a father, I love Mary more. And if having Mary as my fraa means I won't have kinner, then that's Gott's will."

Bishop Troyer's mouth quirked up on one side, and he raised an eyebrow. "Good answer. Also, if it turns out you can't have kinner of your own, you could consider adopting. But that's a question for another day. Horse before the buggy and all."

Reuben sighed. "Yes, but really, what does all of this matter? To have kinner we must marry. And if we marry, she'll be placed under the bann and probably excommunicated. I won't take her family and community—everything she knows and loves—away from her."

The bishop pursed his lips. "You'd be surprised what people will do to be with the one they want. But I don't think it will be necessary in your case. I've thought of a solution. A very elegant solution, if I do say so myself." He looked smug.

Reuben's face blanked. There was a solution? One that wouldn't end with Mary under the bann or him leaving the work he loved? "Okay, I'll bite. What solution is there?"

Bishop Troyer's smile grew bigger. "Why, you must become Amish again, of course."

Reuben shook his head in confusion. "But then I can't drive my truck or carry my phone. How can I practice modern medicine?"

"Because you'll be Beachy Amish, that's how."

Reuben frowned. "Beachy Amish? I don't know them."

The bishop waved a hand dismissively. "They're a relatively new community in this area. Moved up from Kentucky. They use some technology, in a limited fashion. Mostly for their work. But they do have electricity in their homes. They use phones. They. . .drive cars."

Reuben sat back, feeling flabbergasted. "This is a real thing?"

"Yep."

"Why didn't I know? Why didn't Mary know? Why didn't you say something before? Goodness, we've been bereft, believing there was no way forward for us! And all this time, you knew of this?" He was becoming angry. He stood and paced the porch. "I can't believe this! What made you decide to speak up now?"

The bishop looked a bit embarrassed. "Well, to tell you the truth, Dokder, I hadn't thought that far outside the box until very recently. I happened to go to a meeting of bishops, and I met a Beachy Amish bishop. Very nice man. His community is not too far from here. But in our immediate area, there are no Beachy. Not yet. He told me in some places, the Beachy Amish attend newer order Amish churches and live among other Amish without many problems. Of course, there will be some who disapprove. Some of our Swartzentruber brethren, for example, will not acknowledge Beachy as being true Amish. But that doesn't matter. New order Amish have no problem with the Beachy Amish. My community, for example, would not have a problem embracing a Beachy family into our fold." He raised his eyebrows meaningfully at Reuben.

Reuben thought hard. If this was true, it meant he could return to the church he'd grown up in. His parents would be ecstatic. He could continue practicing medicine. He could continue driving to see patients and, in fact, everywhere. And he could have Mary in his life—as his wife!

"Goodness! I just thought of something else! If we were permitted electricity in our homes, that means we could have modern conveniences that would make Mary's life so much easier. Such as a washer and dryer. And there wouldn't be a horse to hitch up. I'll bet Mary could drive. We'd have to see. Bishop Troyer, this could fix everything!" He hurried over to where the older man was sitting, gently rocking, and grabbed his hand in both of his, shaking hard. "Denki! Denki for this amazing information! This is such a gift! I need to go see Mary. Right now. Would you excuse me?"

He was already halfway down the stairs when he remembered he didn't have his truck keys. He turned, ran back up the steps and inside, grabbed them off a hook on the wall where he kept them when the clinic was closed, and then hurried back out and down to his truck. "I'll let you know soon what she says, Bishop! Denki!"

Bishop Troyer sat in the rocker, gently rocking back and forth, watching as the young man threw his truck into reverse, backed out of the driveway into the street, and roared away toward the Yoder farm. He shook his head.

"Hopefully he won't get a ticket or kill himself on the way to talk to her." He chuckled and then considered his empty glass. Glancing at the table, he saw there was still lemonade and ice. Shrugging, he helped himself.

He heard the *clip-clop* of approaching hooves and looked at the street. "Uh-oh. Here comes trouble."

Amelia Schwartz pulled her buggy to a stop in front of the dokder's office and regarded the bishop with an air of surprise.

"Hello, Bishop Troyer." She glanced around, clearly trying to figure out what he was doing there. She saw that Reuben's truck wasn't present and drew her own conclusions. "Ah, I'll bet you're waiting for the young dokder to return so you can talk to him about his shocking behavior! I've seen him over at the Yoders' farm, talking to that young Mary. If you need a witness, I'll step up! We have to keep our young people on the righteous path!"

She looked at him expectantly, and his heart hurt to realize that she was hoping for misfortune to befall the young couple. This woman was part of his flock. How had he failed her? Her heart was dark and bitter. How could God find a home there?

He shook his head. This woman who happened to share a first name with his late wife was clearly unhappy. He'd like to find a way to help her be more content and soften her heart. But for now, he knew he had to shut her down before her gossip did harm.

Finishing his lemonade, he put the empty glass down with regret and stood. He stretched a bit to ease the kinks out of his spine and slowly made his way down to the sidewalk and over to Amelia Schwartz's buggy. She had a smug look on her face, and her eyes glittered with malice.

"You're a bit out of your way here aren't you, Mrs. Schwartz?"

"What do you mean, Bishop? I came to town to pick up some groceries and yarn."

He shook his head at her prevarication. "The most direct path between the downtown shops and your home takes you nowhere near here. I hope you didn't drive over here just to see if you could catch Dr. King and Mary Yoder in a compromising position? Such as sitting on the porch in broad view of Gott and the world drinking lemonade?" he added wryly.

It was lost on the woman, who looked insulted at his insinuation. "Well! Someone has to keep an eye on things."

His brows drew together. He was a patient man and a mild leader, but enough was enough. "Impertinence. I am the one to keep an eye on the situation, as you call it. It is none of your concern. Go home and leave these people alone. They are not sinning."

She sputtered in shock. He wondered when the last time was that anyone had dared call her out for anything. Too long, he suspected. Her late husband had been a well-meaning but spineless man. "Go home and let me do my job guiding my flock."

"But the dokder is not one of your flock! A backslider! He'll lead Mary Yoder astray!"

"That is enough! You'd be best served if you kept your feet under your own table. Go home and we'll forget about this."

"I...I...Oh!" She clucked at her horse and drove off down the street. He watched her go, feeling bad that he'd had to be hard on her. But he couldn't have her challenging his authority.

He rolled his eyes and looked to the heavens. "My Amelia, I miss you so much. You would have known what to say to defuse that woman's venom." He sighed. "Ah, well, on we go."

He'd find a way to mend fences with Mrs. Schwartz another day, while trying to guide her away from such meanness of spirit.

"A bishop's work is never done!" He climbed into his buggy and headed home with a smile on his face, satisfied at least with a job well done for the young dokder and Mary Yoder.

Ten minutes after Reuben sped away from the bishop, Mary was returning from the barn to the house, using her cane for balance but not needing to put much weight on it, really, when she heard a truck engine approaching on the road. Curious about who could be in such a hurry, she turned to look and was surprised to see Reuben's pickup make the turn into her drive, a bit too fast.

"Goodness! What could be the matter?"

He pulled up to the house and shut off the engine, jumping out of the truck before it had come to a complete stop. "Mary! I have to speak with you!"

She put her hand on her heart and took a step back. "Reuben, what can be the matter? Why are you in such a hurry?"

He started toward her but then thought of something. "Wait!" He turned and jogged back to the truck, opened the door, and reached inside. Then he turned and waved something for her to see.

She squinted but couldn't quite make it out. "What is that?"

"An EpiPen! I got two, one for the truck and one for the house, just like I promised!" He returned it to the glove box and then hurried to where she stood. Her eyes grew wide when he stepped closer to her and took her shoulders in his big hands. Her lips parted as she stared up into his eyes, which blazed down at her with a frightening intensity. He raised a hand and brushed it along her cheek. "So soft."

She swallowed. "Reuben, what. . .what are you doing here? You didn't come all the way out here to show me your EpiPen, although I'm relieved you have it."

"No. But it does show that I keep my promises, right? I'll always keep any promise I make to you, Mary. You do know that, don't you?"

"I believe you. But what is this about?"

"I've just had a visit from the bishop, and he told me something."

"Did he accuse us of improper behavior? Has Mrs. Schwartz been gossiping again? Oh! She challenges my determination to be a gut Christian!"

"No, no, nothing like that. Come, sit with me somewhere where we won't be disturbed."

"But we aren't supposed to be alone together. You know this."

"It's okay. We won't do anything improper. But I need to talk to you, privately." He looked around, almost frantically it seemed to Mary, who was becoming alarmed. Then he smiled. "I know! The gazebo! Come, let's go." He started tugging her toward the backyard.

"Reuben! Stop! Talk to me. What is the matter?"

He swung around to face her, frustration written clearly on his handsome face, and opened his mouth to reply, but before he could, the kitchen door opened and Edie stepped outside. "Reuben? What is going on?" She hurried down to the yard and stood next to them, her hands on her hips.

Mary started to speak, but at that moment, Joe and the four boys trooped out of the big barn, where they'd been cleaning tack all afternoon. "Reuben!" Joe exclaimed. "Welcome, but what brings you here? I hope all is well?"

Mary could see that Reuben was growing more frustrated by the moment. "Dat, Maem, perhaps I should go with Reuben and hear what he has to say to me?"

Joe frowned. "But the bishop said you two weren't to spend time together. What's changed?"

"I'm trying to explain that to Mary, sir, if you don't mind? Then I'll fill you all in. May we have a few minutes? I thought the gazebo. . ."

Joe frowned, considering, but Edie nodded firmly. "Ja. The gazebo is outside in plain sight, Joe. What's the harm? Go ahead, but don't keep us in suspense for too long, mind!"

Reuben turned to Mary. "Will you come with me?"

She tilted her head and narrowed her eyes at him. "You seem pretty desperate, but maybe I should finish with the chickens first. I don't think I've gathered the eggs yet."

"Mary, I gathered the eggs!" Simon exclaimed. "You know that's my job!"

She laughed. "I do. I was just joking, Reuben."

Reuben looked pained. "Please, Mary, I'm not in a patient place."

She nodded. "Ja, sorry. Of course I'll sit with you and listen to what you have to say."

Mary took a seat at the gazebo, under rose vines that were still in full bloom. She knew it wouldn't be long before they turned rusty with the coming of autumn. She composed herself and waited patiently for Reuben to speak. He, on the other hand, was not composed. He paced back and forth. He would stop and look as if he were going to speak, and then obviously think better of it, and then pace some more. Finally, she caught his hand and pulled him down onto the seat next to her. "Reuben! You're making me dizzy. What on earth has happened?"

"Mary, it's such gut news, but I'm not sure I believe it. It seems so easy, so obvious, surely if it is true someone else would have thought of it before now!" He waited, looking at her expectantly.

"Reuben, I can't read your mind. What are you talking about? What is obvious?"

"The bishop came to see me. He said he'd thought of a way we can be together."

She gasped. "Can this be true? You wouldn't joke about this?"

"Of course not! He said we can be together, and you won't have to go under the bann, and I won't have to give up my practice."

"But you'd have to become Amish, and then you wouldn't be able to drive or use your phone in your home. How could you continue practicing?"

"Have you ever heard of Beachy Amish?" He waited expectantly.

Her eyes opened wide and her jaw dropped. "Beachy Amish. Of. . .course! Oh, Reuben! Why didn't I think of this?"

"I don't know. Maybe it just wasn't time. We weren't ready yet. But we know now, and we can finally plan a life together. That is, if you still want to?"

She blinked at him, not sure she understood where he was coming from. "What do you mean? Don't you want to?"

"I do! As long as you do."

Mary shook her head, frustrated at his apparent evasiveness. "Reuben. Are you trying to find a way out of this, now that it's more than just wishful thinking?"

"No! I promise I'm not. I just want to make sure you don't want an out, now that it's, as you say, more than wishful thinking. Sometimes people enjoy imagining having something they know they can't have. It's a safe fantasy, because they never really have to commit to it. Now that the bishop has given us this miracle, I just want to be sure you're, well. . .sure!"

"I'm sure. I think I know my own mind at my age! Goodness!"

His lips quivered, and then a smile trembled on them.

"Don't you dare start laughing now!" Mary warned, her eyes fierce. But a chuckle broke from Reuben's lips, which he quickly covered with a hand. But Mary could see his eyes dancing. "You're laughing! Are you laughing at me?"

"No! At us! At this situation! Here we are, handed what we've both been saying for months is our heart's desire, and we're arguing about it like a couple of kids! We're being ridiculous."

She stared at him, at the tears of mirth he was wiping from his eyes, and the absurdity of the situation hit her. Her lips twitched too. He pointed at her.

"Aha! Now you see what I mean!"

"I am not laughing!" she insisted, even as a giggle snuck out. They stared at each other another moment, and then both burst out laughing. Soon, they were laughing so hard they had tears streaming down their faces, and they were hugging each other to keep from falling off the bench.

"Oh! Oh! My family is going to think we've lost it. Stop, my stomach hurts," Mary begged. She reached into her apron pocket for a tissue and blotted her eyes. Then she glanced at Reuben and found him simply smiling at her, joy written plain on his face.

"What?"

"Mary. I just love you so much. And now I have a serious question for you."

Mutely, she nodded.

He reached out and took her hand. "Mary, I would be so very, very happy if you'd be my fraa. Will you?"

"Of course I will, you silly man! I love you too!"

They grinned at each other like kids, and then Reuben leaned forward, stopping when his face was a few inches away from Mary's, a question in his eyes.

"Oh ja, Reuben. I've been waiting a long time for this."

The edges of his eyes crinkled in amusement, but in the next moment his expression became very serious. "Me too," he breathed, and closed the distance between them. He set his lips gently on hers. She closed her eyes and simply enjoyed the feeling of warmth that spread through her. He pulled back and she opened her eyes.

"Mmm, that was nice," she murmured.

"Ja, it was, and I want to do it again! But I don't think that would be a very good idea."

She raised a questioning brow, and he nodded at the yard behind her. "Don't look now, but I think there's a spy—or several—in the bushes."

Mary turned and caught sight of her brieder peeking at them from the nearby azalea bushes.

"Hey, no spying, you guys. Go inside, or I'll tell Maem and Dat about the time you broke all the eggs playing catch!"

There was a flurry of activity, and the four boys scattered back through the yard. Mary heard a high-voiced comment as they fled. "I didn't think she knew about that! Who told?"

Followed by a receding chorus of, "Not me! Not me!"

She giggled. "I saw them of course, out my living room window. They weren't exactly being stealthy!"

"I imagine not." He grinned at her, and she laughed out loud, throwing her head back.

Then she wrapped her arms around him. "I am just purely happy as can be, Dr. Reuben."

He hugged her back. "So am I, Mary."

"I feel as if we've been waiting and praying for a miracle, and Gott delivered it today."

"Ja, He sure did!"

He kissed her again, and she said a prayer of thanks to her heavenly Father, for finding a way for them to be together without compromising their ethics.

They broke apart, and Mary jumped to her feet. "C'mon. Let's go tell my parents."

"Mary! Do you realize what you just did?"

"Aside from getting my first real kiss? We aren't counting the rescue breathing."

He took her hand. "You jumped up from the bench!"

Comprehension dawned on her face. "Ach, ja! Reuben, you were right about the surgery. Thank you for encouraging me."

"I've seen you almost daily and knew you were getting around better, experiencing less pain. But you just jumped right up!"

She shrugged and reached for her cane. "Yes, well, I still need this and probably always will. But my mobility is so much better. My pain levels too! Just as we hoped."

He stood and pulled her in for a hug, wrapping her up tightly in his loving embrace. "I'm so glad." After a few moments, he whispered into her hair, "You know what this means, right?"

She shook her head. "Nee."

"Next summer, you can learn to swim!"

She pulled back in his arms and looked up into his dear face. "You'll teach me?"

"I will. And your bruder."

She sighed. "I can hardly wait. But speaking of my brieder, I'm sure they have already told my parents we were schmunzla."

He laughed and released her before grabbing her hand. "Well, if they think we were kissing and snuggling, we'd better hurry and tell them we're engaged. We have to protect my reputation!"

They hurried joyfully to the house to share their wonderful news.

In the window of the dawdi haus, Hope had watched the happy couple disappear around the corner of the main house. She blinked, then commenced to wash her paws, well satisfied with her life.

Anne Blackburne lives and works in Southeast Ohio as a newspaper editor and writer. She is the mother of five grown children, has one wonderful grandchild, and has a spoiled poodle named Millie. For fun, when she isn't working on Amish romance or sweet mysteries, Anne directs and acts in community theater productions and writes and directs original plays. She also enjoys reading, kayaking, swimming, searching for beach glass, and just sitting with a cup of coffee looking at large bodies of water. Her idea of the perfect vacation is cruising and seeing amazing new places with people she loves.